PRAISE FOR FALLOUT

Rosenfeld's stunning eco-thriller is about acts of sabotage: those we commit against each other, against the planet, and against ourselves. She puts an achingly human face on the love (and sometimes lies) between mothers and daughters, the losses that can buckle us to our knees, and how the only real way to face the future is to unbury the secrets of the past. **Achingly real and totally unforgettable.**
   – Caroline Leavitt, New York Times bestselling author of *Pictures of You* and *Days of Wonder*

Women are made of fire in *Fallout*—women staying awake, paying attention, finding ways to acknowledge and avoid complicity, ways to acknowledge and embrace their individual and collective power. Jordan Rosenfeld helps burn down the patriarchy with this fierce and beautiful novel – **a propulsive, explosive, timely, inspiring read**.
   – Gayle Brandeis—author of *Many Restless Concerns* and *Drawing Breath*

Fallout is truly a rare accomplishment, a page turner with a blistering heart and a powerful sense of purpose. Rosenfeld seamlessly weaves motherhood, grief, environmentalism, family tragedy and hopefulness into a story of redemption. **An equal blend of propulsion and pathos, *Fallout* is a must-read you can't put down**, even as its themes will linger in your mind for ages to come.
   – Laura Bogart, author of *Don't You Know I Love you?*

Fallout is a story of female rage and delayed trauma at midlife, and about the women who will save us from corporate greed and ecological disaster. *Fallout* is more than a gripping eco-narrative from master-of -the-tight-scene, Jordan Rosenfeld. **Women realizing their power and aiming it with laser focus are the roots and wings of this tense novel.** The story is a satisfying page-turner as it rushes toward its surprising denouement – and the truth that new beginnings are always possible.

– Julia Park Tracey, author of *The Bereaved* and *Silence*

FALLOUT

A NOVEL

JORDAN ROSENFELD

RUNNING WILD

To those who fight for a better world through actions, words and heart

CHAPTER ONE

2015

J ustine awakens in a membrane of pre-dawn, a little womb of gray mist, gnawing at yesterday's interview, for a series of articles she's been writing for six months. Her interview subject, if she can call her that, usually appears without warning, and Justine must be ready. She fumbles for her notes by the side of the bed, dislodging a stable's worth of plastic horses her toddler Willa has left there, which clatter loudly to the floor. Her husband Nate mutters in his sleep as she slips out of bed, her feet meeting the cool floor. The woman calls herself Hecate, a Greek goddess, which Justine would have assumed is not her real name, except this is Northern California—she went to school with kids named Galaxy and Whisper. She scoops up the notebook and tiptoes out of the bedroom, past Willa's room with its carnival of nightlights. She thinks of planting a kiss on the sleeping child's head, but opts not to risk a chance waking.

Today she does not go into the office as she told her husband she would. She does not have a proper interview, she muses guiltily; she has an off-the-record...what is it...meeting? Incident? She isn't sure as she slips on a raspberry knit top and her nice black slacks. She has an address she doesn't recognize, and a buzzy sense of anticipation. "I think you're cut from the same cloth as us," Hecate had said. "I think you could be an asset."

Nate will take Willa to daycare—Justine isn't on duty—yet somehow she still feels like a teenager sneaking out of the house when she leaves, tiptoeing out and closing the front door quietly behind her.

Her GPS directions take her to a rural road, to a lone cabinet making shop in a peeling once-red barn that is now a faded, rusty color. Closed up tight, with no sign of life. Next to that is a big open field with a single, doleful cow chewing grass. The cow looks a little mangy—patches of skin showing through its ragged brown coat. Justine shivers in the cool autumn air. The grass is mostly brown from the end of summer, but here and there, tiny green shoots of life from the one rain they've had are peeking through. She almost expects a girl in a gingham pinafore to round the corner carrying a milking bucket.

She is about to turn back to her car, consider that she's been played for a fool, when a prickle of consideration strikes her. Project Nemesis won't exactly post a sign announcing their location. Just because Hecate had walked right into that café months ago—albeit with a black beanie hiding her hair, and dark sunglasses obscuring her eyes—doesn't mean they will hand anything to her easily.

Nate's voice in her head, chastises. *Justine, what are you doing? Justine, you're becoming obsessed.*

Is it obsessive to feel connected to a story, to the energy of this powerful woman and her group? Or is he just threatened by her independence?

Yesterday, by the time she'd gotten the first two paragraphs of her most recent story about Project Nemesis shaped to her liking, Nate and Willa were both dressed and ready, and she was still at the table in her pajamas, pouring her second cup of coffee.

"So...I guess *I* should take her to daycare?" Nate wore a new blue and white striped shirt and his dark red "power tie."

"Please? I'm right in the middle of finishing this," Justine said.

He frowned but nodded. He would do it. He would do anything for Willa, who stood there, curls in a tangle that would require much more conditioner to smooth. The tiny girl swam in her favorite piece of clothing, a dress patterned with big yellow and orange maple leaves with a high neck and long sleeves that went all the way down to her feet. It made her look like a character out of *Little House on the Prairie*.

"That's the dress she tripped in and scraped her knees last time," Justine pointed out.

Nate stared down at her with a pinched expression. "You try getting her to put on something else then. I'm going to be late. And what are your plans for today? Aren't you going into the office?"

"I'm going to do an interview first."

Willa hugged her father's leg, singing her version of "FIVE LITTLE MONKEYS" that was mostly unintelligible.

"You know, Justine, we don't need you to go back to full-time."

She suspected he'd chosen his words carefully, that lawyer's instinct. Need. *They* did not *need* her to go back full-time. Of course *they* didn't. They'd needed her, however, for the past two, well really three years if you counted the pregnancy, to sacrifice sleep and time and mental peace. Their baby *needed* her milk, her touch, her constant, unwavering attention, to be held and rocked and walked—movement the only thing for a full year that would soothe the constant crying. Her husband *needed* her to be a constant source of love and sustenance for both this child and for him. And when sleep deprivation and hormones turned her into a ravaged beast of a person who couldn't bear to be touched or looked at, who stopped showering and cried too much, he needed her to *figure it out.* And she had. She had figured it out. What kept her from losing all sense of herself beneath the skin of motherhood is this—her work, her words. These people she met, with their passions and hungers, their madness, their causes gave her purpose. This is what kept her from splintering apart and becoming the subject of a story herself.

Now, Justine shakes off her bad mom guilt and presses her foot on several half broken strands of barbed wire, and then climbs a rotting wooden fence behind that one. She glances around, sees only another cow, surrounded by a wealth of steaming cow patties she tries to avoid. She walks straight toward the horizon, where all she can see is more grass that rises to a slight hill over which anything may be waiting. She reproaches herself for her typical reporter wear of high-heeled boots and slacks—the kind of clothes that transform her from the mother who can happily cuddle her sticky-handed, nose-running two-year-old, into the journalist who has to keep her at arm's length. Recently, Willa has learned to equate the clothes themselves with her mother leaving and wails at the sight of her dressed for work.

Soon, the meadow grows marshy, and she swears when one bad step coats her nice boot in mud. The meadow curves into a spray of oaks, not quite forest, but providing a little cover. She surveys the hillside, debating whether she can climb it in these boots, and a sudden strain of voices reaches her ears from somewhere farther on. This makes sense—a group of anarchists wouldn't meet in plain sight.

The first time Justine interviewed Hecate in the cafe, there was no preamble, no five minutes of pleasantries. As soon as

Justine had set down her latte and turned on her recorder, Hecate had thrown out her opening gambit, "So, eco-anarchism, what is it? That's what you want to know, right?" Hecate had spoken with an intense, hushed ferocity: "First thing you need to understand: no matter what you think feminism has achieved, nobody listens to women, and certainly not women of color. Especially not men in power. We are little more than objects, still."

"Why reach out to me?" Justine asked. "Of all the reporters out there."

"We enjoyed your profile of Zoe Rasmussen," Hecate says. "My favorite of your lines: 'Rasmussen either does not mind, or is unaware, of the optics of driving to and from EarthWorks in a gas guzzling SUV.' Of course, the wife of an oil magnate is clueless in the face of such irony." Hecate had given out a belly deep guffaw.

Justine doesn't mind the actual hiking into nowhere without a specific destination; the silence, the aloneness, is a reprieve from a house always full of sound—Willa's chatter almost an entity of its own following her around. Now that she finally has a more concrete invitation to an action, she wonders if she hasn't been rash in coming out here. She only has a few hours before she has to pick up Willa at daycare by 4. In the six months that Hecate has been turning up, dropping pieces of wisdom, hinting that Justine could be a "valued asset" in Project Nemesis, to their cause of trying to hold "dirty" energy companies to account, have they really ever promised her anything? She fights a burn of frustration and keeps picking her way across exposed roots and clumps of grass, toward the sound of distant voices that never grow any louder; it is as though a whisper is traveling on the wind beside her the whole way, as light as dandelion fluff. What if it is just her imagination?

She reaches the peak of the hill, which looks out into a low valley dotted densely with oaks and shrubs. There, off in the distance, a tiny curl of smoke rises into the sky, as though someone has lit a small campfire. She pulls out her phone to snap a picture and see if the little compass can give her some sort of help finding this spot again, when, suddenly, she is slammed to the ground beneath someone—too light to be a man is the first thing she thinks—her phone thrown into the dirt away from her.

"Who are you?" A young, deep, but not necessarily male, voice speaks into the ear that is not pressed painfully into the dirt.

"Hecate sent me," she says, spitting out dirt. "I'm not armed, for fuck's sake, can you let me up?"

She presses upward and the person rolls off her. Justine sits up, brushing dirt off herself, and takes in the young person, somewhere between late teens and early twenties. Shaved head, dressed in dark green, long-sleeved shirt, and threadbare cargo pants, and holding a large and menacing folding knife. Slight build, but incredibly well muscled and androgynous.

"Hey, back off. I'm not here to cause trouble. I'm just a friend of Hecate's. She gave me directions here."

The kid surveys her down a serious, proud nose. "Ahh, the journalist. Took you long enough to get here."

Justine appeals to her with palms up. "Well, I *am* here now."

The kid settles into her hips, stands taller, and frowns. She chews her bottom lip like she is grappling with a tough decision. "You dressed for a press conference? What do they want with you?"

Justine keeps her face blank, her posture as open and unassuming as possible. "My keen eye for observation?"

"More like your connections."

Before she can even register the kid's movement, she's

leaned past Justine, picked up her phone and pocketed it in her dusty cargo pants. "You aren't going to need this here."

Justine stands up, dusts herself off for whatever it is worth. "I'm supposed to trust you?"

"What choice do you have?" She doesn't exactly brandish the knife, but she waves it slightly in the air, as though punctuating her sentence.

"Okay then."

"Okay then," the girl mimics. "You walk ahead, I'll follow you and tell you where to go."

Justine doesn't like the feeling of someone at her back, an instinct honed from years of interviewing people she doesn't know very well, sometimes at night, meeting in unlit city streets with keys in fist, head high, peripheral version locked on. Nate never lets her forget that night in the Tenderloin, when a passing junkie threw her up against a building with a pocketknife, demanding cash. He'd been run off by a guy on a bike before she could so much as fish out her wallet.

Why has Hecate made her come hiking out into the valley for the promised...well, what did Hecate even promise, really? A front row seat to an action? A clandestine bit of information?

Hecate spent much of their last conversation on one of her rants. "Nature is feminized, too, right? We call her our mother —which is true, but that doesn't make her any less vulnerable to men's whims. They will literally poison the planet for their own future generations to remain rich and in power now. So, we're not interested in talking about our feelings. We prefer to...get...shit...done."

"What does that mean, get shit done?" Justine had asked, pen poised over notebook, even though she was recording the interview.

"We educate, of course. Grassroots. We've written material."

7

"A manifesto, I know, I read the copy my editor gave me."

Hecate scoffed and pulled back. "The Unabomber wrote a fucking manifesto, not us...Another thing men love to do."

"Valerie Solanas, the woman who shot Andy Warhol, she also wrote a manifesto against men and society," Justine countered.

Hecate shook her head. "If that's the angle you're going to take on this story, we're done here." She began to screw on the cap to her thermos.

"No, no, please, I'm sorry," Justine held out an imploring hand. "I'm listening. I promise."

Hecate set her thermos back down and exhaled harshly before beginning again. "We take information to the marginalized and downtrodden and let them know that energy industries and big corporations do not have their best interests at heart. We plant seeds of understanding that the environmental crisis is a class crisis, a war on them."

Justine wrote down phrases that struck her. *Marginalized and downtrodden. A class crisis.* "We work toward the decentralization of power. Right now, we live in a world where those with the money and the power make all the decisions, allegedly on behalf of the rest of us. But Democracy, despite its best intentions, is failing. All big systems eventually fail—it's not a surprise. We have to find our way back to community-based systems."

"How do you do that?"

A dark eyebrow rose above the mask, the woman's sharp, high cheekbones rising to peaks. "Off the record?"

Justine stopped the tape recorder with that sink of disappointment at being deprived of printable information. "OK, off the record."

The fox-like smile returned. "Acts of sabotage."

"Acts of sabotage? You mean like the, um, poop bombs in oil executives' cars?"

Hecate laughed heartily. "Not my idea. But you have to keep the younger people engaged, sometimes, give them a task so they don't go rogue. Maybe you need a task, too." Hecate reached into her bra and withdrew a tiny, rolled slip of paper that she pressed into Justine's hand. Then she gathered her knapsack and thermos and strode out of the café.

At the bottom of the page where Justine had been taking notes, she had underlined a single sentence so hard she'd ripped the paper. **Decentralization of power…** The paper unrolled to reveal an address.

And here she is. She's never been very good at keeping track of time, but as they pass more and more of the same oaks and manzanitas, dirt now caking her boots, sweat gathering under the armpits of her decidedly bad choice of long-sleeved jersey knit top, without her phone to ground her in time, Justine grows impatient.

"Okay, look, I've got to get my daughter from daycare in a couple hours, where the hell are you taking me?"

"The question is, where do you want to be taken?" the girl answers.

Justine stifles a groan, resists saying, *What is this, some twisted Alice in Wonderland bullshit?*

"I want to know what Nemesis wants me to see."

The girl purses her lips, narrows her hazel eyes. "You know our goals. Our targets. I think you can put it together."

Justine follows the girl's gaze down into the valley below, where she can make out structures down the hillside. There stands a small Rasmussen Energy way station, which provides power to the nearest city and a series of relatively new, gated communities that several environmental groups have protested for years, including Project Nemesis. They claim it interferes with the ecology of wetlands and puts homeowners at risk for dangerous flooding.

You know our goals. You know our targets. Hecate's words of praise for her profile of Zoe Rasmussen ring through her mind.

More like your connections.

Oh! The truth hits Justine.

As Justine stands there, watching the smoke curl upwards, a boom rents the air and she startles, tripping backwards onto her butt. For a moment she wonders if a jet has flown overhead, and then a little plume of black smoke curls upward from down near the plant. Her heart thunders in her ears. The smoke, now more of a steady billow than a thread, is far enough away that she has to squint, but close enough that panic spikes through her.

Acts of sabotage.

Without much thought she turns around and runs back the way she thinks she has come.

She runs and runs, breath exploding in her lungs until she finally has to stop, bent forward, hands on knees. When she can breathe at a steady rate again, she does not know where she is and she has no phone to orient her or call for help.

On her walk in, it seemed that she followed one straight path, but now paths fork off of paths, trees appear where they surely weren't before. She passes one crooked tree. Another tree. All the fucking trees look the same. This is what she gets for not being in her body, paying attention when they'd come in. She can hear her mother, Helen, in her head, chastising her: *You lose yourself, too easily, 'Tine. You need to focus on what matters.*

This *does* matter. Her work matters. Her interests matter. Yet lizards dart before her like they are mocking her slowness. Birds fly too closely overhead like a preamble to attack. The entire forest closes in on her, like something from a fairytale, a menacing presence that wants to keep her from her goal. Her feet have forgotten how to be steady, and she trips over every little surprise in the dirt, keenly aware that time is ticking away, and yet she has no way to chart it. She has to pick up Willa. What an idiot she'd been to come out here unaccompanied, to not tell Nate where she was going. All to stave off his disapproval. Now, he'll be furious if he's called out of work to pick up Willa again, another time, how many times?

"You get so deep into your work you don't even hear her cry," he'd accused more than a few times.

Oh, she *heard* her daughter's cries, but to Justine they became an audible ticking clock bearing down on her, a siren still too many blocks away to be on your own street. How many more words could she get in before the cries turned to shrieks, turned to wails. He'd never understood because he worked away from the house, in a firm full of men. He didn't share her longing to be part of something bigger, to wear more skins than just "Mommy."

Then she thinks of her daughter's big dark eyes, her little lips trembling in an impending cry. She suddenly longs for Willa with a feeling so visceral it is painful, a knife in her gut. It is so easy to miss her daughter when she is away from her, when she is guilty of failing her.

She groans, hot tears of frustration wetting her cheeks when she realizes she's just made a circle around a copse of trees for the third time. She takes a deep breath, tries to ground herself, pay attention, stop letting panic and anxiety drive her actions. She passed that same little cluster of rocks before, so now she takes a different little path to the right. The path is less loamy and more dry dirt here—yes, this makes sense. Dusty dirt has been kicking up all over her pants on the way in. She's close!

By the time she finds the first mangy cow again, just making her out in the approaching gloaming, she crouches briefly, hot tears threatening at the back of her sinuses. The young person she encountered never reappeared, but there, on the hood of her car, sits her phone, looking no worse for wear. She grasps it up like a lifeline, lets herself into her car, gulping down a bottle of water, warm and tasting of plastic.

With a bracing breath, she prepares herself for the string of angry texts she'll find on her phone. Aside from a dozen or so phone calls—phone calls? Why would Nate call instead of texting?—there is only one:

"At Hospital with Willa. Come ASAP. Where ARE you?"

CHAPTER TWO

OCTOBER 2016 (1 YEAR LATER)

Z oe Rasmussen paces, slashes of red power suit like streaks of lipstick across the mirror every time she looks. A good color on her, people have always said. *Phil* always says. He likes her to gleam, to dazzle. She prefers to hide in grays and dark blues like some unimpressed female bird considering a flashy mate. Her closet is full of thirty years of such gifts. Sequins and shimmering things better fitting a teenager. Fabrics that cling and shape, reshape and mold. When they met, she liked the way expensive clothing smoothed away ragged edges, obscured her history of bruises and starvation. Remade her.

Power red also plays well with her mostly male board of directors at EarthWorks, the non-profit she founded ten years ago, which Phil begrudgingly supports. Except when celebrities or liberals promote it. And which, after that profile in the Chronicle put her non-profit on the map, Phil claims, made them a target. Not her. *Them.* Her suit will photograph well, too, for the press packet and social media. Her dark hair pulled back. A chignon. Lipstick a slightly darker version of the suit. Eyes dark-shadowed and mysterious. She will command things: attention, respect, the advantage of being a woman-of-a-certain-age still *keeping herself up*. Because she can afford those syringes full of botulism and surgeons' scalpels to slice away at the excess slipping into gravity's insistent hand.

Despite her gorgeous suit, the coiffed and crimped face glowing up from the mirror, an acid burn scorches the base of her esophagus. She wants to tear open the suit, hear its buttons plink against the glass.

Today she doesn't want to go to EarthWorks' award ceremony. Doesn't want to be seen. This feeling has been coming upon her more often lately. She doesn't understand it. Hannah has already been gone to college a year. *It can't be that. Can it?*

As if he senses her reluctance, Phil pops into the bedroom. She jumps a little. He's put on his own power suit—a shade of blue so dark it's nearly black. Red tie that matches her own suit too perfectly. Jacket tailored to hide his expanding gut. That stupid comb over, like five pale skinny fingers reaching futilely across his scalp.

"You look great!" his tone, too enthusiastic. Grin, too wide.

Her smile must be as half-hearted as it feels.

"The ceremony won't be long," he says.

"I'm sure," she says, more sarcastic than intended. These men love to hear themselves talk. And talk. And talk—all taking personal credit for the new plant and the groundbreaking. He frowns in that way that means he's debating whether to enter argument territory.

"EarthWorks' awards reception is at four. I'll take a car if your groundbreaking runs over," she says.

This isn't the first of his plants; he's made his wealth in oil and coal. This time, however, it's nuclear power. Suited men wearing bright yellow hardhats symbolically, as though these soft-palmed men ever lift a tool. They don't even carry their own golf clubs. They heft nothing heavier than their annual bonus checks.

Her palms are unusually sweaty. *Hot flash? Suppressed anger?*

"I promise. Done by three." He kisses the top of her head, like she's a child.

Her heels pinch, the top button of her suit pants digs in below the belly button. Sweat blooms unflattering stains into the silk of her blouse. She just wants to get this day over with.

She's stalling on finishing her make-up when the house manager comes to her office—Karina, a Russian woman also fifty, like Zoe, but with the dewy skin of a much younger woman that doesn't require a plastic surgeon's hand. Unfair Slavic genetics. Her hair always up in such a tight bun it turns her eyebrows into mountain peaks. Karina doesn't smile very often, but who needs her to smile when she runs the household operations like a multimillion dollar corporation, which, Zoe supposes, it is.

"Justine is here," Karina says. A woman of few words.

Zoe startles. *Justine? Here?* Their friendship started after Justine profiled Zoe about EarthWorks a year and a half ago. Zoe knew immediately that Justine was different from the women she mingled with on a regular basis. Justine cares about fisheries going extinct and invasive plant species choking out native ones. She loses sleep at night because a WalMart is trying to run Mom and Pop shops out of business.

Naturally, Phil dislikes her.

"Karina, please don't let my husband know she's here. Take her to the pool house; I'll meet her there."

It's one thing to go to Justine's house, but a whole other thing to have Justine *here*. Not only because Phil will accuse her of canoodling with "the liberal media," but Justine has never seen Zoe in her actual element—the grandeur, the spiral

15

staircase, the hand-blown glass chandeliers, the eight-car garage and the swimming pool, the multi-person staff. Zoe has kept up a masquerade of living tastefully rich, not obscenely wealthy.

Maybe they wouldn't have even become friends, if not for the death of Justine's daughter. Zoe spent many days curled around Justine a year ago, when her friend could only cry, bringing her food when she could stand to eat again. Zoe likes Justine's small house with its lovely little hand-dug garden. Its imperfectly organized poles of beans and sagging tomatoes. She loves the way the light illuminates small stains on the furniture, scuffs in the hardwood floors. The way things don't match—no fine China, no top-of-the-line culinary equipment; just hand-painted mugs and mismatched plates. She loves her friend's house because it represents small, specific choices personally made by Justine and her husband, money saved and scrimped to buy these little touches that represent the people who live there. Being around Justine makes her feel...real.

Now Justine is here. At Zoe's home. This is what normal friends do. Yet, Zoe's life isn't normal.

She has just stepped outside to intercept Justine, when Phil storms up to her on foot, shaking something in his hand. As he gets closer, she realizes it's his copy of the *Wall Street Journal*. He waves it in her face, a blur of red catching her eye before he thrusts it into her hands. On the front of the rolled-up paper, in thick red pastel crayon, are scrawled the words: PLANET RAPIST. The greasy crayon comes off on her fingers. She can't wipe them on her pant legs, so she reaches down and drags her fingers through the grass.

"What is this?" she asks.

Phil's entire face crimps with frustration. "One. Of. Yours," he seethes.

"Excuse me?" she rears back. Fight it is.

"Your environmental zealots."

She shakes her head, takes a steadying breath, and unrolls the paper. Headlines crow about legalizing marijuana and the aftermath of one California community's losses to a devastating wildfire. But the headline that draws her attention is in a column to the right.

"Just 100 Companies responsible for 71% of Global Emissions, Study Says."

She knows she will find her husband's company, Rasmussen Energy, on that list.

She shakes her head again. "EarthWorks helps low-income people build xeriscape gardens and get access to low-cost solar panels, Phil."

"How do you know those lady eco-terrorists haven't infiltrated?"

"Oh, now you're just being ridiculous! Besides, defacing a newspaper isn't their style. They're more into bombings, right?"

"You don't have to remind me, Zoe! They cost my company a million dollars in damages and hazard pay when they blew up our transformer more than a year ago. I know exactly what they're capable of."

Zoe fights the urge to roll her eyes. "Well, they don't have anything to do with EarthWorks."

Phil's lips have pressed flat, a white worm of rage. "How did...this person...know where we live?" He stabs a finger at the defiled paper.

She shrugs. "The internet, Phil. We live in a digital age. Not so hard to find."

He shakes his head dramatically.

"This is not my fault," she says, voice shrill.

"I have stakeholders to answer to!" A little spray of spittle follows.

Her own earlier rage—did it come with the suit when she

put it on?—resurfaces like a coil of electricity up her throat. "Is that a threat?"

"Oh, for Christ's sake, Zo!"

"I think you should go to the groundbreaking *without* me," she says thickly.

He frowns. "You have everything you could ever want," he says.

At the hostility in his voice, she can almost feel the pen in her sweaty hand, signing that prenuptial thirty years ago. As a woman in love, the prenuptial had felt like just a tiny little inconvenience to have her heart's desire. Because Phil had given his love so freely then, she'd been shocked when, on the way out of the lawyer's office to the car, Phil's father had grasped her tightly around the shoulders and whispered hotly in her ear, "If you ever fuck this up, you'll be lucky to get out with the clothes on your back."

Now, for the first time in thirty years, Zoe feels the edges of that scrawny, terrified girl she'd been when she and Phil had met in the college bookstore. When she still lived in those shitty apartments—her mother passed out on the living room floor with a needle in her arm. Her only possessions a ratty stuffed lion and a cardboard box full of sketches she'd done using burnt matchsticks instead of charcoal.

But she doesn't say anything else to Phil now, just turns around and stomps back inside, clutching the offending newspaper in one hand.

"Give that to Karina, so she can give it to the police," he shouts after her.

She wants to laugh. He feels threatened by *a newspaper*?

As she climbs back up the ridiculously long spiral staircase to her bedroom to change the silk shirt now sopping with menopausal sweat, she burns with the truth of his words. With the power Phil wields, she could make a phone call and see her name emblazoned on a building or highway. She could have her own music label or film production company. She could dine with dignitaries.

Zoe is invited on a regular basis to High Teas and luncheons with Ladies of Great Importance, though she rarely feels like she fits in. Has gotten used to speaking in false tones about subjects that don't matter to her. She has even been photographed once with Michelle Obama—damn if that woman doesn't always have on the best dress in the room—while fundraising for EarthWorks. Phil berated her later. "You've made this political!" he'd said, red in the face, little anemones of spittle blooming at the corners of his mouth.

"It is one fucking photograph," she'd shouted back. It was pointless, foolish even, to argue with him. He could take it all away in a moment if he wanted. And then what? What would she have?

Her mind suddenly darts back to Justine. Her friend is here. *Here!* Waiting for her beyond the gate. Surely Justine didn't toss that paper over the fence? No, even as changed as she's become in her grief, that wouldn't be like her. Zoe takes the elevator down to the pool house, keenly imagining her estate through Justine's eyes, that she lives in a house with its own elevator. And a pool house.

Before Zoe makes it there, however, Karina is back, a couple of frizzy hairs fleeing her otherwise tight coif. "Mrs. Rasmussen, your friend is not in the pool cabana. She insists you come to meet her outside the gate, to her car."

Relief floods her. She won't have to show Justine the opulence of her life today.

When she gets past the gate, Justine is standing outside the passenger side of her car, head held high, long dark blonde hair flapping away from her face. Her cheekbones stand out at hard chiseled angles, her neck a straw, like a gaunt model in a perfume ad. She's thinner than the last time Zoe saw her a couple of months or so ago. Yet there's an odd, lofty tilt to her head, a stoic squint of her eyes.

Justine drives a battered old Subaru Outback. Green, with weathered patches and mud caked on the tires. It's a stark contrast to the polish and gleam of Phil's fleet of Jaguars and Bentleys.

Zoe waves and Justine just nods tersely. She can't remember the last time she saw Justine smile. A motherly pang grips her heart. Her friend is hurting, and she's come here for solace, which Zoe is very good at. She can help a person in pain. Then guilt roars in—it's been too long since she's checked on her friend.

As she closes the gap to Justine, ready to take her in her arms and embrace her tightly, a couple details alarm her—though it's warm, Justine wears heavy green khakis and a woolen turtleneck. Her feet are stuffed into thick, heavy lace-up boots and an actual tool belt. On that are: a knife, the kind Phil keeps for hunting, a flashlight, and some other tools Zoe no longer needs because it has been so long since she fixed anything herself. The passenger door is open, and Justine half leans into it, her hip cocked out at an angle.

"Zoe. Get in. I'd like you to drive." Justine's words are very even, almost monotone, as though she is reciting from a script.

Zoe sees the second thing that alarms her—a hunting rifle —at the same time she realizes the main gate has closed behind her. All her staff are behind that gate, incapable of helping her at the one time when she might actually need something more than a goddamn cup of tea or her silver polished. Justine holds the gun lightly, as though it is a Halloween prop, something she can toss into a closet. As Zoe stands there, practicing words of deferral, how she has a very important awards ceremony in just a few hours, how her daughter is flying home in a few days, Justine's fingers tighten on the rifle.

"I'd rather not have to demand it," Justine says, and raises the rifle slightly.

Zoe finds her body moving around to the driver's side of the vehicle even as some part of her brain resists.

"I haven't driven stick in more than a decade." Her voice comes out thin, scared. *Get it together.*

Justine slides into the passenger seat and props the rifle between her knees, its nose angled in Zoe's direction.

"That's okay. It will all come back to you."

And Justine is right. A thrill trembles below her breastbone when she first puts the clutch into reverse. It does come back to her. There is so much power in controlling the timing of clutch and shift. She backs the car into the street, the stick a living animal beneath her hand. "Where are we headed, Justine?"

"Just go as I direct you." Justine's voice has dropped to a near whisper, like she's at the edge of a crying jag.

"You don't have to point that rifle at me. I'm your friend, Justine. I'll do whatever you like. I'm here for you."

Justine sniffs. "I'm going to keep it where it is for now," she says. "It's just very important that things go as planned."

Zoe takes in a bracing breath. *As planned?* She began her morning as the wife of a wealthy CEO, the President of the Board of Directors of EarthWorks, whose board members are expecting her for the grant-award ceremony in an hour. Now she is...a hostage? If not for the reality of that gun between them, she might laugh.

Sparkling light pops in Zoe's periphery as she drives. The bay stretches out like a luxuriating blue snake. People on sailboats enjoy their days as if nothing is different, nothing wrong. She can almost feel the rocking of the boat, imagine a glass of champagne in her hand.

As they near the toll booths, Justine unfolds a blanket and tosses it over the rifle, sitting loyally between her knees like a beloved old dog. At least it's no longer aimed at Zoe.

"Take the Fastrak lane," Justine says in a small, tight voice. Zoe does as told, the booth making two little approving beeps as they pass through. Zoe has one solitary beat of gratitude— maybe there's proof that she's been in a car with Justine if someone comes looking for her. Which they will in about an hour and a half when the Board, her assistant, and five grant recipients of EarthWorks realize she isn't just running fashionably late. First, there will be a murmur of outrage. Then a ripple of concern. This isn't like her, after all. And finally, eventually, after calls to her cellphone continue to go to voicemail, they will prevail upon her assistant, Bernard, then he will track down Karina. After Karina, eventually, Phil. Even then, it could take a while. He could be at his own groundbreaking for hours, or the cocktail-swilling afterparty, and, now that they are in a fight, maybe longer. And he won't suspect the worst for a long time. The truth is, no one might know that she hasn't just run off to the spa for as much as a full day.

"Justine," Zoe starts, not sure what she is going to say. "I'm your friend, if there's anything you need to talk about, help with…"

Justine's laugh is more bark, angry, scraping the back of her throat. "You haven't called me in months," she says.

Heat climbs Zoe's neck, a wave of shame.

"I know, I'm so sorry. I wanted to, it's just…"

Nothing she says now will make her look good or help her cause. *It's just that Phil doesn't want me hanging out with you? It's just that we are getting too close, the kind of close I haven't felt in thirty years…?*

Justine clears her throat. "Forget it. I have. Anyway, I'm tired of living a safe life. Such a lie, anyway."

Zoe waits for meaning to dawn inside Justine's words, but it doesn't. Her sweaty palms slip a little on the steering wheel. Her pulse pounds in her throat. She drives in silence, waiting for Justine to explain. But she doesn't.

"You've done a lot of good," Zoe says, trying to find some way into Justine's obviously fractured mind. Justine lost a child. *It isn't so surprising that she'd snap. Maybe if you hadn't stopped calling the past few months*, says an accusatory voice in her head.

"I live a hollow life. It stands for nothing, means nothing, contributes nothing."

"Woah, not true," Zoe insists. "You've written award winning articles, cracked important stories, given voice to people. That's more than I can say."

She hopes that her *friend*, the one she shared her darkest secrets with, the one she helped in Justine's own worst hour, will appear from within this disassociated version, reassuring her that, in fact, Zoe does quite a lot. That her foundation and her charitable causes are worthy uses of her time.

"I can see how you feel that way, spending your husband's dirty money." Justine's voice is hard edged.

Zoe inhales sharply. "Well, it's better than me *not* using my husband's money for a good cause. I could spend my days getting manicures and buying Prada purses."

Justine shoots her a sidelong glance as though to suggest that *is* all Zoe does.

The Moscone Center where the awards ceremony will take place appears in her periphery. Her fingers itch toward the door handle—locked, of course. Her mind fills with visions of throwing herself out onto the road, a whipping blur of red like an action hero.

"Justine, I've been preparing a talk I'm supposed to give today, right there. EarthWorks has a grant awards ceremony today. A group of awesome people will be able to lighten their carbon footprint on the world and reduce their utility bills."

Justine laughs, but it isn't a happy sound. "Do you really think a few solar panels are going to save us? If climate change doesn't take us down first, maybe nuclear fallout will do it." Justine waves her hand at the window. "We're so sedated, Zoe. We're padded up by our comforts and our distractions."

Zoe can still smell the lilac soap from her morning bubble bath. Taste the bacon their cook, Guy, made exactly the way she liked it this morning. She can't argue; her life is a fucking house of pillows.

"I don't understand where this is coming from, Justine."

Justine scoffs. "Given your husband's line of work, Zoe, you should know that there are five nuclear reactors in California alone. What about when the big quake hits, snaps those fault lines like rubber bands—do you think we're safe then? Given *your* line of work you should know that climate change is going to, is already, causing catastrophic changes in the atmosphere. Sea level rise. Wildfires. People displaced."

"Hon, we can think of a million ways we're all going to die any time of day, but what good does it do us?"

Zoe risks a peek at the gas gauge—half empty. They'll need to stop eventually. Justine won't risk pulling that rifle out in daylight, will she? *Breathe. Be patient.* She needs extreme patience, the sort she practiced in the years pre-Phil.

Justine shifts in her seat, moves the rifle toward her other leg, pointed away from Zoe, a beat of relief. "You ever ask your husband how he justifies his work? If you can call what he does work, right? I mean, what—plays golf with other planet-rapists? Even Nate is a better person than that and he's a lawyer."

Zoe lingers on the phrase planet-rapists (*Jesus, did Justine throw that paper over?*), but Justine isn't really asking.

"Truthfully, I don't think Phil has any trouble sleeping at

night, Justine. People respect him, kowtow to him, give him everything he wants. But you're right—he's not out there in the nitty gritty. He doesn't inspect oil pipelines or work at a refinery." He is a numbers guy, a man of the money, and oil and coal (and soon nuclear power) has provided him, them, with more money than she could ever have imagined. Even the monthly sum that he deposits into her personal spending account is more money than her mother has or could ever make in her whole life.

She feels suddenly defensive of Phil, too, even though she'd been ready to slap him this morning. "He's just following in his family's footsteps, Justine."

Justine suddenly grasps her rifle again as though it grounds her, gives her purpose, her knuckles white around its barrel. Zoe has a flash of an opposite image—a child tucked between her mother's knees. A knot of understanding tightens inside her.

"That makes you complicit in your easy, comfortable life. A life you chose, as though it could erase your past," Justine says.

Zoe inhales sharply. How is she supposed to argue with a woman holding a rifle, who is the only person she's ever told about the worst night of her life. Sometimes, in moments of stress, she'll have an intrusive thought, picturing that man's body, one moment so full of violent life, and the next unforgivably cold and still.

"Yes, it's comfortable," she says through gritted teeth. She is reminded of the first time Phil took her to his apartment. She could barely breathe inside the walls of her own apartment, dense with cigarette smoke and a layers-deep stench of body odors and shitty fast food. But Phil's home—barely 25 and he owned his own home!—had smelled like a department store, air freshener and new furniture. Everything he owned pulsed with an aura of newness that made her feel dirty in contrast, like it would darken, stain, or wilt when she so much as brushed against it.

Justine laughs suddenly, a slightly hysterical sound, like a child having a private joke. "I guess you'd call my life comfortable, too," she says. "Before."

Ahead of them, the road distorts with heat—summer's last gasp in October always takes her by surprise, even though she's lived in California her whole life.

"Where's Nate right now, Justine, does he know where you are?" *What you're doing?*

"He's sick of me," Justine says, flatly.

"Nate adores you, Justine."

The hard edges of Justine's face suddenly slip loose, as though there is nothing holding her together. "He adored...her."

These words land a punch between Zoe's ribs. Justine goes quiet. Too quiet. And Zoe is struck by remembrance.

"Oh, Justine. Today's the day, isn't it?" She doesn't want to say *anniversary*, as though it is something to celebrate. Exactly a year since they'd taken Willa off life support and she had surrendered to her injuries... No wonder Justine is unraveling.

And you stopped calling, says the voice inside her. *Stopped checking in on her.* They'd been at the precipice of a true, lasting friendship, Zoe suspects. Then Phil had complained, "Why are you always spending time with that woman?" And something about his tone scared Zoe. *That woman.* As though friendship with Justine could peel back the Phil-approved version of Zoe of the past thirty years and reveal the rough-edged version beneath. That girl without any of the comforts of this life. The girl who'd done something unspeakable just to survive.

"Get on I-80 South," is all Justine says, but her voice is thick with unspoken emotion.

Zoe considers doing something dangerous—cutting across

the currently open lanes of traffic, crashing Justine's car into a guide rail. But the image of Justine's already frail body coming apart in the wreckage, ribs breaking, blood splattering, halts her thoughts. There is only freeway around them now. The city spins away behind them.

Instead, Zoe takes the exit onto a spool of road—having hit at that perfect time of day before the lunch rush, free from commuter hell, just open road and sunshine. A part of Zoe lifts up with freedom, euphoria at not having to be anywhere, accountable to anyone.

As they pass the airport, memory slams into Zoe with a fresh pang of guilt. "Shit, Hannah's supposed to be flying home in a couple of days," she says. As soon as she says the words, she regrets them.

"Your daughter is coming home," is all Justine says, as though reminding herself that people still have living children.

If Zoe expects tears or anguish, Justine does not deliver. And that's when the next idea occurs to Zoe.

"Justine...are you still pursuing those...eco-terrorist women?"

Justine makes a low humming sound in her throat, like the precursor to a scream. "Any time women gather to stand up against injustice, they call us terrorists or anarchists. Not that I mind the term—I'd embrace it if people knew what it really meant, which is basically to oppose systems that serve only themselves."

Panic clutches Zoe right at the mid-section, travels up her sternum.

"*Us*, Justine? I remember the article you wrote. What is it called, you won a journalism award for it, 'The Women Are Done Talking', or something, right?"

Justine points—with her hand, thankfully, toward a lane. "Stay in the left lane, toward Los Angeles."

"Did you...get more involved with them, Justine, beyond writing about them?"

Justine is too quiet for too long, and Zoe thinks maybe she's pushed her over the edge, when Justine says, in a small voice, "Not nearly involved enough."

Zoe waits, breathing shallowly, afraid to spook her.

Justine exhales heavily. "They gave me a task..."

"A task? Please tell me you didn't do anything illegal."

"What the hell does it matter to you?" Justine demands.

"Did you throw that paper with 'Planet Rapist' on it over my fence, Justine?"

Justine scoffs. "I found it outside your gate. Thought it needed to go to its intended recipient. Phil's got more enemies than you realize."

"Yeah. Now we're in a fight," Zoe says.

Justine laughs harshly. "Seems the least of your troubles."

Zoe beats back a flash of rage. How blithely Justine can wreak havoc. "Okay. Can you just tell me where we're going, then?"

"You'll see," Justine says tightly and turns to look out her window. Conversation clearly ended.

"Hey, Justine, I need to...I need to use a bathroom pretty soon. And we'll need gas. We're going to have to stop eventually. Are you hungry?"

Justine shivers and leans away from Zoe. "I can't remember the last time I was hungry."

Zoe really looks at Justine then. Though she's hidden inside the bulky turtleneck and khakis, she looks whittled away, carved down to just planes and angles, cheekbones and surfaces. Even her fingers are bony.

Zoe thinks of a time when the high school counselor had called her to his office, handed her pamphlets about anorexia and drugs. *Those stupid assholes.* No one ever asked about her home life. About her mother or lack of nutrition. They took one look at Zoe and decided she must be the architect of her own misery.

"But this car will need fuel, and I'd rather not soil your seats," Zoe persists.

"We've got another thirty miles of gas. Keep going. I'll tell you when to stop."

The gas station Justine eventually picks is a rural, remote little two-pump operation in Coalinga—one of those passthrough towns you don't realize exists until you have cause to stop in it.

After pumping the gas, the actions feel choreographed, as Justine follows Zoe to the bathroom. Zoe is calmed, slightly, to see Justine has left the rifle in the car. Inside the bathroom stall, alone for a few minutes, Zoe doesn't even mind the mold in the corners of the dingy tiles, the yellow stains in the toilet bowl. She could be at the beach, so beautiful is this freedom of aloneness, out from under Justine's oppressive energy. She lets a few anxious tears loose, but stifles the rest. She can't lose control and doesn't want Justine to think she is falling apart.

Desperation must be kept under wraps.

CHAPTER THREE

Hannah stares at her three big suitcases. "Ginormous bougie suitcases," as her roommate Anastasia calls them.

"Your suitcases are as big as my room back home," Ana had teased her after they'd gotten to know each other well enough to joke like that.

"Stop," Hannah says, hot with shame. She hates it when people point out her family wealth. She didn't earn it. She didn't ask for it. It just comes with the package of being "energy magnate" Phil Rasmussen's daughter.

When all her stuff is crammed inside those three suitcases, like now, it's hard to remember what is so important that it required three. Anastasia only has two and they are "College appropriate sized suitcases."

"So, you're really doing this?" Anastasia asks, passing Hannah the now half empty bottle of tequila. Anastasia, petite like a gymnast, but without the muscles, sits on one of the suitcases, like it's a chair, and smooths her hands across its leather surface like a game show hostess from the '70s showing contestants what they can win.

Hannah sniffs, swigs from the tequila bottle, pleased at the way the room goes soft at the edges of her vision, blurry, like a dream sequence in a movie.

"Welcome to your new apartment," Hannah says, pointing to the suitcase Anastasia is perched upon. "I think there's even room for a cat in there, and it's fully furnished."

Ana's impish grin takes up half her face and she snorts out a laugh. "Are you really really sure? I could also just hold onto it for you, for when you come back."

Hannah passes the tequila back to Anastasia, unfolds her hands from one another. "But who knows when that will be!"

Ana smiles again, a little sadly. "Hannah Rasmussen, change maker."

Hannah shrugs. "Colin is, I'm just helping."

"Africa, huh?"

"Kenya, specifically."

Ana frowns. "Is Africa a country or a continent, I always forget?"

Hannah stands up. "Seriously? Africa is a continent, with 54 countries. How do you not know that?"

Ana's face blooms two pink spots. "Not everyone knows everything!"

Hannah shrugs. "I'm just saying that's a thing you should know."

Ana stands up quickly and swigs another shot of tequila. "Well, good luck with your folks."

Hannah has the sense that a minute before Ana would have delivered the statement in a kind and genuine tone, but now she sounds sarcastic.

"Yeah," Hannah plops onto her bed, where one lone green canvas duffle lays waiting, her life pared down to a fraction of before. She's done most of the hard work already—making sure her passport and shots are up to date. She has her letter of resignation from school ready to turn in this afternoon. She gave most of her stuff to Anastasia. Paid for one more month of rent so as not to leave Ana in the lurch.

"Honestly, I don't think it will be the moving to Kenya part that will be the hard sell," she says. The room spins gently overhead like a very slow carousel.

"Yeahhhhh," Ana says sleepily from the floor where she lays sprawled. "It's the environetal, enviro, envir...fuck, I'm drunk."

"Environmental NGO," Hannah says, liking the way it rolls off her tongue, slick with tequila. "Climate Corps." Her boyfriend's father started it.

"You should have just become a stripper," Ana says. "Or like...a Democrat. Your father would be way happier."

Ana laughs hard at her own joke, and, despite herself, Hannah starts to laugh too, until tears are running down her face and her stomach hurts, forgetting the things her dad will say to her when she tells him tomorrow. Her mother will probably be proud, but in an obnoxious overbearing way in private, and calm about it publicly so as not to further piss off Dad. After all, here Hannah is, essentially following in Zoe's footsteps. She can imagine her parents already:

"Why so far?" her mother will ask.

"You're cut off," her father might say, but Hannah has already planned for that. She's been putting away every dollar that doesn't go directly to food and textbooks, and her birthday and Christmas money over the years has added up. Now she's going to prove that she can survive in the world without her father's purse strings.

She just has to make him understand.

CHAPTER FOUR

Once off the freeway, Justine instructs Zoe to pull onto a dirt road that looks like something from a bad horror flick. Unpaved and thick with rocks. Unpopulated. What should be pretty landscape menaces her with looming, nearly leafless trees and rocky ground. Justine uses the rifle to motion Zoe out of the car, then walks behind her, rifle aimed at Zoe's back. Justine keeps looking at an old school pager in her hand, muttering to herself. Her friend has good and truly lost her shit. Zoe pictured Justine taking her to the site of some toxic corporate dump to rant about corporate ills, not tromping through trees and scrub that snag at the cuffs of her good, red suit. She'll need more than a dry cleaner after today; she'll need a tailor.

Zoe walks in a slow-motion sensation of dreaming. Surely she'll wake up and find herself in a menopause induced nap any minute now. But her heels pinching blisters into her toes, and heat gathering in her armpits, are all too real.

Fear returns, a slithering presence up her spine and into her belly. What does Justine possibly want with her?

"Where are we going?" she asks after a while.

Justine doesn't answer, so Zoe turns back to look at her. Her friend's face is alarmingly blank.

"You'll see."

She lets herself be urged forward into a denser tree canopy. Oaks and pines give off a holiday scent she might find lovely under other circumstances.

Zoe eventually grows lulled by their meandering until her smart watch buzzes with incoming messages. She doesn't dare look at her wrist. It's freeing not to attend to the texts, in fact. The walking takes on the quality of a meditation, if one could meditate while facing down potential harm, in heels and a suit not meant for this terrain. Just when she's begun to slip into mindless thought, she hears...*birdcalls?* But the calls are too structured, too human. Justine is bringing her to...*someone? Multiple people?* A fresh gout of sweat slicks Zoe's armpits. If she kicks off her heels, can she outrun Justine? Zoe tries to conjure herself of thirty years ago with reflexes of steel, borne of necessity. That girl could thrust a knee in a man's groin in a matter of seconds, and probably have disarmed someone as frail as Justine, too. But if Justine doesn't mean *her* harm, might she turn that rifle on herself?

Justine pushes her through a dense set of bushes, which scrape and grasp at her suit jacket. There, Zoe stumbles to a stop, finding herself staring at a small circle of women in black, in Zorro-style eye-masks.

Justine's face shines the moment she steps into that clearing, her eyes wide, like a child presenting a piece of art to a teacher.

"What is this bullshit, Justine?" says a woman with dark hair and brown skin, pointing at Zoe.

In contrast to the women in their comfortable, earthy-toned clothing, Zoe suddenly wishes she'd worn a dark suit, something that doesn't scream "look at me."

"Tsk tsk, Hecate," says a woman with a long red braid and friendly green eyes, "Judgments."

Hecate's head snaps toward the redhead. "Oh, Artemis, don't get on my case with your 'calling in' right now. I'm not judging her *as a woman*. I'm wondering who wears a suit into the woods? Is there a cocktail party I wasn't invited to?" The woman called Hecate cocks her head appraisingly. Little flyaway hairs sprout from her dark bun like tiny snakes. "Jus-teeeen," she says, sing song. "What have you done?"

Red-haired Artemis frowns and looks curiously back at Zoe, then over to Justine. The rifle is slung over Justine's shoulder, toward her back, and now manages to look no more threatening than a purse. "Mrs. Power Suit doesn't look like she chose to come here on her own."

She fucking kidnapped me, Zoe wants to say. *She's had a mental breakdown and I'm the collateral damage.* But she doesn't know just what sort of women they are, though she has a feeling she knows *who* they are. Can they see for themselves what is happening to Justine?

"I know I'm late," Justine says. "I should have done this a year ago, but...I got sidetracked."

Zoe isn't following any of Justine's words. Done what? And sidetracked? Is that seriously how she's referring to Willa's death?

Hecate's sharp eyebrow carves upwards again. Appraising. Possibly...proud? Zoe's tongue is glued to the roof of her mouth. Worse, those places where the suit rubs up against her —armpit crevices and the grooves between thigh and groin and the small of her back—are instantly, unbearably scorching.

"Oh my fucking god," Zoe flings her jacket off in a motion that pops buttons and has Justine clutching her rifle.

Artemis watches impassively, but Hecate cackles. "Ha,

well Justine, I will say there's no better soldier for a cause than a woman in the change of life. I recall it well, myself."

"I am not a fucking solider," Zoe says.

Hecate raises a brow. "No? So what are you then?"

Zoe opens her mouth to answer, but Artemis jumps in. "Zoe Rasmussen. Founder and CEO of EarthWorks, an environmental non-profit that gives grants to low-income people for solar panels, energy efficient appliances, that sort of thing," she says, with scripted fluency, as though she is reading off a teleprompter screen. "And, the wife of Phil Rasmussen, CEO of Rasmussen Energy."

Hecate literally rubs her hands together and laughs out loud. "Soooo, you convinced her?"

"Convinced me?" Zoe shoots Justine a look, but her friend is actively avoiding making eye contact with her. "She...threatened me. Kidnapped me."

Justine manages to keep her face maddeningly blank, like Zoe has seen Phil do whenever the press accosts him.

"Kidnapped?" Hecate barks. "I don't see any handcuffs, any ropes. You don't look injured."

Zoe narrows her eyes at the women. "She's been carrying that rifle ever since she demanded I get in her car and drive her here."

Hecate makes a *tsking* sound with her lips and Zoe wants to smack them right off her face. This rage feels both new and unfamiliar, as well as ancient and primal.

"So let's review—you got into a car willingly with Justine and drove her here. But you were...kidnapped?"

Zoe chokes back a shriek of frustration. The radiant heat is still pulsing in waves through her. Sweat drips down the back of her neck and low back, and the underarms of her blouse cling moistly to her sides.

To look at Justine, she does look incredibly harmless. Gaunt and thin and fragile and standing in half a slump. But what can Zoe say in her own defense? Every other time in her life she's been on the pointed end of a gun, it was loaded. You don't take your chances.

"What do you want from me?" She asks the question of the air.

"To do something meaningful," Justine says firmly.

Hecate and Artemis shoot each other a loaded gaze Zoe can't read.

"Really? Running a non-profit that helps people isn't meaningful enough?"

Hecate smiles tightly. "Some might say you're patching a hole."

"Excuse me?"

"Your non-profit fills a need that shouldn't exist in the first place. Everybody should have access to clean energy and power cheaply and affordably. They should be able to power their homes and cook their food without it causing them to go broke, no?"

"Well, of course, but..." Zoe begins.

"So, your organization, which largely gets its money from big donors who are part of the problem in the first place—corporations and billionaires who need tax write-offs—fills a few tiny holes here and there. Maybe even a lot of holes. But it does nothing to get to the root of the problem. It's kind of like recycling. It's great that we can reuse some of the plastic waste we make, but it does little in the bigger picture—there's more plastic out there than we'll ever be able to reuse, and it's choking the oceans and we'll probably drown in it soon enough..."

Zoe puts up a hand. "I get it."

Artemis flips her braid over a shoulder and shakes her head. "I don't think you do."

Zoe zips her lips shut. She's glad when they turn their attention back to Justine.

"So, why now, Justine?" Hecate asks. She squints at Justine as though she is hard to see by looking directly at her. Or maybe, Zoe considers, Hecate knows about Justine's daughter, and is treading lightly.

Justine's eyes drift out of focus. She looks through Hecate, not at her. "I want to burn it all down," she says so softly that Zoe isn't sure she heard her correctly.

Hecate and Artemis lean in, too. "What's that?"

"I want to burn everything to the fucking ground!" Justine almost shouts.

Hecate only smiles wider.

Zoe has to fight from emitting an audible groan. *Could you burn shit down on your own time?*

"That's my girl," Hecate says, pulling Justine in for a hug, rifle and all.

Justine lets herself be hugged but stands limply in the larger woman's arms, eyes still searching the horizon behind her as if she can see something the rest of them cannot. She looks so broken Zoe's empathy resurfaces.

And that's when Zoe's Apple watch buzzes with more texts.

All of the women jump at the sound, surprisingly audible in this quiet forest.

Zoe points to it. "EarthWorks has an awards ceremony I am supposed to be at. They're wondering what happened to me, I'm sure."

"Do *you* ever wonder what happened to you?" Artemis asks.

Zoe frowns. "Should I bother to ask what you mean?"

"Are you proud of who you are, Zoe? The life you live?"

Zoe opens her mouth, unsure of what she's going to say.

She's proud of EarthWorks. She's proud of Hannah. Hannah...
who is supposed to be coming home this weekend. *Fuck!*

"Well, go ahead and text them back that you won't make it.
Then give me that." Hecate puts out her warm brown hand.

"What? I can't just text them I'm not going to make it.
People are going to investigate my whereabouts eventually. My
husband is already pissed at me after our fight this morning."

Hecate clapped her hands together. "Perfect! You had a
fight, and you disappeared to cool off."

Zoe frowns. "That's not like me. I would never abandon my
responsibilities at EarthWorks. My staff knows that."

Justine shakes her head slightly, as though disappointed,
and that animal rage hisses and spits inside Zoe again.

"You're a woman in menopause," Hecate says silkily. "You
aren't exactly in control of your emotions right now." Her tone
is ironic, but Zoe sees where she is going with it.

Zoe presses her palms to her sweaty temples, yearning for
them to be cool.

Hecate gestures at her to send the text. "If you think about
sending out a plea for help, it might get you rescued, but it
won't get you off our radar," she says.

Is that a threat? Zoe supposes it is, though she feels less
threatened by the forceful woman with her dangerous smiles
than by the cool weapon over Justine's shoulder. With shaking
fingers Zoe taps out a simple text to her assistant, Bernard.

*Won't make ceremony. Proceed without me. Will explain
later.*

Of course Bernard does not simply take her explanation for
an answer.

WTF? Bad optics, Z.

Hecate holds out her hand. "Give it, please."

Artemis raises an eyebrow. "You said please. How polite."

Hecate laughs and nods. "You're right! It's time for me to go back into the wild, clearly. Becoming too civilized for my own good."

With that, she stomps over to Zoe and snags the watch right off her arm in a swift motion that leaves Zoe's wrist red and stinging. Then she lays the watch on the ground, hefts up a sizable rock, and before Zoe can argue, brings it down with a sharp crack.

"Heeeeey!" Zoe cries.

Hecate turns to Justine with a furrowed glare. "Sweetheart, we will cut you a little bit of slack given...all you've been through. But if you ever make a mistake like that again, we're done, do you understand?"

Justine gapes at Hecate as though unclear what she's done.

"I'm sure she's got *find my phone* activated on all her devices?" Hecate says. "Easy for them to figure out where she is, where she's been."

Zoe presses her sweaty palms to her eyes, wishing this was all one of those hormone inspired nightmares, from which she'll thrust up in a pool of her own sweat, heart a wild tattoo against her chest.

"Let's get out of here," Artemis says.

"Where are we going?" Zoe asks, embarrassed at how her voice shook.

Hecate stands, smooths some of her wild curls away from her face. "To burn it all down. With your help, of course."

CHAPTER FIVE

Justine can feel Zoe's loaded gaze on her as they walk along forested trails where the turning of the seasons is evident in the musty scent of oak mulch, pine, and leaf mold. No sign of rain, though. In her childhood, it would have been damp and moist by now, at least one heavy rain having sloughed away the scrim of summer-cracked dust.

She can't believe she did it, brought Zoe here. A year too late, but then, Nemesis has not turned them away. A chord of guilt tugs at her. No one surprised her more than Zoe after Willa's death, with her kindness and dogged showing up. Zoe never demanded anything of Justine, simply brought her food and companionable silence. For a time. Until that fucker of a husband got wind of their friendship. It has been months now since Zoe called. Maybe she'd just made a project out of Justine. To prove to herself that she was decent.

Though Justine's thighs are weak beneath her, she likes this walking, exerting herself. She wants to use up what is left of herself, spend it like the last gallon of gas to get somewhere she can finally put the whole burden down.

"Where are the rest of us?" Justine asks.

Artemis pivoted back to look at Justine. "Us?"

"You," Justine quickly amends.

Hecate stops short, and Zoe, who stares at the ground as she walks, grunts as she almost bumps into the woman.

There is something in the way Hecate stands, strong on the earth, planted in her powerful hips, that makes Justine feel as though Hecate is readying to charge her. She backs a step away, feeling vulnerable, momentarily forgetting that she still carried the rifle on her shoulder.

"Justine, sweetheart...may I remind you that partnering with Nemesis is an earned right? This is not the fucking Girl Scouts where you get a badge just for showing up. Just because you dip your toe in the waters does not mean you're *in*."

Justine fights the urge to hang her head. Bringing Zoe here isn't enough. Of course not. She should have known that. Still, she wants to clutch herself and cry like a little scolded child. She lifts her chin higher, inhales sharply and nods.

Zoe looks between them with that assessing gaze, part pity, part curiosity, maybe some fear. Justine wants to shake Zoe. Where has all this rage for her friend come from? Zoe was the only one willing to brush right up against the edges of the worst thing that ever happened to her. She can remember the surprising strength in Zoe's arms when she'd curled around Justine and held her like a mother in that bed when Justine could only lie there, leaking tears, too tired to actually sob. But she'd stopped calling, and Justine has felt her friend's absence almost as keenly as her daughter's.

Now, though, the sight of Zoe makes her hands feel full of static that wants an outlet. When she'd pulled up to the grand estate Zoe called home, she had to clamp her knees together to stop herself from scaling the fence, putting bullet holes into the walls of the pool house. It just seemed so...much. So unnecessarily much. Why did Zoe get to have everything and then some?

"Justine?"

Zoe's voice derails her thoughts.

"You're shaking," Zoe says softly. As Zoe's slim-fingered, manicured hand gently reaches for her, Justine shouts, "Don't touch me!" so loud that Zoe startles backwards.

Artemis makes an annoyed sounding scoff and storms over to them. She grasps Justine by the bicep, hauls the rifle onto her own shoulder, and points ahead of them. "Walk, both of you. Now."

Without the rifle, Justine feels light and naked. She doesn't dare look at any of the women in the eye. She *will* prove herself. She will make herself the most useful tool they have ever had. She will give everything she has to give.

They walk single file through brush that grows thicker and less easy to pick their way through the deeper into the woods they get. Justine has never admitted, even to herself, how much she coveted this very feeling, of being part of a group, a cause, back when she first encountered them.

Zoe suddenly groans and stops abruptly. She yanks off her heels and tosses them into the brush.

"Nuh-uh," Hecate whirls around. "You can't leave those here," she says. They'll think we dragged you out here and disposed of your body."

Zoe's eyes go wide, but she obediently scrambles after them, tucking them under her armpits instead. The cuffs of her fancy suit are already caked in dirt and trailing leaves.

"How much longer are we going to walk?" Zoe asks, voice starting out sharp, but quickly dropping in tone as she catches Hecate's dark-eyed gaze.

"As long as it takes," Hecate says, in that tone that means she is not having anyone's shit.

As they walk, dodging branches, tripping over unseen logs, Justine loses track of the time. She's become very good at that over this past year, in fact. She'll find herself in some part of the house with no memory of having gotten there, looking down at a sink full of dishes, or standing outside at the garbage cans, uncertain of what to do next. Everyday tasks seem so pointless. Eventually Nate grew frustrated trying to get her to keep up the essentials of self-care. Even her mother, Helen, a woman who expressed her love pragmatically, through actions, stopped appearing with her mountains of Tupperware every other day. Just as well, Justine simply tossed it all into the compost after her body refused to eat it.

Now someone is calling her name. She shakes herself slightly and looks up to find them all standing in front of a dark green van. Zoe and Artemis are stripping off leaves that have been used to camouflage it.

Hecate bends down toward the ground. "Well fuck," she says matter-of-factly. "Those sons of bitches."

Artemis drops to a squat beside her, saying, "Shit." Then she moves around the van on all four sides, muttering under her breath.

The tires are all flat as the ground, and from the front left tire protrudes a knife so massive Justine can't help but imagine it as a tool of murder—something to lop off heads. Her hands tremble slightly and she clutches them together.

Zoe has gone so still, if not for that garish slash of red she makes in her suit, she can almost blend in with the scenery, like some wary animal.

Artemis grips the knife in two hands and yanks several times.

"You shouldn't touch that," Zoe says. "It might have DNA evidence on it."

Hecate laughs, which makes Zoe purse her lips and narrow her eyes.

"She thinks we'd call the police," Hecate says to Artemis.

Artemis's wide, thin lips curve into a half smile. "Of course she does."

"I don't see what's so fucking funny!" Zoe says shrilly.

Artemis extracts the knife and inspects it. Its hilt is tied with something. *A bandana?* Artemis unwraps it and holds it up. *A confederate flag.*

Hecate's sneer is so full-bodied her lips look like they will peel backwards off her face.

"Who did this?" Justine asks gingerly, aware that she is not *in*. Not yet.

"Defenders of Freedom," Hecate says in a tone one might reserve for stepping in shit.

"Who?" Zoe asks.

"White nationalists," Justine says. "I wrote about them, don't you remember?"

Hecate shakes her head. "Call them what they are, dear. Nazis. Fascists. The only thing they actually defend are their own dicks. And why? Because we are a threat to them, of course."

Zoe gapes.

"Don't look so offended," Hecate presses on. "You've probably dined with them, yourself. Shopped with their wives."

Zoe's mouth hangs open, a retort forming, Justine can tell, but Zoe wisely chokes it back.

"Page base camp," Hecate says to Artemis, who is already extracting something from a deep pocket in her cargo pants. She pulls out an old-school pager and types.

"What's with the old tech?" Zoe says. "Didn't know they still existed before today."

"We stay as simple as possible," Hecate says.

"Why are you a threat to those...Defenders?" Zoe asks, slumping down on a half-rotted log.

"The least you could have done is told her a thing or two about us before you brought her here," Hecate says to Justine, then to Zoe: "Being empowered women is all it really takes to get on their radar. But one of our past actions targeted a member of their group's company for dumping toxic waste into a local stream."

"By past actions, you mean...a bomb?" Zoe asks.

Hecate frowns. "Hardly a bomb. Just a little fecal explosion. In his car. His very expensive car."

"With white leather seats," adds Artemis, with a snicker. "Who has the audacity to get white leather in a car, anyway?"

"Huh," Zoe says, looking torn between a chuckle and a gag of disgust.

Justine bets that Zoe's husband has white leather seats in several of his cars.

"Anyway, I don't think Justine *intended* to bring me here," Zoe says. "I don't think Justine knew what she is doing."

"I definitely know what I'm doing," Justine says, louder than she means. "I would have brought you sooner if not for..." She chokes off the words, unable to speak the awful truth, waiting for the reality to hit Zoe, but her friend just sits taller, chin tilting high. Zoe manages to seem every bit the untouchable wife of Phil Rasmussen rather than the scrappy survivor she'd revealed herself to be in those awful months after Willa's death.

"You know what it looks like to me?" Zoe spits, "You don't need a cause, Justine, you need a good grief counselor."

Justine grasps for the phantom rifle that now hangs over Artemis's shoulder. Hecate's eyes don't miss the motion, though; she watches like a prison guard.

Justine stalks over to Zoe and grasps her by the arm,

yanking her to standing. She expects Zoe to cower, but she finds steel in the woman's eyes.

"Try me," Zoe says softly.

Justine's hands clench into fists, her whole body coiling for action, when the sound of tires over ground startle everyone to alertness.

Hecate shoots a look at Artemis, who now holds the rifle aloft, like she means to shoot it. "No way they got here that fast," Artemis says, and Hecate scrambles for the van. She throws its back open. The insides have been tossed. Gear and food and clothing are scattered haphazardly across the insides.

"They took our weapons," Hecate says.

Justine remembers that first conversation with Hecate, her assurance that their acts of sabotage did not include violence against people. *Is that still true?*

Artemis clenches her teeth. Hecate digs into her boot and pulls out a tiny gun that looks almost too small to be real, like a toy.

"Get in the van, ladies," she snarls toward Justine and Zoe, and they do, the doors thrown shut just as a truck rolls up into the clearing, spewing exhaust and loaded down with men.

CHAPTER SIX

Justine crouches beside Zoe, staring out with a honed alertness. Zoe can barely breathe, heart thundering, hot flash receding. Now she's just clammy, craving a shower. The truck spills out more men than it seems possible.

"So many beards," Zoe says, sotto voce to keep from panic, teeth chattering. The men are all dressed alike: white T-shirts, dark green Army fatigue bottoms, hate sharp in their eyes. They form a semi-circle around Hecate and Artemis, who stand with backs to the van, chins up. Several of the men shoulder big, black rifles, mass shooter style. The kind Phil's second amendment purist friends love more than their wives.

"Fuckers," Justine mutters.

Zoe's legs are dead logs. Breath a hot, clawing sensation in lungs squeezed to straws. She is breathing heavily, loudly.

"Zoe, you need to keep it together," Justine says. Her voice comes through as if from down a long tunnel.

Old images flash, jag through memory: a door splintering open; a man's booted foot; houting; her mother's limp arms; the man a blur of black and green, storming into her room, grasping her by the hair, dragging her out back, to the silent woods behind her house; the copper slick of blood in her mouth; wrestling and coiling and trying to scream beneath hands that encircled her throat; explosion; blood in her hair, on her face, everywhere.

A hand on Zoe's shoulder nearly makes her scream and brings her back to the present. She chokes it back beneath the hand that slides, light but sure, across her mouth. "Zoeeeeee," Justine whispers harshly. "Quiet!" Justine points.

Through the sliver of window glass, a man, tall and scraggly, sharp and angular, looms down over Hecate, a finger in her face. Behind him, his ragtag militia holds their rifles at the ready.

Five deep breaths, eyes closed, she calms her slamming heart a bit. "Who are they?" she whispers. "What do they want with...your friends?"

"Not sure. Maybe they think they can stop Nemesis."

"Those AR-15s say so," Zoe breathes.

Justine smiles—Zoe can't fathom asking her mouth to do such a thing right then. "They have no idea," Justine says. "If they killed all of us today, Nemesis will keep on going."

"Don't say that!" Nausea unspools inside her.

As though the words have summoned the men, the van doors are suddenly thrown wide. Zoe blinks against the light, against the dead-eyed stares of the sneering men.

"Get out," one man barks.

Zoe is momentarily jarred by his vivid green eyes but then drawn to stains on his white shirt. *Food? Blood?* She can't tell. Zoe and Justine both stay where they are.

"I said, get OUT!" he shouts, but doesn't wait, reaching for Zoe's arm to drag her.

Animal rage erupts. She slaps his hand off and leaps out. Just as quickly, his open palm meets her cheek with a stinging slap. The daylight dims and suddenly she is all fists and nails, swinging and punching and fighting for her life. Shouts and clamor, and feet crunching on leaves, then rifles are cocked and trained on her face. Strong arms at her waist, at last, and Hecate hauls her back, holding up one hand toward the men, a mountain militia gunning for a fight.

When Zoe's vision returns, she sees blood and tries not to gag. *This isn't real,* she reminds herself. *Nothing you can't undo.* Just a scratch down the man's cheek, bleeding in one long line onto his white shirt.

"What do you want?" Hecate hisses. "You going to shoot us? Rape us?"

"Hah!" a stocky man with a salt and pepper beard barks out, "Who'd want to fuck you dykes?"

Artemis shakes her head slightly, but says nothing.

"We hear that you've got a plan involving something to do with the new nuclear power plant going in. We want to make sure you know that your little band of commy dyke bitches aren't getting anywhere near it."

The new power plant? Zoe's heart pounds. *Rasmussen Energy's plant?*

Hecate raises her hands in a gesture of supplication. "Do you think if we had a plan that you would know about it? You came, you saw, you put us in our place. I think your work here is done," she says firmly. She wields her words like a nun with a ruler, never showing fear. Zoe admires that.

Suddenly, the sound of another vehicle from somewhere off in the forest, then the shriek of a police siren. Faintly in the distance, but hard to tell which direction it is coming from, or where it is headed. A spike of hope surges in Zoe.

"Spencer," the stocky man says to their leader. "Let's go. We know where to find these bitches."

But Spencer has narrowed his eyes on Zoe. "Why are you

dressed like that?" He points at her power suit pants, her silk shirt, both grimier than they were a couple hours ago, but a stark contrast to her companions.

"Part of our training is to help women see how ridiculous and impractical fashion is," Hecate says quickly.

Spencer shakes his head. "Nah. You're somebody." His finger, a fleshy gun, aims at Zoe. "I know you from somewhere."

If these men were anyone else, she'd rally them to rescue her from these radical women. She'd plead with them to take her away. But not *these* men. Her grandparents didn't escape Hitler for her to walk right into some Nazis' hands.

"I thought we already determined that I'm a commy dyke," Zoe hears herself saying, before thinking *oh shit*.

Spencer raises his rifle like a hammer, but now the sirens grow louder, closer. Zoe dares a rush of relief. *Is someone really coming to help us?*

"Spencerrr!" The stocky man growls again. "Let's *GO*."

"Fuck's sake, B-dog. Relax."

But when the sound of tires grows all that much closer, Spencer presses his lips together and flashes an "OK" sign at his men, who all retreat into the truck.

"We'll find you again," Spencer says to Hecate and Artemis. "And we'll find out who you are." Finger at Zoe.

Their truck peels away. Then not long after, another van screeches into the clearing. Zoe is ready to collapse with relief, expecting cops, when three women launch themselves out of the van.

"Thanks for putting on the siren, Calliope," Artemis approaches a short woman with hair so blonde it is nearly white.

Calliope grins, revealing deep dimples. "Works every time. Everyone in one piece still? She hurt?"

She points at Zoe, who follows the woman's gaze down her

blouse, which is splattered with blood. She looks at her hand, then, too, recalling the feeling of the man's flesh beneath her manicured nails, and shudders to find a tiny bit of skin stuck beneath it. She gags, drops to her knees, and spits up a tiny bit of bile.

"All in one piece—except for the firebrand there who tried to take Spencer Miller's face off with her fingernails," Hecate says. Something like pride fills Zoe for a moment.

Artemis smiled wide. "Who *is* the firebrand?"

"That's a story," Hecate says smoothly, looking at Justine.

Calliope's bright blue eyes follow Hecate's and widen. "Justine?" she says softly. "Well, hello again."

Justine's lips lift as though in memory of a smile but don't quite make it to her eyes. "Calliope," she says lightly.

The woman who follows Calliope out of the van is dark skinned and languid. Tall, imperious, and commanding in her presence. If anyone looked like she should be wearing a red power suit, it is her. "What did the douchebag Defenders want this time?" this woman asks.

Artemis shakes her head. "What do they ever want, Persephone? To piss on us. To protect the interests of white men and their power."

Persephone scowls. "What do they know? They have to know something or they wouldn't be showing up trying to intimidate us."

"Perhaps they think we're going to show up with buckets of blood or chain ourselves naked to some fences after we knock down a few posts?" Hecate says.

Persephone smiles. "Oh, well, then. They'll be disappointed, won't they? You're not going to tell us who the firebrand is?" Once again, all eyes on Zoe.

"This," Hecate lays a hand on Zoe's shoulder, "might be a

magic key I'd been hoping for a year ago. But everything takes its own time."

Zoe shakes her head. Softly at first, then harder. *What does she mean "magic key," and why a year ago?*

"Do you believe in fate?" Hecate asks Zoe, with that laser-eyed look of intensity.

"No. I believe in free will," Zoe says, voice thick.

"In Greek mythology, the fates are goddesses who wove the tapestries of men's lives as they so desired."

Zoe shrugs. "In my memory, Greek myths are full of male gods doing what they want with women."

"Not in the story that we're writing."

"I didn't ask for this. I didn't come here of my own volition. Is that really what you want? Someone who's here by force?"

Persephone steps up then, pierces Zoe with her dark eyes. "My ancestors came to this country by force. Enslaved, in chains, those who made it alive. None of them wanted to be here. But here we are. Sometimes, you have no choice but to make do with where you are. You can try to make something better of it, though."

Words choke in Zoe's throat.

"We're going to need all the spares," Hecate says to Persephone, pointing at the flat, slashed tires.

"Idiots," Persephone mumbles, but she gets straight to work. With the help of the silent third woman with shaved head and serious green eyes—*not a woman, still a girl,* Zoe decides—they roll out three tires from the back of the van and throw down a jack. Persephone sets to hefting up the van. The silent one stands ready to hand over the first tire.

"You're going to need more than three," Justine says dryly.

Hecate glares. "Can you make a fourth tire magically appear? Three is what we've got—it'll get us out of here, is all that matters."

"Then what?" Justine asks.

Hecate stares at Justine as though she'd said something offensive.

Persephone works at getting the lug nuts off, muscles straining against them. There was a time when Zoe could change a tire single handedly. Had to do it almost weekly, her mother borrowing whatever car some hard-up junkie gave her as collateral. Now she simply makes a phone call and someone does it for her.

Persephone hands the hub cap to the silent one. "Ariadne, you want to do the honors?"

The silent girl's eyes go wide. She falters a moment then nods and takes up her place putting on the tire. Her petite size barely matches the gargantuan tire.

Persephone rises and dusts off her pants, then stalks toward Justine. "You should go home, Justine."

"No. I want to be useful," Justine rasps. "Use me. Please." Her face collapses in on itself.

Persephone shakes her head slightly. "I don't think you're ready, Justine."

Justine shakes her head, her eyes like dark pits, her hair flying madly around her face. "I brought you...her!" She points at Zoe. "And who else among you has as little to lose as me? You need me. I can help you."

Zoe looks away from the stark desperation in Justine's face, a strange pressure in her chest.

Persephone shoots a look at Hecate, something seeming to dawn on her. "Oh shit, this is her, isn't it? The Rasmussen wife."

Despite the gentle way Persephone speaks, Zoe bristles at being described thusly. She bites her lip until she tastes blood, but keeps her lips clamped tight. Much of her life has prepared her for keeping her mouth shut. The first part, when anyone could slink through her mother's door seeking a score. The second part, where she cannot speak poorly about her husband, his company, his stockholders.

"However, she doesn't seem terribly interested in the cause," Artemis says. She tugs at her braid. "It's a nice idea, but I don't think it's going to work. We don't have the right leverage."

Justine's face grows stoic again, just like when she came to Zoe's home this morning—like she's pulled on a mask.

"I have some leverage," Justine says softly.

She won't look at Zoe, and suddenly Zoe's fingers tingle. Then shake. She jams them into her pants pocket, but her body isn't satisfied with stillness; she sways a little.

"Justine, don't..." she warns. She'd told that secret to Justine in confidence, in the darkest hours of Justine's own grief. A shared awfulness to combat the loneliness.

"She killed a man," Justine says, point blank, matter-of-fact. "Zoe killed a man in cold blood. But because of her husband's money and power, they got her off, wiped it under the rug, sealed her record. Though I'd guess it could be dug up if you know what you're looking for."

"How dare you," Zoe says, her voice a low rumble.

Persephone puts a bracing hand on Zoe's shoulder. "Easy, killer."

Zoe wants to bite Persephone's fingers.

"You had no right to share that," Zoe spits. "No right."

Justine still won't look at her. "I imagine Phil Rasmussen has a vested interest in that information never going public. They both do. It's a house of cards."

Zoe's nausea returns when she sees all the women are... smiling. *Leverage*, Justine dared to call it.

Hecate angles herself toward Zoe, her fingers curling around the small pistol still in her hand. Artemis turns her way, too, knuckles going whiter as she clutches the strap of the rifle. Persephone's grip on her arm tightens the second Zoe decides to run for it. She brings an elbow up into Persephone's shoulder with a satisfying smack and breaks away.

Zoe spent her early years sizing up exits, keeping vigilant for the quickest, fastest, or least painful way out of a space. Familiar adrenaline fills her as she thrusts forward, aiming for the break in the trees just past Justine. Justine is the weakest link, her body and reflexes likely dulled from this year of little more than lying in bed. Indeed, the sheer surprise of Zoe rushing past her is enough to make her stumble to the side, where she tumbles into Hecate, who thuds to the ground. Zoe sized Hecate up earlier: *not a runner*. It is Persephone's powerful footsteps she suspects are bearing down on her. The seams of Zoe's pants split, the top button pops open, but she doesn't care. Twigs and rocks drive into her bare feet, but she is too purposeful to feel any pain. She lunges for a break in the trees and finds out too late it is more forest-like, denser, harder to run through. She has to pick her way, zigzagging left, right over, and around, breath heaving in her lungs. She vaguely feels the scrape of tree branches along her arms and face, but doesn't stop.

Until the report of a gun sprays wood from the trunk of a nearby tree. She drops to her knees and crawls, her vision going blurry, reality and memory overlapping. The roots of her hair prickling. His hand firm, lifting her hair like a leash, pulling it out in chunks as she screamed. She screamed, but nobody came. She screamed until her voice left her.

A shadow materializes into Persephone, and the last thing Zoe knows is the slam of something hard against her skull.

* * *

The last time someone had laid a hand on Zoe, she'd been nobody, just Phil's unsavory girlfriend, the one his parents kept trying to talk him out of dating.

"Calm down, just calm down," Phil had said through the phone. "I can't understand you."

"Help me, help me, helpmehelpmehelpme," she'd breathed, intoned like a mantra, a prayer. Left the phone hanging there like a witness, after she could say it no more.

How long she'd waited, bent and rocking, until she heard his voice again, "I'm here. It's okay." His body followed voice. He was really there.

"Just tell me what happened?"

But she couldn't tell. Could only point. Blood and bone and brain matter. Had to turn away and gag. Phil's soothing hands on her back. The feeling of water on her body, through her clothes, where Phil told her to stay. Warm until it ran cold. She tensed at the sound of another voice, but Phil reassured her gently. "We're going to make this disappear," he said. "Like it never happened."

Sometime later, he came again. She'd scooted back as far as she could get against the wall, but Phil hushed softly, "Hey, don't be scared." His words were soft, but still she cowered at the back of the shower. She couldn't feel her hands, only a slow steady throb between her eyes.

"It's going to be OK. I promise."

How could it ever be OK again?

CHAPTER SEVEN

Hannah's mom really hates surprises. No surprise birthday parties—they'd learned the hard way after Zoe fainted in front of 150 guests at her 40th—no sudden changes in plans, no springing a wild idea on her last minute, no matter how awesome. Hannah only hopes showing up several days earlier than she'd planned won't count as one of those unhappy surprises. Because the other surprise, about quitting school and flying to another continent for an indefinite amount of time, is definitely not going to sit so well, either. Maybe her mom will be proud, but the conflict it will cause with her dad won't do Hannah any favors.

No one is home, anyway. Well, not unless she counts Karina and the six or so other staff members that run the operational aspects of the estate and business. She parks in the back lot so no one will see her rental car when she arrives. Slips upstairs by the back stairwell, and closes herself into her musty room. She's only been off to the Art Institute of Chicago for one full year, but already the bedroom, with its bright colors and floral designs, feels smaller, its magazine cut-out collages, cliché. It is a happy room. So weird that the art she finds herself making now is none of those things. Shadows and hollows and interiors where dark things lurk. *Some psychologist would have a hey-day with me.*

And her parents will have an even bigger one when she tells them what she's come home to say. She practiced whispering it aloud: "I'm quitting school. I have this opportunity to travel to Kenya to focus on climate change."

She preempts her imagined retort, "Hey, you never thought art school was a real career option anyway."

Her imaginary father presses his lips tightly together and growls, "I didn't raise you to quit on things!"

She shakes her head. She doesn't want to argue with her father for fake or for real.

She sets down her duffle bag, and then goes looking for Karina or Jared, her father's assistant, to get some idea of a schedule. Maybe she'll swim some laps. Fix herself a meal. Watch a few hours of Satellite TV. Maybe she'll sneak into her dad's 30-seat movie theater and steal one of his Cuban cigars. She hasn't done those things in years, but coming home to an empty...well, she thinks, house *is never the right word, is it? Mansion? Villa?* Whatever, finding it empty always leaves her feeling strangely alone—lonely—like one of those orphans from a storybook whose wealthy relatives take them in after the sudden and mysterious death of their parents. Only a few of her private school friends can come close to understanding this level of wealth.

There is no sign of Jared in his office, but there is something strange on her dad's desk. It takes her a moment to realize it is just a newspaper. Scrawled in thick red pastels, *Planet Rapist.* She can't swallow for a minute.

"You look for something?" She whirls. Karina's Russian-accented voice, so sudden and sharp in the silence, scares her.

Karina is dressed in a light gray cashmere sweater dress, her graying hair pulled up into her signature top knot bun.

"Was just wondering when my parents might be home."

Karina has an odd, pinched look. She doesn't answer right away. "You have talked with your mother?"

Hannah shrugs. "No. A couple days ago. She isn't expecting me until Saturday."

Karina nods slightly, her eyes darting left to right.

"What's wrong, Kari?"

Karina purses her lips. "Is nothing, I'm sure."

Hannah looks pointedly at the paper on her father's desk. "Really? Nothing?"

Karina nods slightly. "Mister and Missus had fight. About that." She points at the paper.

"Ohhh." Hannah can imagine the scope of the conversation —her father blaming, her mother defensive.

"Her assistant, he says she no showed for EarthWorks awards ceremony."

Hannah takes a step backward. "What? She would never not show up to something like that."

Karina frowns. "She is so angry," Karina says. "With your father."

Her parents have been getting along worse and worse the past couple of years. But she can't imagine them divorcing; that seems like more work than either of them would want to bother putting in.

"She is very...emotional lately," Karina carries on.

"Hormones," Hannah says knowingly. "Still, should we be worried? That just seems so unlike her."

Karina looks down at her hands for a moment, then back up. "In my change of life, I almost killed a man...with my car."

Hannah widens her eyes. "Wow. Did he...is he OK?"

Karina lifts one side of her mouth in an amused smile. "He was...very fast runner."

Hannah doesn't know what to say for a moment. Then Karina laughs, a silly, girlish cackle that always jars with her serious face. Hannah can't help but laugh along.

"Well, I was going to surprise her..." Hannah says, but Karina shoots her sharp eyes, and Hannah holds up her hands. "I mean just by getting here early. I wasn't going to jump out and shout *boo* when she comes home. But I'll try calling her. OK? She'll pick up for me."

Karina's face softens into relief. "Yes, please tell me if you learn something."

Hannah nods. Her mother doesn't seem like the running-over-husbands or the running-away-from-responsibilities type, menopause or no, but disappearing is totally not like her. Hannah pulls out her phone and calls her mother. But it goes straight to voicemail.

So she plops down at her father's desk and turns on his computer. Her father has a carefully curated selection of alerts about his companies, most of it detailing promotions, awards and deals signed by the men he does business with. Today, however, the news section is pages long, and at the top, all of them about the same thing:

--100 *Companies Responsible for 70% of Harmful Emissions*

--*The* 100 *Companies Driving Climate Change*

--*To Halt Climate Change, Look No Further Than These* 100 *Companies*

She flinches, thinking about a close friend from high school, Willow—a name she gave herself when she decided she'd pursue environmental studies in college—asking her, "Does it bother you what your father's invested in? That your entire education is financed off the dirty money of Big Oil?"

Oh, she thinks about it all right. As a younger kid, she'd been unable to put a name to the dread that always overtook her at bedtime, keeping her sleepless and restless. A school counselor pointed out to her mother that Hannah was carrying the weight of the world on her shoulders, afraid of an apocalypse that she felt sure was imminent. And as a teen, she'd discovered that oil companies had known about climate change and suppressed crucial info. That was part of what had driven her mother to found EarthWorks. Because her father always had the same pat lines.

"The world doesn't run on good intentions, kiddo. We need energy to do everything you take for granted, and not just driving gas guzzling cars and flying airplanes. Hospitals run on energy. Schools need electricity. Transportation brings food to people in food deserts, you understand? Until we find a more profitable form of energy, the world's going to keep running on petroleum-based industry."

"We have solar, and wind and stuff," she remembered arguing, determined to back him into a corner, to admit he was wrong.

He'd only smiled at her in that way that made her want to kick him in the shins, all teeth, eyes a little heavy with pity for her stupidity. "Kid, they're just not practical."

"You mean there's too much profit in the other things!"

But that was all she had in her. Her father knew the limits of her knowledge, sensed her defeat. Actually patted her on the head, like a much smaller child. "It's good to start becoming aware. At your age, it's necessary, even. You'll learn that ideals don't make the world go round, however."

And now here she is, literally preparing to go round the world based on ideals. Based on Colin's ideals, at least. He is persuasive, and probably a better person than her, and...*hot*. She gets a little lost in the thought of his long dark hair, that shoulder-length surfer look, that stupid grin when he looks at her.

She scans the paper again, with its blood-like pastel crayon. *Did someone affiliated with EarthWorks do this? Is that why her mother isn't answering her calls?* She can imagine the things her father might have said to her mother—saying her organization was inciting terrorists. Can imagine her mother's proud face pinching with indignation. Maybe Zoe said a few choice things of her own before stalking off, vowing not to speak to him for several days. But not showing up for her own ceremony at her beloved non-profit? *Never.*

Hannah calls her mother's assistant, Bernard. He answers right away.

"Hannah! Sweetie, good to hear from you."

"Have you heard from her?" Hannah asks.

Bernard sucks in an audible breath. "She sent me a really weird text saying not to expect her at the ceremony and then, *nada.*" A hum of voices murmurs behind him. "It doesn't seem like her."

"I just flew home. Karina told me. That's totally out of character, right?"

"Your mother never no-shows."

"Do you think something's wrong, should we call the police or something?"

"Oh honey, I don't think it's anything like that. I'm sure she has a reason, but she has some serious answering to do."

"I don't know, Bernard. You don't think someone related to EarthWorks would...."

Bernard is silent again, only the faint din of voices behind him on the line for a moment. "Honey, I think you shouldn't worry, but do tell her to call me ASAP the minute you see her, will you?"

Hannah sighs and says she will, hangs up the phone, and

then finds she can't sit still. There isn't anything to unpack in her room. She pulls out her passport and runs her fingers across the gold lettering. There are a handful of stamps in it: Switzerland, France, Singapore, New Zealand, places she's been able to tag along for some of her dad's business trips, and a few family vacations where her parents usually drank too much and got loud with friends who had no children.

She texts Colin over WhatsApp: "So excited. 7 days and counting."

It's night in Kenya, so she doesn't expect a reply. She'll probably wake up to find a message from him.

She expects to hear the echo of her father's voice in some distant part of the house, and just the thought of it makes her hands sweat, her heart to race. But no matter where she seeks him out, he isn't there. She isn't asking anything of him, anyway, so there is nothing he can do to her. He can't cut her off or refuse to pay her tuition. Really, she has nothing to lose. Well, there is her future inheritance and her father's respect. She starts to lose her nerve. *Maybe I should just go, and let them know when I'm already in Kenya. Maybe I'm just setting myself up for unnecessary drama.*

She is so stuck in her head mulling this thought over when the sound of her dad's song programmed into her cell blurts out in the stillness, startling her. *Jeez, it's like he has a sixth sense for me.*

"Hi Dad," she says into her phone.

"My girl!" he says. "I thought you weren't coming home until Saturday?"

She looks around the room with an uncanny sense of being watched. "How did you know...oh, right, the door camera."

"What's up?" Her father has a laser sense for trouble. "Did something happen? What brings you home early?"

"Oh, um, no, I haven't. It's just..." *Spit it out, Hannah. Get it over with. Rip the bandaid off.*

"I'mgoingtoKenyawithColinandnotgoingbacktoartschool." She blurts it out so fast she is pretty sure it's unintelligible.

She can picture him raising that critical brow. "You're going where, what?"

She takes a deep breath. "Kenya. Colin's NGO. He wants me to work with them. I want to do something more important than I'm doing now. Art school is..."

"A waste of time. I told you that," he interrupts.

She isn't going to argue with him because at least he isn't yelling about Kenya. Yet.

"I'm not asking you for money, Dad."

She can picture his lips pressing into a tight line. "Good. You wouldn't be getting it. But I never thought you would stay in art school."

The words are so sharp and quick she almost doesn't feel the sting at first.

But he doesn't burst into an angry diatribe like she expected after that. "Let's go grab a meal and talk this over," he says instead, so calmly, so kindly, she stares at her phone. "I'm going to send you a car, okay? Just go hang out by the garage."

"I don't know, Dad, I could use a shower and..."

"Don't worry, kid. I'm not mad, okay? I'll meet you...."

She doesn't have a chance to answer him, though, because the window behind her shatters with a crack so loud she thinks it's her own skull breaking apart, and her father's office erupts in flames.

She screams and drops to a crouch, thrusting her hands protectively in front of her face. She can hear her father shouting on the other end of the line, "What is that?"

"Something just exploded. Fire," she cries, her brain spinning, her body flooded with adrenaline.

"What?" he says. "This is not..."

When she moves, shards of glass like vicious snow patter down all over her head and shoulders. She doesn't know how long she sits there, frozen in shock, until Karina bustles in, shrieking, and then her strong hands roar into the void. Karina is hustling her out of the office, down the hall. She hears other staffers shout, someone activates a fire extinguisher.

"Come," Karina urges, breathing heavily. They take the spiral staircase down into the parlor.

She is vaguely aware of other people around them—her father's staff has such high turnover she rarely recognizes anyone. The young men dashing around her have the soft faces of boys her own age, college boys—*how did they get these jobs?* She is vaguely aware she is in a filmy state of shock. But before Karina can get her outside, another young man barely older than her, dressed in khakis and a white polo shirt takes Hannah's arm and says, "I've got her."

Karina nods, and then the man pulls her toward the parking lot where her father's security team keeps a fleet of cars. He waves someone down—dressed in black like some wanna-be secret service officer. Hannah fixates on his piercing green eyes, which are all she can see—he's got a bandana around the lower half of his face. Smoke, she realizes. There's a lot of smoke in the air. He waves—his eyes friendly, his posture assertive.

"Come with me, it'll be okay," he says.

Hannah gulps back tears. This is just so wrong. They've never had a security breach in all her life. She thought that gate was as reliable as an armored car. *Where am I even going?*

"I'll take you to the Hilton. We'll get you a room. Everything'll be okay," he says.

Hannah moves to get into one of the big black Escalades parked in a row, but the man shakes his head. "I've already got one outside the gate. You'll see we can't drive easily out right now. Come on. It'll be okay. He takes her elbow, firmly, and guides her past the pool house. Past the rose gardens and the tennis courts.

She gasps when they reach the front gate. Huge black smudges mar twisted metal. Small embers of flame still scorch the ornamental grasses that are now a smoking mess.

The security officer taps on his Apple Watch, and then a van pulls up. Not a big black Escalade, but a nondescript white van. Before she has time to think about what is happening, he shoves her inside, right onto the floor of the van, and leaps in after her.

"What the hell..." she manages to get out before the security officer pushes her across the floor of the van, and trains a black gun on her. "Don't scream," is all he says.

Scream? She can't even breathe. She glances at the driver. A woman from the look of her long, blonde hair.

When she can catch her breath, she demands, "Who are you?"

The woman turns over her shoulder to glance at Hannah quickly. She catches only an aquiline nose, full lips. "Project Nemesis. You may have heard of us?"

"The...eco-terrorists?" Her mom's friend, Justine, had written several articles about them. They had engaged in some acts of sabotage to draw attention to environmental causes. But...*kidnapping?*

"Why me?"

"Leverage," the woman says, and the man laughs.

CHAPTER EIGHT

Zoe's head throbs hot then cold. She fears touching it, the world swimming into a blurry view. She feels misshapen, warped. But she forces her fingers to the bulging shape and finds it cold. Lumpy. Frozen peas, she guesses.

She blinks to find focus. After a few times, the room materializes clearly. A homey bedroom. Simple lamps with plain shades cast a woozy yellow light. Tapestries hang on one wall—hand woven, like something similar she once bought in Mexico.

She tries to sit up, swaying with dizziness.

"Give it a while," says a voice, vaguely familiar. "Here." A hand reaches out, puts something to her lips.

"Ginger. Chew it. It will help."

She turns toward the source of the proffered root, takes the fresh slice into her mouth and sucks. It burns, but steels her. The pale face and red hair of Artemis slide into view.

"We're sorry about that." She gestures at Zoe's head.

"You didn't seem sorry when you were shooting at me," she manages to say.

"Hecate wasn't shooting *at* you. Just trying to slow you

down. She's an excellent shot. If she'd wanted you dead, you'd be dead."

"What *do* you want with me?"

"We want a more just and civilized world," Artemis says.

"I'm not asking for your vision statement," Zoe says, groaning against the throb. "What do you think I can do for your...cause?" She tongues the burning disc of ginger to the other side of her mouth.

"You are in the unique position to have influence over a powerful player in the energy game. Someone who can influence policies. Regulations. We need that."

Zoe laughed, weakly. "To my husband, I'm just a wife. I'm not an influencer. I hold no sway."

"You hold more than you think."

Zoe tries again to sit up, dizziness subsiding. The bag of peas slides from her head. Her arms feel too weak to lift it back up. Artemis leans forward, and Zoe recoils into the headboard.

"I'm not going to hurt you, Zoe." She picks up the peas and presses them to Zoe's head.

"So, if I want to go home again, I have to make you some kind of deal or you'll blackmail me?"

Artemis doesn't answer. Zoe pushes her hand holding the peas away. "I'm fine, leave it," she says.

"You already believe in doing the right thing, Zoe. Earth-Works is cold, hard proof of that."

"Because my husband *tolerates* it."

"You're a powerful woman. You're not some kept pet of your husband's. You have agency, Zoe."

Zoe laughs, but it makes her head throb. "You don't know much about me. Just the parts of my resume that connect to my husband. You really don't know."

Artemis shifts slightly. Opens her palms. "So, tell us. Help us get to know you, and we can help each other."

Zoe pressed her lips together. "I doubt that," she says.

"You're afraid, but you don't have to be."

"What choice do I have?" Zoe says.

"I don't want you to help because you have no choice, Zoe. I want you to understand why."

Zoe closes her eyes, her head a carousel slowly spinning. Chews the ginger. "It won't matter," she says, then spits the ginger into her palm. "Whatever I do is going to tear my life down. My husband won't allow that... and how will it affect my daughter...?" She knows she is rambling. She opens her eyes. "Saying yes to you means burning down my own life."

Artemis stares at her, silently for a moment, then plucks the chewed piece of ginger from Zoe's palm and tosses it into a nearby trash can. "Sometimes that's what has to happen for the greater good."

"How?"

"How much do you know about your husband's company?"

"I don't sit in on business meetings if that's what you mean, but I know enough, and I get it—it's an industry that fights for its survival."

"So, you know about the company's lawsuits over toxic dumping...?"

"The company is reforming their practices," Zoe says, knowing she is spewing a hollow line.

"Mmm-hmmm," Artemis says dryly. "How about the lawsuits by multiple women and people of color for being passed over at promotions they earned, when less experienced white men got them instead?"

Zoe opens her mouth to defend this one, too, but can't, because in truth, she did not know.

"Or the current federal investigation for bribing key Republican congress members to pass legislation to bail out failing plants?"

"None of that has been proven," Zoe says, more firmly than she feels. The litany of her husband's company's crimes in one fell swoop is hard to hear.

"How about reducing and relaxing standards for renewable energy and energy efficiency programs. That one should hit rather close to home for EarthWorks, no?"

Zoe is good at not showing hurt or outrage, but that one lands hot between her ribs. She puts a hand to the lump on her head in the hopes Artemis might think that is the reason for her heavy breathing.

"What do you want from me?"

Artemis sighs, rubs her hands over her khaki clad thighs. "We want your husband's company to take active responsibility for some of its crimes, rather than paying off lawyers to settle it. But I'll let Hecate fill you in on the rest."

Artemis stands up and holds out a hand. "Come on, let's go eat."

Zoe refuses Artemis's hand but rises, unsteadily, to her own feet. Stomach hollow, temples throbbing, she follows.

Artemis draws her into a small, conjoined dining room/living room in a humble, bare bones little house. A group of ten or so women sit eating at a long table over bowls of food. The scents travel from her nose to her stomach in a punch of sudden hunger. She recognizes imperious Hecate and regal Persephone and the slight, silent, bald-headed one from earlier —*Ariadne?* The rest are new faces. As she approaches, some women switch from English to Spanish, perhaps to keep her unknowing. The faces stare up at her curiously. A mix of ages and ethnicities.

Justine sits by herself in a beat-up easy chair, hands cupped around a mug, staring out the window. She doesn't appear to register Zoe's presence. A good thing, with that tension between them.

"Sit, eat," Hecate waves her over with startling nonchalance, as though she did not shoot at her hours before. Persephone, too, smiles at her, as though she didn't chase her down. Leave it to women to attempt to murder each other one moment, and then break bread the next.

"We're sorry for earlier," Hecate says, waving her over. "Sit, sit, please. You must be starving."

Zoe eyes the seat Hecate proffers. Persephone glances at her, eyes homing in on the lump that is half of her forehead now. To her credit, she winces. "That looks painful," Persephone says.

Zoe frowns. "You think?"

Persephone's smile is a slash of white; she traces her long fingers over her own forehead. "You should have seen the one Hecate gave *me* some years ago."

Hecate barks a laugh. "Come on now, she's going to get the wrong idea. We're not a fight club. We leave that to the men."

The women around the table laugh. Zoe slides into the chair beside Hecate.

Another woman, all black ringlets and eyes, with a scar that travels from chin to eyebrow, ladles beans and rice onto her plate. She slaps down a warm tortilla, its sensuous scent filling Zoe's nose. She douses it all in salsa heavy with cilantro, squeezes on some lime. Zoe closes her eyes, inhales. Once she's taken her first bite her body relaxes a bit, muscles softening out of fight-or-flight, heartbeat slowing to normal.

"I gave her a bit of the rundown," Artemis says. "About Rasmussen Energy and its laundry list of bad behavior."

"Did you mention the part about its need for a change in leadership? Starting with the entire C-Suite?" Hecate asks.

Zoe suddenly can't swallow her bite. She reaches for a napkin and spits her mouthful into it.

"Hey!" Ariadne, green eyes almost glowing in the light, points at her. "We don't waste food. You eat that."

Zoe flushes, filled with nervous laughter, but none of the women are smiling. She puts her face back into the napkin, tries not to gag on the partially chewed food. Rice sticks in her throat, and she coughs so violently it brings tears to her eyes.

When she can breathe again, she glares at Hecate.

"You want Phil to step down from his own company?" Zoe laughs. "You're mad."

"We've been called much worse," Hecate says.

"How the hell do you think I will convince him to do that? He'll think I've lost my mind. Or tell me to go get medication."

"That's the worst case scenario, Zoe? He laughs at you while you continue to live a life of wealth and power? How terrible for you," Hecate says.

From across the room Justine scoffs. "You aren't going to get anywhere by talking," she says.

The women's heads pivot toward Justine. She sits with arms splayed, gaunt and dark-eyed, like a battle-hardened warrior Queen.

"*You* are the ones who told me that men don't listen to women talk. *You* are the ones who showed me the power of action. What's stopping you now?" Justine spits.

Hecate narrows her gaze sharply on Justine. "We have to also keep our eyes on our goals. In this case, negotiation might get us there sooner."

Zoe shakes her head. *The last thing this group of wild women needs is a rousing speech.* "I'll do it. I'll talk to him. I have no idea what to say but I'll...try."

Justine shakes her head, disgust lacing her features tightly together. "Talk talk talk."

Hecate nods, eyes far away. "We'll help you craft the right words," she says to Zoe.

The right words. What could those possibly be? She just wants to go home. Go back to normal.

Hecate turns. "Since we last met, Justine, we've eased off our little acts of sabotage. We realize that all it does is organize forces against us. We've been spending our energy lifting up the downtrodden now, trying to shift the seats of power."

"What about your plan for the power plant that those Nazis are talking about?" Justine insists.

Hecate shakes her head. Zoe thinks she looks sad. "Just because we've stopped all that doesn't mean we want anyone to *know*. We have a reputation to uphold. A little anxiety, a little intimidation is good."

Justine groans. "Zoe's husband's company has a stake in that plant. They just had their groundbreaking."

"Enough!" Hecate thunders, slamming a hand down on the table, rattling mugs of freshly poured tea, which slosh out their contents. The entire room grows quiet. "You're here by our good graces. And if you want to do good work, then get back to your job, Justine. Maybe Zoe can dig up the dirt. Maybe you can write about it."

Justine curls in on herself, crackling with a malevolent energy, an explosion in the making. "I don't work for the newspaper anymore."

"And that's a damn shame," Hecate says. "But I'm pretty sure you could remedy that if you wanted to."

Justine simmers in what looks like unspoken fury to Zoe, but doesn't reply.

* * *

After the meal, Zoe helps the women clear the table, scrape food into containers, wash the dishes. Her own hands embarrass her, lotion-smooth, fresh French manicure. Not a single woman has fingernails longer than a sliver. No nail polish. One woman is even missing her middle finger altogether.

When was the last time she washed her own dishes? Staff sees to that. There was a time, in the decades before Phil, when she had to peel crusted dishes off sticky surfaces. Soak dried and rotten bits of food from their interiors. Kill roaches and hold back ant armies all by herself.

* * *

As she is falling to sleep that night, a thought pulses in the darkness. *Hannah.* Her daughter is coming home soon. Hopefully all this bullshit will be done by then.

She sleeps surprisingly deeply that night, and wakes refreshed, despite the throb in her temple.

She keeps expecting a dark turn, to be locked in a shed, tied to a tree, tortured for information. Instead, they invite her to eat a savory breakfast of eggs and sauteed vegetables.

"Why is my husband's company the sole focus of your energies?" Zoe asks in a lull.

Hecate stares at her with something that almost looks like respect. "Persephone, tell us why you joined Nemesis?"

Persephone raises one elegant brow and sets down her fork. "My sister worked for your husband's company for ten years. One of the first and only Black women they hired. There are fewer than five Black employees, by the way, in a company of several hundred. Did you know that?"

Zoe shakes her head, hot with shame.

"She watched promotions come and go. Had it out with her boss, HR, was continually told that promotions went to those who earned them. Then a man *she* hired was promoted over her after only a year. Then *that* man became her manager. And he had a nasty habit of making both racial and sexual slurs out of earshot of anyone who could intervene. He made her job a living hell, but she was too stubborn to quit. HR needed proof to follow-up, and all they had to go on was his word versus hers. I told her no job was worth that abuse, but she was determined to prove a point."

A hush has fallen while Persephone talks. Zoe realizes she is holding her breath.

"One night, her manager came to her house. Nobody knows what was said between them." Persephone stopped a moment, swallowed hard. "The last text I got from her was simply, 'Jim is here. WTF.'" The muscles at Persephone's jaw flexed. "She died by suicide the next day."

Hecate does not pause, does not allow time for Zoe to process this horrible story, or what it all means. She simply says, "Artemis?"

Artemis is mid-bite. She takes an uncomfortably long time to chew and swallow.

"Cancer," Artemis says, almost cheerfully. "My parents and my brother. Their well water was being slowly infiltrated with toxic chemicals from illegal Rasmussen dumping. They all died within two years of each other."

"Would you like to hear more?" Hecate asks.

Zoe is sick to her stomach. She looks at her hands and shakes her head. When she finally looks up, she catches Justine staring at her.

* * *

Hours later, Hecate's voice rises, sharp and angry from the other room. "Fuck!"

Zoe moves toward the living room, then stops. *Should I go?* Zoe hangs back in the doorway, where she can hear but not see.

"Are you sure?" Hecate again.

The blonde named Calliope has returned. "I'm sure. Got it off the police scanner."

Hecate slaps a palm down loudly on some piece of furniture. She swears in loud Spanish.

As if they sense her eavesdropping, Hecate and Artemis both turn toward Zoe at the same time.

A shiver of dread passes through her. "What?"

"Someone broke into your estate. An explosive took out your gate. A Molotov cocktail went into your husband's home office."

"What? Is anyone hurt?" Zoe's heart races.

"No injuries reported. But it sounds as though someone might have been...taken hostage," Calliope answers.

Zoe sinks into the nearest chair. "Not Karina, please." She won't be so sad for one of the soft-cheeked young men her husband rotates in and out—lackeys from prep schools whose main goal in life is to be rich.

"They're pinning it on us," Calliope says, low. "They put out a statement already!"

"What the fuck?" Persephone is on her feet now, pacing the room. "Those small brained little piles of puke."

Zoe's brain can't process the information. Who has been taken hostage? Is this tied to that defaced newspaper? A stab of panic. *Please say it isn't someone connected to EarthWorks.*

"Who...did this?"

Hecate grinds her teeth together. "Those pieces of shit who followed us to the woods yesterday. Defenders of Freedom. They must have figured out who you are, all right, and they are using it against us. They're pinning this on us."

Zoe feels like she'll puke up her food. She braces herself as though she'll fall, though she's sitting down.

A crackling sound rents the sudden stillness, voices

sounding tinny. Zoe looks up. Sees that Calliope still holds the police scanner.

"Witness says hostage is a girl. Might be the daughter."

Every head in the room whips to Zoe.

"Hannah? She isn't supposed to be home yet." Zoe's voice sounds so small.

There is some muttering among the women that Zoe can't make sense of, her mind padded with shock. Then Persephone brings forth an iPad and they call up a news channel, propping it up on the table where all can see.

There, holding court as he does so well, stands Phil behind a podium, flanked by police.

"Two hours ago, my home was bombed, and my daughter was taken hostage," Phil begins, his voice effectively thick with emotion. Zoe just stares, only realizing she is sagging into the woman next to her when strong arms help her back to sitting.

"My wife also appears to be missing. We have good reason to believe we know who did this. They call themselves Project Nemesis..."

A collective gasp of fury goes up through the room around Zoe.

Phil continues, laying the emotion on thick. "They have targeted my company in the past, causing us millions of dollars in damage. And now they've gone after my *family*. They've gone after the head of an environmental non-profit, when they claim that as their cause. They will stop at nothing to get to me."

He pauses to wipe sweat off his brow. Zoe has a reflexive urge to comfort him, assure him all will be okay as she's learned to do in thirty years of being Phil Rasmussen's wife. But just a beat later she wants to throttle him. He has no proof this was Nemesis.

"They will not get away with this. We are offering a reward

of $100,000 for any information on the whereabouts of any of the members of the terrorist organization known as Project Nemesis," Phil concluded.

Persephone closes the window and all eyes turn to Zoe.

"What the fuck just happened?" Zoe says.

"Your husband did what he does best," Hecate says, eyes hard and narrow. "Threw us under his big, energy-guzzling bus."

CHAPTER NINE

The women cluster around Artemis and Calliope, murmuring, gesturing, talking. Justine's legs shake. She can't stay sitting here any longer. She needs to walk, to run, to do something.

"They don't get to do that," Justine hears herself saying. "They don't get to threaten us. They don't get to *use* us like that."

Hecate's gaze is a lance, piercing her. She can read the silent thought again: *You're not one of us, not yet.* But Hecate isn't frowning at her for once. "You're right."

Now Zoe lifts her head. "Not us. *Me!* They have *my...* daughter." Her voice is a rasp, as though she is choking back screams. "It can't be her. She isn't coming home until Saturday. Damn it, Justine, I should have been there."

"They're big babies," Persephone says. "All talk."

"They're not all talk," Justine says, rising. "*They* took action. While we sat around here and did nothing, *they* did something."

Zoe's brows pinch together. "If Hannah isn't supposed to

be home yet, then how could they have known she's there. Why take *her*?"

Hecate sighs. "Honey, for an intelligent woman you sure are stupid sometimes."

Zoe whirls on her. "Excuse me?"

"Let me guess...your daughter and you, you look alike? Those idiots can barely tell their mouths from their assholes. I have no doubt that Hannah is close enough."

"You're saying they meant to take...me?"

"Lucky you. Your husband has inspired the white nationalists," Justine says. Zoe glares at her, but Justine presses on. "He has had a vendetta against Nemesis, and frankly many environmental groups, for years, publicly. You said it yourself, he all but accused you of being complicit because of your passionate EarthWorks supporters," Justine nearly shouted. "Your husband is happy to jump on any opportunity to disparage Nemesis."

Zoe presses fingers to her temples, as though trying to understand.

"So, why are we just sitting here?" Justine demands.

"Justine," Hecate says warningly.

"Activate the flock," Hecate says to Persephone. "All birds in the sky, got it?"

Persephone nods and strides out of the room.

To Justine, Hecate says, "Justine, here's your first task. Take her home." She points to Zoe.

Zoe lifts her head, eyes wet, relief showing on her face.

"What?" Justine asks, heavy with disappointment.

"We're going to help her get her daughter back in one piece, and she's going to help us work on getting information we need. And then *you* are going to do something with that information."

"But what if she..." Justine starts.

"She's not running anywhere," Hecate sneers. "She lives in a gilded cage. She can't leave. Plus, we all know her dirty little secret now, right?"

Hecate's words appear to land like a punch, given Zoe's falling expression.

"What am I going to tell my husband, the police?" Zoe asks softly, almost to herself.

"You took a couple days to cool off, remember? You're *hormonal*. You shut off your technology. You knew your assistant had the ceremony under control," Hecate says, as though reciting instructions. "You didn't hear about the bombing or your daughter until you emerged from the woods or wherever you went off to clear your head."

"You can get Hannah back...safely?" Zoe asks.

Something catches inside Justine at Zoe's words. She can almost feel small, phantom hands on her face.

* * *

"No go, Mommy." Willa's insistent voice.

"I have to, sweetie," Justine had knelt down, tried to will patience into her legs. Tried not to kiss and run. "Mommy has important work to do." Could almost hear the sound of Nate's eyes rolling up in his head.

"'Tine, just try to keep time in mind," he'd said, swooping in, scooping up the little girl who giggled and nuzzled against her father's neck. The perfect father. Justine had loathed him for that at times, for the ways it made her own mothering seem fractured and messy. She'd resented his ability to always show up, "make time," be patient, while she'd be dragging herself through a sleep-deprived morning, snapping and grumbling, and always desperate to get out the door, to inhabit herself, alone, again.

And then she'd gotten that wish, if it had been a wish, one of those unconscious, unspoken thoughts you should never put out to the universe, to be alone more. To not be needed so much.

* * *

Suddenly cool hands are on the back of Justine's neck, soothing words muttered in her ear. For half a beat she thinks it is Zoe again, come to find her in the shuttered bedroom, with sweet smelling essential oils and soup. Justine sits up with a gasp, a half circle of women squatting before her, expectant. Zoe stands across the room, looking dead-eyed and pale, which matches how Justine feels inside. She nearly fainted.

"You need to eat," Hecate says, peering down with her beautifully weathered face and hazel eyes.

Justine just shrugs, as if to say, "what is the point?" Death has already marked her.

"Warriors need strength," Hecate says. "Warriors need energy and fuel if they are going to get shit done, right *mi hija?*"

Justine knows she is being patronized, but Hecate could just as easily dump her back on the side of the road for any reason. She has to make herself valuable, worthy.

"OK."

With the wave of Hecate's hand toward one of the other women, food is unwrapped and unpacked from the kitchen. Then warmed and delivered to her in a steaming little burrito. The scent turns her stomach. Justine eats while trying not to inhale. She eats to sustain herself because she doesn't want to enjoy it. Days for sensual pleasures are behind her.

"Persephone and Artemis will take you back to your car, Justine. And you'll drive Mrs. Rasmussen home."

Zoe's head snaps toward them at the sound of her last name, eyes narrowing.

"How will you keep in touch with me?" Zoe asks, her voice tight. "How will I know that you're helping Hannah?"

Hecate stands up and hands her an older smartphone. "The app on there is called Signal. There's already a contact in there. 'Carol.'" She makes air quotes with her fingers. "You use that to communicate with us. "You keep it on you at all times."

* * *

Hecate insists both Justine and Zoe be blindfolded again as they leave the safe house and make their way back to Justine's car. Justine likes the feeling of moving through darkness; it soothes something inside her. There's a strange freedom in no longer worrying or wondering or waiting. No fear that if you look away too long, the worst might happen. It has already, and that's where she lives now, inside the cold hollow of the worst that can happen.

Zoe fidgets at her side, sighs heavily, cracks her knuckles.

When at last the van screeches to a stop, Hecate says, "You can remove your blindfolds."

It's that perfect time of evening where night creeps like gray velvet over the horizon, drawing a shroud around them.

Hecate hands Justine a pager. "We'll let you know when it's time to act, Justine." She turns to Zoe. "As for you, you cooperate with the police about your daughter. You do not speak a word about what has happened to you over the past 48 hours. You tell them you lost your shit. You went for a wilderness vision quest, whatever rich white ladies do under pressure. You fell and hit your head. You did it and you are sorry you scared everyone. And meanwhile, you look for information that can help...convince your husband that a change in leadership is needed."

"Don't you think it's suspicious I disappeared right before my daughter has been..." Zoe chokes back a cry. "What if Phil makes something of me going off with Justine? He knows she wrote about you. He's already so paranoid about anything to do with my work, and anyone affiliated with it."

Hecate shakes her head slightly. "Correlation is not causation, got it? And let's be real. You're the wife of one of the wealthiest men in the country—do you think they're going to believe that *you* arranged to work with a, as they see us, terrorist group, to kidnap your own daughter? That *you're* really a radical?"

Justine isn't sure, but it looks like hurt flashes across Zoe's eyes.

Zoe shakes her head. "Just *find* her."

"Don't worry," Hecate says. She takes Zoe by the shoulders and squeezes her. "Be something more, my dear. Think bigger than yourself, okay? You can do some real good in the world."

Zoe nods tightly.

"Actually, don't take her home," Persephone says suddenly, before Zoe gets into the passenger side of Justine's car.

Even Hecate stares at her.

"Take her to the emergency room nearest her house," Persephone says.

Justine cuts a sharp glance at Persephone, while Zoe absently rubs the lump on her head.

"It's the best cover story."

Zoe nods, to Justine's surprise, seeming to think out loud. "I hiked by myself in a menopausal snit. I fell, knocked myself out, am probably concussed. Got confused."

"Yes, good. Good," Persephone approves.

Then the women wave them off, and Justine gets back into

her car. It feels like months ago, not two days, that she'd first set out with intent to bring Zoe to Nemesis, to fulfill that suggestion of theirs from a year before. It's shame that washes over her now when she thinks of that rifle in her hands, pointed at her friend. How she'd demanded Zoe get in the car. At the moment, it had felt urgent, necessary. Now, she has no rifle. Zoe isn't afraid of her anymore. Anxiety hums beneath Justine's skin. She's done a terrible thing, and now things are spinning out of control. If the Defenders didn't come upon them in the clearing, would they have bombed the Rasmussen estate, would Hannah have been kidnapped?

Justine extracts the keys from the wheel well where she stashed them, then slides slowly into the driver's seat. She puts the keys into the ignition, but does not turn it on, angles herself toward Zoe to say something like an apology.

Zoe holds up a hand. "Don't." Then she closes her eyes, hunches deeper into the sweater Hecate gave her to replace her damaged suit jacket, and leans against the side of the door as if going to sleep.

"I don't know what I was thinking," Justine mutters.

Zoe lances her with a sudden gaze. "You weren't fucking thinking. Because of you, my daughter is in danger!"

Justine could break apart into shards, crumble under the weight of Zoe's gaze.

"I'm sorr—"

"Don't!"

The hospital soon looms into view. Zoe doesn't even wait for Justine to come to a complete stop, just snaps open her door and leaps out, stumbling slightly as the car continues to coast, then slams it hard again.

Justine lingers, watching Zoe trudge into the ER. When she is out of sight, fatigue slams into her, her foot on the gas pedal a thousand tons. She can't go home. If not for the weight of the pager in her pocket like an iron anvil, tethering her to earth, she might slip away entirely. She misses the days she could come home tired and collapse onto the couch for a foot rub and a debrief with Nate. She misses their easy banter before, but after...her mouth grew heavy trying to make conversation. Words felt like weights that took every bit of energy. In the easy angles of his face, she saw too much Willa. His very presence was a reminder of what they'd lost. His disappointment that she wouldn't go to therapy, a palpable entity. And so he'd agreed to move out. To give her space. To give her time. For what, she didn't—doesn't—know. Nothing is ever going to return to how it was. There is no going back.

Now, she takes deep steadying breaths. Remembers that she packed her computer and phone in the trunk. Orients herself. Retrieving the phone, she searches for the nearest Motel 6. She has to drive to the next city over, since one so well-to-do apparently can't be bothered to offer a cheap night.

Mid-week in October, she finds a room with no problem and ignores the feral gaze of a man smoking in front of the next room. She buys a granola bar from the vending machine because Hecate was right: Warrior women need fuel. Even if she is no warrior, nothing more than a limping grunt, a tool that can be useful before the end of its time.

The room is cold. The sheets starched to stiffness. It holds nothing more than worn wooden furniture and a TV.

She sets up her computer, uses her phone as an internet hotspot, and logs on.

She's written about them before, but it's been some years. This west-coast counterpart has stayed just on this side of trouble, lining up at Black Lives Matters marches in their white t-shirts and baseball caps like something giant birds shat upon the earth, but nothing to make news about.

She takes a steadying breath before making her way to the

places that internet trolls called home, a place she's spent some time years before for a story. *Storm of Pride. White is Right.* Websites that made her feel dirty just typing their URLs into her browser. Reddit. 8Chan. Deeper in, if you know where to look, links lead to chat rooms with sub rooms.

She searches for keywords:

Project nemesis

Eco terrorist

Greek goddesses

Her first round of searches brings up nothing useful, and she turns on the TV and zones out to a nature show, where lithe large cats hunt for prey in a dusty tundra. *What am I even thinking? I am useless.* Her one big gambit to bring Zoe to Nemesis landed with the grace of a Condor. In truth, she never really had a plan, just a hope, that something about Nemesis would free her from this purposeless place, this lethargy that borders on something much worse. When those men found them in the wooded clearing, those bearded faces bearing down on them behind cold eyes, she was genuinely afraid. In over her head. *Who wants to fuck you dykes?* She remembered the one called Spencer saying, and it gives her an idea.

She types: *environmental dykes, dykes, Greek dykes* and a page of chat loaded to life before her eyes.

Subject line: **Operation Secure the Future**

Before she can follow the thread deeper, her phone buzzes, startling her. It rarely rings anymore, except for telemarketers. The caller ID tells her it's Nate. It's like he has a sixth sense for when she's about to dig into something. One part of her wants to answer. But what will they talk about? He'll ask the same questions: "How are you doing? Do you need anything? Do you want to have dinner?" And she'll feel guilty for lying. Guilty that there's nothing she needs from him, that she doesn't want to have dinner. She still loves him, but the sight of him is an agony.

"How long are you going to avoid me? Avoid her memory?" He'd asked one of the last times he called. And she had hung up. There was no answer. Not one he would like. Not one she was proud of.

She does not pick up.

Instead, she returns to her laptop screen.

Opportunity to teach some perspective to some enviro-dykes. Who's in?

Men (or so she assumes) with names like WhiteKnight45 and BloodNHonur, Europa88, jumped on the bandwagon quickly.

It takes two straight hours of scanning through lines of self-congratulating promises of vigilante justice before she finds what she is looking for: a location that sounds like a part of town she really doesn't want to visit. One night of sleep, and she'll see what she can find. One way or the other, she'll prove herself valuable to Nemesis again.

CHAPTER TEN

Hannah's had nightmares like this many times. Someone grabbing her. Always in black. Faceless. Sometimes he had a gun, sometimes just his tight grip on her wrist or shoulder. In every dream, the certainty that it is really real this time slowly gives way as a gun turns to something almost laughable: a drumstick, a tree branch, an elephant trunk. There is always that sweet moment of relief when the dreaming mind takes over, assuring her this is just a fabrication and she'll awake into freedom.

She keeps waiting for that to happen now, but it won't, because this scene is not hazy at the edges the way a dream is. Still, she hopes that her wrists, now bound in a plastic zip tie, will break apart to find it merely a shoelace, a rubber band.

The people keeping watch over her all wear cloth gaiters draped around their faces, red, like an army of superheroes gone bad. There are five women. All of them blonde, every single one, none of them naturally. A long blonde braid or a blonde updo or a blonde bun poking out of each beanie.

She's been shoved to the back of a garage, made to sit on a

greasy couch. She figures that she is in a former mechanic's shop from the smell of oil and the car jacks and tools scattered haphazardly, like workers simply threw down their tools in a hurry before this group arrived with her.

"Just do what we say and nobody will hurt you," says the man with the beard, the man she'd thought was security, who led her into the van. He sounds like a villain in a bad TV show.

She can't stop her shallow breathing that makes her head spin a little. Her heart thunders in her chest and sweat gathers between every crevice.

This has something to do with her father. Someone wants something from him. She can't stop thinking about the red-smeared newspaper. *Planet Rapist.*

"Hey, you need to use the bathroom?" One of the blondes materializes before her, kneels down.

She shakes her head. "I want to go home."

The woman's blue eyes crinkle. *Sympathy? Annoyance?*

"Who are you?" Hannah asks.

The woman smiles. "I thought he told you. We're Project Nemesis. Maybe you've heard of us?"

Hannah frowns. She's heard of them. Mainly from her dad's rants about them. He calls them terrorists. Her mom's friend Justine wrote about them...they have a message about democratizing energy or something, holding big energy corporations accountable.

"I pictured you differently," Hannah says.

The woman frowns.

"Didn't expect you to have highlights." She waves to the woman's freshly streaked hair.

The woman's eyes narrow. "Don't believe the hype," she says.

Hannah scans the room for possible exits.

"You know what, I do have to pee," she adds as Blonde Number 5 starts to walk away.

The woman sighs, but helps Hannah up and leads her to a cramped bathroom that is little more than a closet. Hannah grimaces at the stained toilet bowl, the smell of urine strong in the room. She holds up her bound arms. "I can't wipe like this." The woman sighs heavily, pulls out a pocket knife—*pink!?*—from her crisp new khakis and cuts open the zip-tie handcuffs.

Hannah shuts the door. There is no window big enough to escape through, so she just sits down on the closed toilet lid and puts her face in her hands, trying to think. *Are they going to try and ransom me to Dad? What do they want?* She wishes she could get a message to someone, anyone. *If only Colin was here.*

She doesn't know how long she sits in there when three sharp raps against the door startle her out of thought. The door is flung open. It's the man who escorted her out of her home, glaring down at her. He doesn't seem to realize his gaiter has slipped and she can see almost the entire top of his face.

"Just finished peeing," she says, holding up her hands as though to show she hasn't grabbed the plunger as a weapon.

The man scowls at Blonde No. 5. "I told you to keep eyes on her at all times."

Blonde No. 5 shakes her head. "I'm not going to watch her pee, for fuck's sake. And look—she can't get out that teeny little window." She points over Hannah's head.

He glares, then reaches in and grasps Hannah by the wrist, hard. Despite her desire to stay stoic, she squeals at the pain of the small bones grinding together. He drags her back to her spot on the couch.

"We are not fucking around here, lady," he says harshly, and though some part of her has the urge to laugh at him, she quickly catches sight of the butt of a gun poking out the top of his pants and shuts her mouth.

"What do you want?" Hannah asks. "Money? My dad's got plenty of that."

The man smirks, shakes his head. "We don't need your daddy's money."

For the first time Hannah feels a stab of true fear. If they don't want money, what could they possibly want with her?

CHAPTER ELEVEN

Time passes for Zoe in slashes and pulses, like strobe lighting. *Slash*: a nurse runs stinging solution over abraded skin. *Pulse*: a protein bar in her hand she can't eat. *Slash*: A phone in her hand, ringing Phil. *Pulse*: Someone is there for her. Minutes or hours she doesn't know. Can't think much past the lament in her head: *HannahHannahHannah.* *Let her be okay.* No one to pray to, she has a void of religious faith. Her Jewish grandparents are just a whisper of memory. She thinks about the higher power of her mother's NA meetings. *Our father, who art in heaven...* That will have to do.

Phil doesn't even come in person. He sends his fucking driver, Fernando. She is happy to see Fernando's warm face, bald head hidden under a little fedora, but, *really? Phil can't even be bothered?*

"Are you badly hurt?" Fernando asks, wringing his hands, a gesture sweet, almost childlike. He touches the spot on her forehead beside the big white bandage pasted there.

"A little concussion," she assures him.

"I just have to take it easy." Fernando holds out a Peet's mocha and her phone.

So many missed calls.

The ones from Hannah on Thursday make her stomach clench. Those from her assistant Bernard, and Richard, the VP of EarthWorks, and his assistant, and Phil, and...Hannah, her sweet words prick tears to the back of Zoe's eyes.

Mama, I came home early, don't be mad.

Mama, why aren't you picking up?

She's sick with shame. There was a time not so long ago that Hannah told her everything, when they talked every day. Because she'd refused to be the hands-off mother who let her child be raised by a nanny. It was normal for mothers and daughters to separate when they went off to college. So why does it bother her so much that Hannah didn't tell her in advance that she was coming home? If she'd known, she could have been there, when—her head hurts, and she presses her fingers to her temples, trying to breathe through the throbbing.

Only when they make it home, when she sees the twisted metal of the exploded gate, the police tape, the security car parked out front, does it all become real to her. *Did those Defender assholes really do this? For what? To make Nemesis look bad? Does Phil really represent something they admire?* That makes her queasy.

A security guard halts Fernando, makes Zoe get out and walk inside with him.

"I understand you've had an accident," the guard says. He is short, stocky, face crusted with a five o'clock shadow that probably grew back too soon.

"I had klutzy feet," she says evenly.

He only says, "Detectives are waiting inside with your husband. They'll want to ask you some questions."

She surprises herself as she reaches out and grasps the officer's arm. "Does anyone know anything about my daughter?"

"I'm not the one to ask, Ma'am. You can talk to the detectives."

She is "Ma'am" again. Like armor over something tender and vulnerable that awakened there in that house full of women. She tries to steady her wobbly legs.

The officer leads them downstairs, to the study Phil uses as a meeting space, with a long mahogany table, fancy caned chairs, and modern art. For a moment the room looks alien, as though she has been brought to a place she doesn't live.

Two detectives, Phil, and Karina are seated there like a panel of judges about to sentence her. Karina's eyebrows shoot heavenward with relief at the sight of Zoe. She stands, but the detective waves her down. Phil blinks up at Zoe, eyes roving straight to the bandage on her forehead.

Zoe waits for Phil to say something. His face is hard, but his eyes are moist, aggrieved. She can't tell if any of that is for her, or if he, too, can only worry about Hannah. Phil opens his mouth, but the angular, thin detective with a pronounced cleft chin speaks first.

"Mrs. Rasmussen, please sit. I'm Detective Steve Hollohan. This is Detective Ruth Meyers."

From Zoe to Ma'am to Phil's wife. Mrs. Rasmussen, wife of the Energy Executive, suddenly feels like a wire around her neck.

"Your daughter..." Hollohan begins.

"Has been kidnapped, I know," she finishes.

Hollohan's eyes narrowed on her. "How do you know?"

She remembers her phone. *Zoe where are you? Hannah's gone...missing. I'm really fucking worried.*

"My assistant, he texted me."

Hollohan's mouth compresses just slightly. "Your husband

says you've been...missing for the last day and a half. Can you tell us where you went? What happened to your head?"

Zoe looks at Phil briefly but can't read the emotion there. She passes a hand over the gauze at her head. Tries to remember what Nemesis asked of her. Her heart pounds in her chest.

"My husband and I had a fight a couple of days ago."

"About what?"

Phil looks away, grinds his jaw.

"Someone wrote some nasty things on a newspaper, and threw it over our gates..."

Hollohan nods as though he knows what she's talking about.

How to describe our fight without making Phil look like an asshole?

"I run an environmental non-profit. Our supporters can be zealous. My husband is in the energy business. Sometimes these things are at odds."

The female detective shoots Phil a loaded glance that makes Zoe want to laugh.

"He might have suggested that my organization is to blame for the newspaper."

"I see," Hollohan says. "And because of that you left for... two days?"

Phil's smug and angry gaze spears her. Zoe looks at her hands. Her manicure is chipped on two nails and dirt lines two fingernails. She clutches that hand in the other.

Hecate's words ring in her mind. *There's no better soldier for a cause than a woman in the change of life.* "I've been going through some changes," she says. "Hormonal changes," she adds quickly. "Sometimes my feelings are erratic. I can behave...impulsively."

Detective Meyers raises an eyebrow. "So, you behaved...

impulsively...when you disappeared without a word to your assistant, your husband, or your estate manager?"

Zoe exhales hard, puts her head in her hands, trying to paint a picture of regret. "I did. I was angry. I was just...I don't know, fed up. So I took off."

"Without your car or your phone?"

"When you're running off in a fit of pique you don't go hunt down the chauffeur, you know?"

Meyers definitely smiles that time. Zoe isn't sure if the woman is on her side or merely entertained at her expense.

"So..."

"I called a friend to pick me up. Asked if she wanted to go for a little getaway."

"Which friend?"

Zoe takes a deep breath. "Her name is Justine. We drove down to the central coast, camped for a night, and then took a hike that was a little too aggressive for my level of fitness. I tripped over a log, went down hard, and hit my head. Concussed myself mildly, and soon realized that I'd had a hissy fit and that it was time to come home."

Zoe glances briefly at Phil whose lips are white with the force of his compression.

"Your friend just left you at the hospital?"

"I told her to. She lost a child last year, and hospitals are triggering for her. What about *my* daughter?"

Now Meyers speaks. "Whoever your daughter went with..."

"Took her," Zoe amends. "Whoever took her..."

"We don't have a lot of information yet, Mrs. R—"

"Zoe. My daughter wouldn't just go off with...with someone who bombed our home!"

"How do you know that?" Meyers asks, leaning in closer.

"Kids go off to college, get caught up in stuff. It's an idealistic time. Maybe she's part of it."

Zoe rears back. "Are you *kidding* me? You think my daughter perpetrated an act of terror on her own home? Are you crazy? Phil, did you not just go on public television and announce she was kidnapped? What the fuck is with this line of questioning?"

"Calm down, Zoe," Phil leans in. "We have to look at this from all angles."

She turns on him. "Oh, I bet you love this. It helps with your theory that everyone who wants to save the environment has to be out to get you."

Phil shoots her *cease and desist* eyes, but that roiling primal rage has seared its way up her spine again. Next comes the heat that makes her want to crawl out of her skin.

"I can't believe we are wasting time talking about a stupid fight my husband and I had while our daughter has been taken!" She has to believe that Nemesis will make good on their promise to get Hannah back. She can't give anything away about where she's been. Incriminate herself.

Meyers puts out her hands. "I promise you, we've got detectives on this. Your housekeeper..."

"Estate manager," Zoe amends.

"Right, estate manager, Karina, gave us a description of the man your daughter was seen leaving with. Your cameras at the gate caught an image of a man walking your daughter to a van. Your husband says he's never seen him. We want to show you the image to see if it's someone you know or have ever seen, okay?"

Zoe is breathing hard. Sweat beads up beneath her bandage, armpits. She wants so badly to hold it together, but the heavy hair of the sweater Hecate had given her is smothering her. She shucks it off and fans herself with a brochure that's lying on the table.

Hollohan opens a folder and pulls out a perp sketch. Zoe's breath hitches like silk on a nail. Though she can only see the top half of his face, thanks to a bandana tied lower, she thinks she knows exactly who it is. Those small eyes, that stupid haircut with the shaved sides. The one the Defenders of Freedom had called "Spencer." She'd watched him hold a gun on them in that clearing. If she tells them that she recognizes him, she'll have to tell them all the rest, about having contact with the real Nemesis, about why she didn't report where she's really been. She has to run on faith here that these detectives will find him. And Nemesis will find Hannah.

She has to.

"No," she says. She swallows down a quaver in her voice. "I've never seen him before."

CHAPTER TWELVE

Justine sends one text through the Signal app, chokes down half a protein bar from the 7-11 and changes into darker clothes.

For the first time in months her body is electric. She knows that it is all a trick of excited chemicals pumped at the brain's signal into her blood: adrenaline and cortisol and maybe even some endorphins. When the rush fades she'll be back in this forlorn skin. But this is as close to alive as she's felt in a long time.

She waits a half mile away from the address she's scraped from the bottom of that horrible chat room, where she texted Nemesis she will be. She waits ten minutes. Then twenty. Starts pacing after thirty. What if they don't show? *You should call the police*, says the voice of reason she barely recognizes anymore. Yes, she should. For Zoe's daughter, Hannah. The tall, serious-eyed art student she met only once. The one time they'd met, Willa had dashed right into the teen's arms, as if she knew her, held up her favorite board book *The Belly Button Book*, and demanded that Hannah read it to her.

If she calls the police, though, she can't prove her worth to Nemesis. Can't make them see that they need her.

The sounds of feet cracking on twigs snaps her to attention. All she has for a weapon now is a stupid hand-held taser, gaudy pink like a huge eraser, a gift from Nate when he was so worried about her always running off in pursuit of a story to places where she might not be safe.

She crouches beside her car, running the pattern of self-defense moves she learned, also at Nate's insistence—*eyes, testicles, knees*. Use the sharp parts—*elbows and fingernails*.

A familiar whistle lets her muscles relax. Justine whistles back and Persephone and Artemis materialize through the trees, Persephone all eyes and teeth, Artemis ghostly pale. They quickly pull up masks that cover the lower half of their faces.

"That's it? She only sent you two?" Justine asks, tasting defeat.

Persephone smiles, and suddenly the trees behind her seem to boil as dozens of dark-clad figures emerge into the night. They wear masks and hoodies pulled up—everything black. Even their hands are covered in black gloves.

"We might have mentioned there would be some white supremacists on hand," Persephone says.

Justin gapes. "Who are they?"

Persephone just spreads her arms wide. From a case slung over her shoulder she pulls out several rolled up pieces of soft plastic. Signs, Justine realizes, as she unfurls them: *Save the Planet. Fossil Fools. The Dinosaurs Thought They Had Time, Too.*

"If anyone interrupts our progress, we are all just coming back from a climate change vigil. LED candles in the pack," she gestures over her shoulder.

Justine's lips curve into a brief smile.

The black clad figures use the trees on the side of the road to stay less noticeable as they walk. Justine's GPS homes in on one of a handful of tattered warehouse-style buildings. A junk shop. A vacuum repair store. A mechanic shop that is no longer in service. *Your destination is on the left,* her GPS warns.

Justine points, nods, pulls up her own hoodie and moves. The dozen black clad figures follow behind her, darting across the road, remarkably silent for a group. At a backwards glance, Justine catches Persephone hanging back, sliding several steps into the trees, while Artemis joins Justine, following behind her very closely. She can't tell if the woman has a weapon on her. Doesn't know if she hopes she does or doesn't. *The Defenders will have guns,* she is sure of that. *What about these figures at my back?*

Dread fills her. *What was I thinking?*

As they close in on the back of the garage, she peers through one grimy window where a light flickers within. A crashing sound behind them makes her drop into a crouch. She only calms her thundering pulse when she sees the retreating tail of a raccoon take off past the metal trash can. Rising up again, she peers into the room. Through the grimy window she can only make out the silhouettes of people inside, and tires, abandoned car jacks, and even an entire car bumper littering the mostly empty warehouse, one that has been long out of business. Not as many people as she feared. Maybe half a dozen, most of them gathered around an old TV set. She can't tell if one is Hannah.

She gestures for Artemis to look, too. Artemis peers in, frowns at Justine. "Is it them?" she whispers.

Justine doesn't trust the small number of people when she expected a crowd. It feels like the rest of these men could be anywhere—watching from the trees, crouched behind derelict cars. Goosebumps rise at the back of her neck, but she stops herself from whirling around to look behind her.

"Let's circle around," Justine whispers. Crouching below the line of sight, they sneak around the side until they reach the back of the building. No circle of men sitting outside drinking. No trucks parked here.

The massive garage door itself is closed, but Justine moves toward the office door, one hand almost on the knob, when a hand comes down on her shoulder. Justine almost screams, but clamps it back, turning, heart thumping, to find Artemis holding something out to her. A gun. Even though she took that rifle with her to pressure Zoe, she'd never have used it. And right now, she doesn't want to touch the weapon in Artemis's hands.

"Not loaded," Artemis whispers.

Flooded with relief, Justine grasps it and turns the knob, walking as quietly into the room as she can, somewhat bolstered by the bodies behind her.

She takes one steadying breath, and then does her best to remember method acting from a couple of college courses. Digs deep for the part of herself that can be commanded and storms into the garage shouting, "I've got a gun, hands up."

The people clustered around the TV lift their heads in unison, blinking, as though this is just part of the show they've been watching, rendered in 3-D. Justine is surprised to be looking at the faces of all women. Youngish women, so much blonde hair spilling out of caps and hoodies, gaiters and bandanas pulled down around their necks.

"What the fuck?" says one with bright red lipstick.

"Where's Hannah?" Justine says, aiming the gun at the lipsticked one.

The woman sneers at her, like a cheerleader talking down to a geek, and Justine storms right for her. The woman jumps up, stumbling backwards out of her chair, while the others just stand there, hands dangling helpless.

"I told him to leave us one fucking gun," says Lipstick Lady.

"Where's the girl you kidnapped?" Justine shouts.

"*We* didn't do anything," says Cheerleader Blonde.

But Justine hears it then, a muffled banging, toward the back of the shop. A small room, a closet or bathroom. She waves in the group behind her, and as the small mass in black slides smoothly into the room, one of the women screams. The black clad figures pour in and surround the blondes. Justine rushes to the little door. It sticks at first, but she gets it open, and finds Hannah in there, seated on the toilet, eyes red rimmed, as though she's been crying.

Hannah stares up, wide eyed at Justine, fear blanking out her features until recognition dawns, but also confusion. "You're...my mom's friend?"

"Yep. Come on, we've got you." Justine lifts Hannah up by the arms. Her hands are bound with plastic zip ties. It's stuffy in the room, and a sheen of sweat coats Hannah's brow.

The Blondes are corralled between black-clad bodies, the screaming one laid flat on the ground beneath one of their knees.

"Who are you?" Artemis demands of Lipstick Lady.

"We're...we're Project Nemesis," she says with a whimper. Artemis howls a laugh.

Justine hurries Hannah over toward the exit. She is already beginning to swell with the feeling of accomplishment. She has done something significant. She's proven her value.

"What's going on?" Hannah asks Justine as they hurry back out into the night, along the side of the garage, and past half of the black-clad group that had gone in behind her.

"We're rescuing you."

"Who are you with? I don't understand any of this," Hannah says, her voice sounding so much younger than her 19 years.

"It's a long story."

Right as they step out into the road, to dart across into the trees, a roar of engine and the blinding flash of headlights throws open panicked floodgates inside her. Hannah screams and...stops...just stops, as a truck barrels down at them.

Justine uses what little strength she has to shove Hannah onward. "Go. Run!" she shouts.

Hannah recoils in horror from the grasp of a black-clad figure who pulls her into the night, and then the world erupts into light and noise. Shots are fired into the sky, men shout, feet stampede upon pavement and someone rams into Justine's side. She hits the pavement beneath a solid body, striking the ground so hard she hears and feels a crack that resounds all the way through her skull.

From the ground, Justine thrusts a knee upwards into the man's groin and hits home. Using everything she has, she shoves him off her and scrambles to her feet, temple throbbing. Artemis squints after her from the trees, brows furrowed. *Come on*, she seems to be saying. *Now*. But Justine can't get her legs under her fast enough. The world is swimming around her, blurring together. She takes a few more stumbling steps, but then a man's guttural voice lances her. "It's that bitch from the other day." A hand takes her ponytail in his fist and yanks. She flies backwards with a cry of pain.

Artemis, Hannah, and Persephone slip into the darkness beyond the trees while the violence chugs around her—a blurry yin-yang of black clad figures grappling with white-shirted men. She finds it amusing that the good guys are in black, the bad guys in white, the trope turned on its head. Or maybe only she is. She is blinking up at the stars, then she is flying, lifted skyward by hands that dig too deep into her ribs. She imagines herself like a piece of radioactive metal, wishes she could poison him with just a touch.

"We got this one."

She laughs. Each ripple of laughter makes something catch painfully in her torso, something tweaked or broken, she isn't sure.

"What's wrong with you, fucking bitch?" says the man who now hoists her over a shoulder.

"Nobody's going to come for me," she keeps laughing. "You'll get...no ransom..." Laughter. "No reward. Nobody will bargain for me. I'm completely worthless to you."

She's carried back into the garage where the Blondes are pouting and dark-eyed. One of them has a blackened, bloody nose. The man drops Justine at her feet, cement a painful kiss all along her left side. "She's all yours."

Bloody Nose Blonde smirks down at Justine and pulls back her foot.

CHAPTER THIRTEEN

Zoe sits alone for a long time after the detectives have shown themselves out. After Karina goes home, Phil wanders off, stone-faced.

She feels like a trespasser in her own home. Same as all those years ago when Phil had brought her home to his folks. The nose ring and the tattoos she'd since had lasered off had drawn his mother's eyes all night, like a nervous tic. She'd wanted to laugh. Those were only the visible signs of what made her different from Phil, from Phil's family. His mother couldn't see the other marks, nobody could, because they weren't inked or impressed or bruised on her body anymore. They were like those shadows inside an X-ray scan that reveal cancers lurking below a pristine surface.

"And what about your mother?" Phil's own mother, Betsy, had asked. "What does she do?"

That Zoe of long ago had answered, "She's dead" with such ease, Phil's hand had tightened in surprise on her knee. Whether to reassure her or to keep her from digging deeper into her lie, she didn't know.

"Oh my dear, I'm so sorry. Phil didn't tell me." Betsy cut sharp, disapproving eyes at her son.

Zoe looked down at her hands, pretending grief. She just wanted to hide from that woman's predatory blue eyes. "I asked him not to. I wasn't even sure I would tell you myself. Not exactly get-to-know-you conversation."

An obnoxious flurry of condolences had followed, better than the alternative, the truth: that her mother was a heroin addict who often opened up both her home and her body to pay for that habit.

She deflected the conversation about her father by complimenting Betsy's china plates. There was no good way to fake that she'd never known him. Didn't know if he was a love long gone or a ragged customer who had found his way into her mother's home and bed.

* * *

Zoe's bladder routs her out of unwelcome memory. She stumbles toward the nearest bathroom but finds herself confused. The staircase doesn't seem to be where she remembers it, and the light from the art deco chandelier makes her temple throb. She feels for the wall, a blessed sturdiness as the room swims slightly in her eyes.

Her name is spoken softly.

She opens her eyes to realize she is slumped on the floor against the wall.

Phil stands—solemn. She searches for the sharpness in his eyes. *How long ago did we fight? A lifetime?* He puts out his hand and helps her up.

"Bathroom," she says. He leads her to it, around the staircase, down the hall.

When she emerges, he is leaning against the opposite wall, arms folded.

"What happened?" he asks. In the dim light of the sconce, he looks strangely young. Lines swept into softness, comb-over hidden in shadow. She'd been in love with him once.

"Our daughter has been kidnapped," she says.

"Maybe. That's not what I'm asking, Zoe."

Her spine feels like it could conduct electricity, followed by a jagged bolt of heat so intense, light flashes behind her eyes. "Maybe? You can't be serious. Our own daughter wouldn't sabotage her home and just...leave! If you think that, then you don't know her at all."

"You've seen the friends she's been keeping since she went off to school. You'd almost think she doesn't grow up in this house," he says bitterly. "And kids change when they go off into the world. I told you art school would make a radical out of her."

Zoe clenches her jaw so hard it shoots pain spiraling up and through her head.

"Plus, what's this bullshit about her dropping out of school to go to Africa with that stupid boyfriend of hers?"

Zoe snaps her gaze to his. "What? What are you even talking about?"

He raises an eyebrow, looks smug. "She didn't tell you."

"Tell me what?"

"The whole reason she came home early is to let us know she's dropping out of art school and traipsing off to some African country with her boyfriend's NGO."

Words form at the back of her throat but never reach her mouth. *Boyfriend?*

"How is it I know more about our daughter for once than you do?"

Zoe chokes back an "oh you have no idea," that she wants to

spit in his face. But she can't dull the sting of Hannah not confiding in her. Doesn't like to admit that her daughter has been pulling away for some time.

Phil's face softens again. "Where'd you go, Zoe? We fight. That is not even close to the kind of fight that would make you take off for several days. What the hell's going on?"

Zoe shakes her head, but that makes the room sway. She presses a hand to her forehead, remembering the lump there. Phil's eyes dart to it, droop, his tone gentling suddenly. "Let's get up to bed," he says.

She doesn't argue. Fatigue comes on like a dentist's x-ray vest laid heavily atop her chest. He takes her arm and helps her up the stairs. So many stairs.

She is out of breath by the time they reach the bedroom. Phil helps her shuck off the clothes, eyes narrowing. "Where'd you get these?" he asks.

"Justine," she says.

"Feeling sorry for someone does not a friendship make," he says, sinking down onto the bed.

"Jesus, Phil, do you hear yourself? Every word out of your mouth is some kind of criticism or paranoid suspicion...of your own daughter, of me, of my friends. I'm sorry I worried you... but if this explosion hadn't happened, would you have even noticed I was gone?"

Phil presses his face to his hands. And then, to her great surprise, Phil tears up.

Zoe is shocked into stillness.

"What..."

"I'm sorry," he says, and her mouth falls open. She can count the times he's apologized for something on her fingers in their 30 years together. "I've been stressed about the new plant, and that article did us no favors, and that newspaper, and you've just been...different, lately. I was angry, and I figured you just had your own kind of fit and I didn't believe that anything bad could have happened to you...much less Hannah."

Zoe exhales a breath and sinks down beside him.

"It's just menopause," she says, though that doesn't sound right. "It makes me feel...like I've been reshaped on a potter's wheel and thrown into a kiln. I'm in the cooking phase now, and I don't know what I'm going to look like when I get out."

Phil wipes his cheeks, smiles. "Nice metaphor."

She smiles back. "Our daughter is not a revolutionary or a radical. She's just a young woman figuring herself out. I'm *scared* for her. Aren't you?"

Phil sighs. "I just don't want to let myself believe there's real reason to be."

"There's always a reason to be afraid, if you just look around. But I also don't want to live like Justine, whose loss is so deep, so tied to guilt that she feels she has very little to live for."

"Why are you still friends with that woman?" Phil asks, but he asks it softly, his arm sliding around her middle.

She sighs. Wants, in that moment, for him to be the Phil she fell in love with, the man she could tell anything to. The man who didn't even flinch at the bloodied body on her mother's floor. She could tell *that* Phil about Project Nemesis, and together they'd work out a plan.

She pulls back enough to look him in the eye.

"Phil, I'm tired of feeling like a part of your life that you and your business partners tolerate. I'm tired of feeling bad for caring about things like the climate and justifying to *my* people, the ones that count on me, believe in me, and hold me up as a role model, that I'm not a hypocrite for being married to you."

The words sound much harder than she intended.

Phil pulls away slightly, lacing his hands together and biting his lip. "You must think I'm a really bad person," he says. "I don't."

He shakes his head, eyes focused inward as though arguing with some part of his own mind. "Do you want to give this all up?" He waves his arms around the room, but she knows he meant all of it. The estate, the staff, the never having to worry. Except, she does worry, all the time.

"Why does it have to be so...much?"

Phil stands up and she sighs. A monologue will follow as he paces. "I find it very convenient that you only start questioning your lifestyle after you take off on a lark with your radical friend."

"Justine's not radical. She's a journalist."

"Same thing."

"Oh, for fuck's sake!"

"Do you not remember how life was for you when we met?" he spits.

She throws up her hands. "Oh, here we go. How you *saved* me."

He narrows his brows. "Whatever you want to call it, when we started dating you were living in a hovel. A cross between a crack-hotel and a squatter's paradise, where you triple-bolted yourself into your room at night in the hopes that your mother's drug-seeking johns didn't rape you."

Her rage flares. "Don't you think I remember every last moment of that life? That *night*? Guess what? I left that red suit you like so much in the woods where we...hiked. I tore it off and left it there like an old skin."

"Oh yeah?" Phil stands and stalks to the closet. "Fine." He flings open the doors and begins tearing clothes down by the handful, suits and blouses slipping to the floor. Then he goes and tosses them into the bathtub of the master suite. She hears him turning on the water. Then the sharp smell of bleach fills the room.

How can she tell him that his tantrum is all for himself? She literally doesn't care if she ever wears those clothes again.

"You're acting like a child," she calls after him.

He pounds back out into the bedroom, his shirt splattered with drops of water. "You never have to wear them again."

"You could have donated those," she says. "You didn't have to ruin them!"

He points a thick finger at her. "You have everything you could ever want, and you want more. You treat me like some kind of criminal when what I do powers people's jobs and lives. That's my big crime—I make it possible for hospitals and office buildings to run, for people to take public transportation and get to work. What a terrible human being!"

His voice is loud enough that she wishes he had closed the bedroom door. She hates having their personal shit aired out in front of the staff.

She looks away from him. She wants to throw in his face all that information Artemis and Hecate told her. The lawsuits, the discrimination, the toxic dumping. She puts her face in her hands. She's gone so far from what she told Hecate she would do. Soften him up. Make herself useful to him, get information, maybe even—*ha, as if*—convince him to step down.

She takes a big gulping breath of air and sucks back down all her own righteous indignation. "I'm sorry," she says, weakly, probably unconvincingly. "Maybe I need a menopause support group."

Her apology takes all the huff out of Phil's rage, and with his deflation, his posture sags. He suddenly looked so much older than his 55 years. "This is stupid," he says." He looks to her almost pleadingly.

"Yes. Let's stop this, please."

Phil returns to her side on the bed, slides an arm around her. "They'll find her," he says.

Zoe leans into him, fighting the urge to cry. She wants Phil to be the weak one here. She holds him to her breasts. "We'll get through this," she says. But suddenly she wonders if she means she and Phil.

Hours later, after Phil has fallen into his usual sound sleep, and her own insomnia kicks in right on cue, she seeks out the phone Hecate gave her, downloads the Signal app.

She sends one text as Hecate instructed. "Active."

Then she goes downstairs to make herself a snack—the last food she had eaten was the savory tortilla full of rice and beans in that homey little cottage. Is it weird to regard that brief stretch of time as pleasant? *You were kidnapped, attacked, threatened and blackmailed. Wow, you know you're unhappy when all that equals a good time,* she thinks, laughing out loud between bites of cheese and crackers.

The phone buzzes in her pocket. She pulls it out and finds a text from CatLvr8. It reads:

caged bird free

She almost drops to her knees in relief.

CHAPTER FOURTEEN

What Hannah likes so much about going away to college is being out from under the constant watchful eye of her father's staff. The people that drive her places and lurk, even when her father swears it isn't at his request, on dates and even down the street from parties. And, though it makes her guilty to admit, she likes the distance from her mother. Her always-there, always-in-her-face, always-hovering mother. Being trapped with this horde of annoying Blondes and their mindless chatter, their constant vigilance, is like a nightmare version of the life she left behind.

With the men and their guns gone, she feels bold, and turns to the women prattling on about stupid TV shows and shopping tips. "Don't you have anything interesting to say?"

"Excuse me, Girl?" says the blonde-in-charge, the one whose lips are stained a perfect brick red that doesn't falter over the course of hours.

Hannah shakes her head. "I don't know how you can stand each other."

Blonde-in-charge stands up with as much menace as a puppy trying to bark fiercely.

"What the fuck do you know about anything?"

Hannah smiles. "Why are you even hooked up with those assholes? You let them push you around? Run the show? Don't you have any self-esteem?"

"Shut her up!" says Bun-top-Blonde, taking off her hat and straightening out her messy bun.

"We know trash when we see it," Blonde-in-Charge says.

Hannah thinks of several retorts that point out the net worth of her father and the passionate concerns of her mother, but figures both will make her sound pretentious.

"Up!" Blonde-in-Charge says as she pushes Hannah into the tiny bathroom where they'd left her for so long earlier, she actually fell asleep seated atop the toilet. At least it's quiet in there.

Then, sometime later, the room erupts into noise again, but no gunshots, thank god, and when the door bursts open at long last she is looking up into...a familiar face. A friend of her mother's, *Justine*, and something clenches in her midsection. *Is my mother involved in this, somehow, too?*

Justine hustles Hannah out of the garage and into the street where lights are bearing down on them with so much noise —*are those gunshots?*—her legs fill with sandbags.

She just wants to close her eyes against the light, suddenly —strangely—remembering the time her best friend Sasha took her to see a slasher flick, and she was so frozen in terror that she just curled up in her seat with her hands in front of her face rather than calling her mom to come get her. Later, she knows, this will all come rushing back out onto the canvas in some form she will be able to explain, but for now she is taken by cold terror. Snapping out of her thoughts, Hannah heaves her out of the way of an oncoming car, pushing her into the arms of another woman with a long, red braid.

And then a man is barreling down on Justine, and, though Hannah screams and reaches out her hand in an attempt to save Justine, the redhead pulls her into the woods. They are running. They run for how long she can't even tell, until her legs throb and her chest burns. Until a dark car pulls up alongside them, and they jump into the vehicle like characters in an action movie.

* * *

Now she is comfortably seated on a tattered but comfy couch in a little house somewhere. They made her wear a blindfold during the drive to get there. The walls are hung with tapestries and handmade pottery sits on shelves and side tables.

A lovely Black woman with hair closely cropped to her scalp is seated opposite Hannah while another, pale-skinned girl her own age hands her a ceramic mug of water.

She chugs it.

"Hi, Hannah, we just want you to know you're safe here. You can call me Persephone," the Black woman says.

"Who are you? How'd you find me with those...people?"

"We're a concerned group of women. You might say we're friends of your mother's."

"Might say...but aren't?"

"That's really up to your mother," Persephone says. "We have similar goals, but our methods are slightly different."

"*You're* Project Nemesis. The real ones, aren't you?" Hannah leans forward now, her blood bubbly with excitement. "Women eco-terrorists?"

"We're not terrorists. *Anarchists* might be a better word. We believe in decentralizing power and yes, protecting the earth, the climate, because it's our home, because it's the right thing to do, and because the people who get hurt the most when we destroy it are the poor, the marginalized, the already oppressed."

"Wow," Hannah says. "My friend Ari would die if she could see me now. She is all about this kind of thing."

Persephone doesn't smile. "This isn't a game, or some club you can join for college credit," she says. "We aren't some flash in the pan trend you can hashtag. We're a network, you might say, a movement."

"No, I get it. I totally don't mean to, like, downplay it or anything."

"Good." Persephone runs the flats of her hands across the knees of her navy cargo pants. "So, here's the thing, Hannah. We made your mom a deal. We'd help get you back, and she'd help us."

Hannah shrugged. "Okay."

"But we think it's going to be hard for her to keep her end of the bargain. She's not going to want to go through with it because, like all acts of true justice, they're hard. It's hard to work against the system, any system."

"Okaaaay."

"Basically, until we can get greater assurance that your mom is going to help us, we'd like you to stay with us."

"Ohhh," Hannah says. "So, I'm not exactly free to go?"

Persephone cocks her head. "We'd prefer it if you'd consider staying with us as doing your part. Being part of our effort for the greater good. You, who were raised with everything you could ever want. You have a lot to give, Hannah."

"It's funny you say that," Hannah begins, thinking of the very thing she came home to tell her parents. "I'm leaving for Kenya in a week—my boyfriend works for a climate NGO—it's really important that I go."

Persephone's face remains impassive, and Hannah wonders if she offended her. But Persephone finally speaks. "That's good, Hannah. You've already got your heart in the right place even if your methods need a little work. Thing is, we could use your help *here*. There are needy and suffering people struggling with the impacts of climate change here, in our country."

The cold seep of dread fills her. What has she gotten into?

"If I help you now, will you let me go in time for my...trip?"

Persephone smiles again, but it doesn't seem to reach her eyes. "We just need you to do something for us. Record a little video and send it to your parents. You'll tell them that you're okay, that you've found a cause you believe in that's really important, and that they should not worry about you. You'll contact them soon. All they have to do is go on with life as usual."

Hannah leans back into the soft couch. "And...what if I don't want to do all that?"

Persephone nods, as though she's already considered this. Around her, the women who've been sitting nearby like chatty girlfriends at an afternoon tea stand up forming a phalanx around her. "Then your chances of going on that trip are pretty slim."

CHAPTER FIFTEEN

Justine lay with her head on the foot of Willa's hospital bed, her body tucked awkwardly into the chair. Nearness was her only option—even if the rise and fall of her daughter's chest was artificial, she wanted to be in the same room to share the same air. Wanted to feel her limbs in the sea of tubes that pushed her away with their inhuman tangle. Would have crawled in and stayed in that bed if the tutting nurses would just leave her be. But they didn't leave for longer than a few minutes at a time, and pulled her away from Willa when she climbed in to hold her daughter. Now that it was maybe too late, she wanted to take back every moment of time she'd spent away. Give it all back. Redeem every hour for a new one.

Nate, too, came in like a ghost at her back, but she didn't turn to find him. Didn't reach for him, and he stopped reaching for her. Sometimes she found him across the bed looking at her with an expression like confusion. As if he wasn't quite sure where he knew her from, as if she couldn't be the woman he'd married. And maybe she wasn't. Maybe she had stopped being that woman from the moment they conceived this other person, despite all her doubts and insistence that she was not mother material. Despite all his assurances that she was. Her own mother was hardly maternal, she'd argued. She'd had no great model. Helen was a woman of great independence, forced into single motherhood when Justine's father died so young.

In between great gulping waves of grief came a sharp, cutting rage. He had wanted her to be a mother. He had insisted. And look what it had wrought.

* * *

The room around her floods with cold.

It takes her a long moment to realize it is not the hospital air conditioning but the shock of something being removed from her body. She is not in the hospital. She is on a cold cement floor. She blinks against blinding light. Her ribs and sides ache so much she cries out when she sits up. Bearded Man leers down at her with a shit-eating grin.

"Morning, sunshine. Hope you've enjoyed your stay." He holds a stained blanket he must have wrenched off of her.

The smell of old oil and bitter coffee hits her nostrils.

"You in a little bit of pain?"

"I think your girlfriend broke one of my ribs," she says, investigating with cautious fingers the hot, bruised spot on her side.

He makes a mock pitying face. "Ohhh, I'm sorry. Would you like me to get you some medicine for that? Maybe bandage you up?"

Justine lays back down. "I don't care what you do with me," she says flatly.

Her tone must be convincing. Bearded Man frowns as though disappointed. "I bet your family is worried about you," he says.

"I have no family," she says, pushing Nate and her mother's faces out of mind. She is no good to them. "If you're hoping to use me as a bargaining chip for something, you're out of luck," Justine says. "I told you, I'm worthless to you."

He sneers, stands up, and kicks a wrench near his foot. Justine flinches for the impact, though it spins off away from her.

"Jesus, Brock," says one of the Blondes hunkered down on the couch. She is sipping coffee out of a mug with a Hungarian Crosstar on it.

"No surprise you have no family, who the fuck would care about you?" Brock says testily.

"Agreed," Justine says. Every time she takes the punch out of his words, the lines at his eyes and mouth ratchet tighter.

"I do think those Nemesis ladies might have a use for you, though. I think they might come back for you."

"I doubt it," Justine says, fearing she isn't as convincing this time.

"Mmm-hmmm," Brock says. "We'll see about that."

"You're not very good at this, are you, Brock?" Justine grinds out.

Brock is suddenly on her, knee pressed to torso, right over her aching ribs. She can't stop herself from shrieking at the bright hot pain.

"What's that, bitch?"

"Crime," she says, panting. "Kidnapping and assault and all that. You showed us your faces. You left a trail of evidence. You kept me in the same location, for crying out loud. Even I'm better at crime than you."

Brock's hand curls into a fist, but suddenly the Blonde is at his side, holding onto his arm. "She's right. We ought to get the fuck out of here. Just leave her. She's useless to us."

Brock shakes his head, appearing to be thinking. "Not entirely. Not to those eco-bitches. And we need them."

Blonde sighs. "Fine, but we gotta get out of here."

Justine can walk, though every step and breath is like a lance through her side, but Brock hefts her up like a child—her ribs a bright, hot throb of agony. His fingers dig in extra hard into her ribs and behind the tender flesh of her knees, but she doesn't try to struggle, just takes small, shallow breaths, reminiscent of labor. The pain is bracingly sharp, all encompassing. He slings her into the truck's backseat and makes her lie half curled fetally on the floor, where every bump and rattle of the truck sends shards of pain through her side. She wishes he'd just thrown her in the back so she could leap out and end it all on the freeway.

She doesn't know how long they drive, is too woozy with pain to chart the turns of the road or get a sense of the direction they are going. The pain keeps her tethered to a body that she feels less like inhabiting every second.

She begins to make up her mind on this drive. She's done something useful, even if it isn't what she had in mind. She wishes she'd put a greater dent in the cause. But Hannah is safe. Now, she is going to make things hard for these assholes who defend a strange interpretation of freedom.

When the truck comes to a stop, and Brock leans in to help her out, with a bracing inhale she musters a reserve of force and kicks, hard, boot meeting his face. Pain grips her torso but adrenaline drives her forward. He falls, spluttering blood, backwards onto the pavement. Justine climbs out and jumps down right onto his torso. Though her weight is sleight, she feels something snap beneath her boot heel, hopes it is a rib in kind as he howls.

Blonde-in-Charge doesn't notice what is happening until it is too late. Justine darts around the back of the truck and takes advantage of her surprise, knocking the woman down as she sprints, accepting the throbbing pain in her side as a reminder that she is still alive. She doubts she will make it very far before they tackle her and beat her beyond recognition, but she doesn't care. She barely makes out that she is running through a bland suburb of homes so alike they are indistinguishable.

Running until she can barely catch her breath, as though one lung has shrunk to the size of a straw, she realizes someone is shouting, and she collapses, hitting the ground only vaguely aware of the scrape of pavement through her thin pants.

* * *

Justine wakes in a soft bed, under dim lights. A familiar face smiles from a bedside chair. The room smells like rosemary.

"Hecate," she rasps. Her voice has mostly gone.

"Justine. I'm sorry, hon. It takes us longer to come back for you than we intended. Had to track you down. Got a broken rib, I think. We almost took you to the hospital, thought maybe your lung was punctured, but your breathing evened out. How do you feel?"

Justine smiles. Barks a laugh. "I really thought they were going to kill me."

"Not today, darlin'," Hecate says.

Justine smiles, then winces and grasps her ribs. "Owww."

"Sorry," Hecate pats her shoulder. Rib fractures usually heal pretty quickly. "At any rate, we want you to know that we are grateful to you. You put yourself on the line for us."

"Hannah's safe?"

"She is. She's here, in fact. We thought her mother was a soldier for the cause, but I wonder if her daughter is a better fit."

Justine inhales as deeply as the pain will allow, finds

Hecate's eyes and locks on. "Please don't say I have to go home again. You know there's nothing left for me there. I can be of more use to you. Nate, he...we're not..."

Hecate nods. "Well, you're not going far with that rib, sister."

"Hey, I knocked out a man twice my size with these messed up ribs."

Hecate cracks a wide smile. "You did do that, my girl. Indeed."

CHAPTER SIXTEEN

Z oe wakes to the perfume of a good medium roast coffee and the sounds of Phil swearing loudly. She stumbles out of bed, pulling on her luxuriously soft robe and slippers. She's still a little unsteady from the concussion, but the throb in her head is tolerable.

She finds Phil in the kitchen, phone in hand. His eyes are slits, his cheeks blooming red.

She is afraid to ask, but he looks up the minute she enters. "I. Told. You." He holds out his phone, shaking his head wildly back and forth as though truly bewildered.

"What?" She takes it. A video sent by text from a number she doesn't recognize, Hannah's face frozen mid-sentence. Zoe's finger trembles as she hits the little play triangle and her daughter's sweet face, those almond-shaped, dark brown eyes framed by messy dark curls, speaks. They look so much alike that sometimes Phil complains his genes didn't make much of a dent.

"Mom, Dad, I'm so sorry if I've worried you. I didn't know that they were going to bomb the gate, I swear. And they promise there won't be any more violence. They just wanted to send a message."

Hannah closes her eyes briefly, and Zoe knows she is choking back tears. She wants to reach through the screen and hold her daughter.

"And the message is that we can't keep living like this—stripping the earth of her resources so that billionaires can make more billions, while the...um...while the poor and the working class..." she trails off a moment, casts her eyes toward what must be the person holding the phone...for her line, her cue.

Zoe could combust with fury. *How dare they use my daughter like this? They rescued her from the Defenders of Freedom only to twist her to the agenda Project Nemesis?* But she can't say any of that in front of Phil.

"While the poor and the working class get poorer and sicker, too. Please don't come looking for me. I'm safe. I'm not in danger. And we promise no more violence. If Phil...Dad... steps down as CEO of Rasmussen Energy...if the entire board is replaced."

Phil makes a half-roar of indignant rage. "We?" he shouts.

Zoe turns toward him, beseeching. "This is *not* her idea. You can't possibly believe that."

"So, what the fuck do they think happens if I resign, if everyone leaves and we're replaced? Different players, same game!"

Zoe closes her eyes. "Maybe you could throw them a bone. How many times has your company been approached to lower rates, to offer subsidies to the poor?"

"I do not negotiate with terrorists, Zoe! The cost of energy is the cost of energy. If we go making it free to everyone then how is that fair to the people that have to pay?"

"Maybe none of it is fair," Zoe says. "The whole system."

Phil grips his head like he wants to snap his own neck rather than have this conversation with her. "How did this become my life?"

"Let me save you the trouble; it's all my fault, isn't it? If only you hadn't let my leash out so far, let me satisfy my little liberal cravings, none of this would be happening, right?"

Something shifts in Phil's eyes. "Is that really how you see me? Having a chokehold on some...leash?"

Zoe shrugs. "It feels that way sometimes. More and more lately. There was a time when we were in on everything together. But as your companies have grown and grown, it's always about your stockholders and your board...what I do is just an embarrassing thorn in your side."

Phil inhales. His next words take her by surprise. "How long since you've heard from your mother?" Zoe halts in place. Too long, truth be told, but she isn't going to let him pin her mood on that.

"That's not what's going on with me, Phil."

"Are you sure?"

Zoe looks at her feet, dark veins webbing her pale skin, toe polish in need of a refresh. "It's been a while."

"Do you want me to send Fernando out to look for her?"

Zoe inhales, shaky breath giving away more than she cares to. "No. I will go look for her myself."

"Not alone," he says sternly.

"None of those people are going to hurt me," she says sharply. "They're too sick or weak, most of them."

"Still."

Zoe closes her eyes. "Fine," she says. "Fernando can take me."

There is a long pause, then Phil says, "What are we going to do about Hannah?"

Zoe turns at last to look at him. "Let the police find her."

"That video...we have to show it to the detectives."

"No!" Zoe's voice is loud as a gunshot in the silent room. "No. It incriminates her in something I don't believe she has done."

"This is a criminal investigation, Zo. And what if she's been...brainwashed or confused by these people. Maybe she really isn't okay?"

"I'm sure she's fine." Zoe tries to steady her voice, which is just at the edge of shaking. "Just at that idealistic age. If it wasn't this she'd be sitting in a tree somewhere or saving the whales. You can't show this to the police until we know more."

Phil shakes his head slowly, like he's building up steam to begin shouting. "You know something."

Zoe isn't quick enough to make her face impassive. "I know as much as you do."

"No." Phil shakes his head. "You're not freaked out enough. It's almost like you really do know that she's okay."

Zoe keeps shaking her head, but Phil advances and jams a finger in the air at her face. "You tell me what you know, Zoe. If you..."

"Jesus, Phil, there is no conspiracy against you, okay?"

"Really? Between these terrorists' violent vendetta against my company and that hit-job profile of me in *Mother Jones*, you don't think I have any reason to be paranoid?"

"You're a public figure. We both are. That's par for the course," Zoe insists.

"I'm turning that video over to the police," Phil says. He snatches up his phone and storms toward the stairs.

Zoe runs after him. "You can't—don't do that. What if it puts her in real danger?"

Phil's lips compress to a tight white worm of outrage. Zoe is so used to that version of his lips sometimes she finds the sight of his face at rest puzzling.

"What. Do. You. *Know?*"

Zoe shakes her head but says nothing.

"Zo, if you're sitting on something, you need to tell me."

"I don't know anything, I'm just going on mother's instinct," she insists.

Phil jams the phone in his pocket. "I won't show the detectives *today*, but I can't promise about tomorrow," he says, and strides out of the room.

When he's gone, she uses the signal app:

What the hell? Video made things worse. Phil threatening to turn it over to cops.

The reply doesn't come until she is showered and changed. She reads it and wants to smash the phone into the terracotta tiles.

Whatever it takes.

* * *

Later that day, Zoe insists Fernando drop her off on Market Street in the city and promises she'll text him when she is ready for pickup. He is only reluctant, she suspects, for fear of reprisal from Phil, but there's relief in his eyes. As he pulls away, a part of her wishes she hadn't told him to drive off as she surveys the street. She'll never get used to the contrast of business-suit clad people stepping over—literally over—these ill and uncared for people in the street.

One man is daubing baby wipes into a weeping open sore at the end of a stumped foot, a needle protruding from in between the toes of the other foot. He mutters to himself and she tucks $50 in his jacket pocket as discreetly as possible.

"Who called the angels?" he says as she scans the street for signs of her mother.

She has to walk slowly and carefully, stepping over human

excrement, trash, and soiled, tattered belongings. She weaves amongst these poor lost souls, looking for the ones whose eyes are the least glazed.

She has a pocket full of twenties and a photograph of her mother. She picks a young woman wearing a ski suit over a ragged thermal t-shirt who is pouring water into a bowl for a small Chihuahua with a little pink collar and bow.

"Hi, hey, can I trouble you to look at this photo and tell me if you've seen this woman? Goes by Tamara or sometimes just T?" She holds out the photo in one hand and the twenty, rolled into a tight little tube, in her other.

The girl's eyes shoot straight for the twenty, then to the photo. "Yeah, maybe I've seen her."

"I'll give you the money either way," Zoe says. The girl chews on her lip. "I can't really tell. Lots of old people come and go out here. Some of 'em don't come back."

Zoe passes her the twenty like she is sharing a cigarette. The girl palms it and hides it in her clothes so fast it looks like a magician's trick. "I can't say for sure."

Zoe nods and moves on. Looks for any faces that might be familiar. At various junctures her mother has befriended little clusters of others, called them "road family" and they hang together for months, even years at a time. But it has been a while since she's done that.

She nudges a sleeping woman awake, and the woman screams and pulls her knees against her body so reflexively Zoe feels sick to her stomach, wondering what this woman thinks is about to happen. She holds her mother's photo up and the money, again thinking absurdly of all the space in her home that could fit these people. She's long had a fantasy of bringing them home by the dozen, bathing and tending their wounds, halted by the imagined look on Phil's face if he walked into such a scene.

She fights back the urge to vomit at her own hypocrisy—she so easily could be one of them—and stumbles through the crowd. An old man packing a pipe full of the tobacco scraped and salvaged from cigarette butts he is busily peeling open, lights up at the sight of her mother's face. "Hey, that's Big T! Where she at? Ambulance come take her away some time ago, and I hadn't seen her since."

"When? Do you know how long ago that was?"

She peels off $60 and holds it out to him. "I'm her daughter, and I'm worried about her."

The man raises his eyes to the sky as though looking for an answer in the clouds. "I can't say, Miss. Coulda been a day, coulda been a week. Not exactly on top of the calendar." He knocks a knuckle atop his bald skull.

"Thank you, I appreciate it."

"No, thank you, Miss!" He smiles a mostly toothless smile as he takes the proffered cash. "She sure is a good lady," he calls after her.

Leave it to her mother, even under the direst and bleakest of circumstances, to make people like her.

She knows which hospital is most likely to take in the homeless. She texts Fernando to pick her up, and spends the remaining minutes waiting, passing out what remains of her cash to the people who are conscious enough to receive it.

Then they speed off toward the hospital.

* * *

The intake nurse does a double and triple take at Zoe. It only requires a swivel of the head to the cast of destitute people around her to realize she is a far cry from what they usually see around here in her clean pink blouse and pressed slacks, $600 booties without so much as a scuff mark. Yet, as a girl, Zoe had spent countless nights herself in clinics like this, slapping her mother's cheeks to keep the blue from her lips and fingertips, to keep death from creeping in like a fast frost. Or herself, for a broken finger after punching one of her mother's visitors when he climbed into her bed "by accident," and that time she stepped on an abandoned needle, and they had to cross fingers and hope she hadn't contracted any disease.

That was before she'd begun to tempt fate herself, putting the needles in her own arms on purpose, until her mother caught her and busted open her lip in rebuke. Only then did her mother play at sobriety for a time.

"Yes?" The intake nurse says at last, when it's Zoe's turn.

She holds up her mother's photo. "My mother, she's homeless. I haven't heard from her in some time. I have reason to believe she might have been taken here in distress?"

The nurse's eyes soften with pity, but her mouth tightens, as though fighting any compassion for what she deals with every day.

"Name?"

Zoe proffers all the information and waits, time condensing to a blinking red light on the phone beside the nurse who is click-click-clicking at her computer.

"She was here. Discharged her a few days ago, though."

"What did she come in for?"

The nurse cocks her head. "I can't tell you that, hon, you know that." But the nurse waves a hand around the room as if to say, *You know why.*

Zoe wants to stomp her foot like a little kid. *Do you know who I am?* But she calms that reaction. How many times has she just decided to stop caring, to forget entirely about the woman who was little more than her vehicle into the world? At the very least her mother could remain in the same place long enough that Zoe could put to rest her guilt with a new jacket and a hot meal. Tamara manages to withhold even that satisfaction.

She makes her way back to the street, finds Fernando, and gets into the car feeling like a failure several times over. She won't be able to convince Phil to make any changes in his company. She can't protect Hannah. She can't help her mother.

As they are pulling away a familiar face emerges from the bustle.

"Stop!" Zoe shrieks.

Fernando grumbles that he can't stop where he is and she has to wait until he reaches the next block, while her mother's form drifts further away.

"Damn it!" Zoe pounds the seat cushion.

Two blocks later, he turns and lets her out with a sigh, and Zoe dashes back down Market Street the way she'd seen her mother go. The booties have a slight heel, which makes running precarious, and someone shouts after her, "Slow down, bitch," but she doesn't care. She reaches the street vendor where she saw Tamara, but she isn't there. She shucks off her cardigan and wraps it around her waist. Just that little bit of movement has made her skin crawl with heat again.

And then, as though she'd been there all along, Tamara is just standing there, in front of her, scarfing down a hot dog.

"Mom," she calls after her. Tamara doesn't so much as turn at the sound of Zoe's voice. "Tamara! Big T," she shouts, louder, afraid Tamara will run off in the crowd again. Her mother's head whips toward her. She squints, then widens her eyes, and moves toward Zoe with purpose.

There is good color in her mother's face, despite a sizable band-aid on her cheek. Her formerly auburn hair has thinned to the point of baldness at several spots on her scalp, and it's a lot grayer, but the overall quality of her skin is not too bad. What's more, she has on a shiny down coat, the kind that well-heeled skiers wear at their mountain resorts, and a fresh pair of weatherproof muck-luck boots. Her eyes are clear and bright.

"Zoe," she says, through a mouthful of hot dog.

"I heard you were in the hospital," Zoe says by way of greeting.

Tamara shrugs. "Almost as good as a vacation." She laughs. "They fed me three square meals, gave me a nice shower, and pumped me full of anti-bi-otics."

"You do look good," Zoe says.

Tamara raises her eyebrows, as though to suggest that "good" is pushing it. "I'm feeling better than I have in years."

Zoe never asks if she is clean, or for how long. There is no point. "Where are you sleeping these days?"

Her mother's eyes dart away. "Here and there."

"Our offer stands, Mom. There's a studio for you. Everything you need."

"Awww, no, you know I like to wander. Don't want to get stuck behind some gates."

The relief comes first, followed by a grappling hook of guilt. Sometimes she lies awake at night thinking of her mother shivering out here in the cold, at the mercy of others, and can hardly breathe. But they haven't lived together since Zoe was 20 and she's not sure how she'd deal with having her around.

"Let me take you for a meal," Zoe insists. "I've got a fresh sleeping bag for you in the car, some clothes."

Tamara waves the wrapper of the hot dog in the air between them. "Already ate. Got what I need right now. New stuff just gets stolen, anyway."

Zoe's body becomes a shrieking instrument. Anger plays one chord, pity plays another. She thinks of that saying about how mothers can push your buttons the best because they installed them in you.

"Okay then." Her mother smiles at her. She's lost significantly more teeth than the last time she'd seen her. No point in asking if she wants a trip to the dentist. A nice set of dentures. They'd probably be traded for cash or drugs anyway.

"But if you have a few bucks, I'd appreciate that," her mother says then, all wide innocent eyes and demure smile.

Zoe's chest feels unzipped and disgorged of its contents. It's easy to give freely to the strangers who expect nothing, but it makes her feel dirty, this exchange with her mother. Still, isn't this what she came for? *How can I help and judge her both at once?* Her lips try to smile but stay stuck in a pursed grimace. She fishes out an envelope tucked inside a pair of gloves. Too much cash for Tamara to be walking around with, but this is what she can do. So, she hands it over, and Tamara takes it, tucking it away inside her big canvas coat.

"Don't you worry about me; I don't worry about you," her mother says. It is supposed to sound like a compliment, Zoe suspects, to show confidence in her ability to take care of herself in the world, but it still stings. "Everything you've got, you got by yourself," her mother had said right before her wedding to Phil. That brief, halcyon period when Tamara got sober out of spite, because she wanted to hold her head up high in front of Zoe's in-laws ("Surprise, my mom's not really dead!" had been a fun conversation).

Zoe fights back tears, accepting her mother's brief hug, watching her turn slowly and walk away.

She is struck anew with surprise when Fernando pulls through the busted gate. She's once again taken over by that feeling of displacement, as though she shucked some essential part of herself off those two days with Nemesis. With that thought she has a sudden craving—almost physical, as familiar as that pulse of need for a drug—to be back in their midst, planning something formidable.

Instead of heading for the house, she watches Fernando

pull into the back lot, and then she turns and heads back out of the gate, and down the road toward the street. She pulls out her phone when she is out of any chance of eye or earshot from the house and opens the signal app, typing:

I want to see the caged bird

She doesn't expect an immediate response, so opens her Lyft app and hails one.

Ride-shares often have trouble finding her on these twisty backroads, so she hangs out beneath the closest stoplight and waits, shivering slightly against the sudden chill of late autumn afternoon.

The Lyft finds her and she is halfway to her destination by the time she receives a return text.

Bird is well cared for.

She groans, texts:

Not worried. Want to talk. Want to help.

The response comes:

U r helping.

She mimes strangling the phone.

Not making headway. Need brainstorming.

Her Lyft driver drops her off at a bookstore cafe where she used to take young Hannah for hot cocoas heaped with whipped cream.

Where are you?

She relays her location.

Give us one hour.

She tries to kill that time leafing through magazines, pretending that she is waiting in anticipation like some besotted girl on a date. Yet her eyes refuse to take in the images she sees. She chews at her cuticles until they bleed.

"Hey!" A young girl with a bright smile and a peach beret atop dark curls suddenly points at Zoe. "You're Zoe Rasmussen, aren't you?"

Zoe startles slightly. It isn't totally out of the ordinary to be recognized in town for EarthWorks related news, though it has been a while.

Zoe raises her eyebrows, bites a lip. "And who are you?"

The girl plants her hand on her hip but doesn't give her name. "How do you do it, I have to know?"

"Do what?" Zoe asks. *Juggle all the balls of being a professional woman, wife, and mother*—she expects something along those lines, a mentoring speech for an aspiring young entrepreneur.

"Live with yourself. Your husband's company is in the middle of, like, a shit ton of criminal lawsuits, and on the list of top 100 major contributors to the greenhouse gasses that are making climate change worse, no?"

"I'm sorry," Zoe says, putting down her magazine. "I'm just heading out." She turns on her heel and makes for the exit, but the girl calls out to her friend, "Jennifer, get over here."

Zoe hurries faster, head down, refusing to make eye contact with any interested eavesdropper.

The two girls catch up to her at the exit. "You're running

away from a simple question? I mean, it's hypocrisy. You run this environmental non-profit, but the very clothes on your back come from dirty money."

Her spine tries to send a warning, heat licking upward. That supercharged sensation spreads outward, bringing with it a rage that is almost supernatural. She wouldn't be shocked to shoot fire bolts of electricity out her fingertips.

"You just wait," she seethes. "Life is all ideals and empowerment right now, but don't worry, you'll sell your soul, too, for some sort of illusion you think will bring you happiness, and then you'll wonder what the fuck you've done, but by then it will be too late, so you'll just try to mitigate the harm. There's nothing you can say to me I haven't said to myself a thousand times over."

The girl stares at her, momentarily speechless, but then her friend elbows her and she remembers the act of speech. "So why don't you...like...walk away, or something? Do something different?"

Zoe looks back over her shoulder as though she can see her home, and Phil presiding over it, a King who doesn't realize his reign has ended.

"Maybe I already am!" she says, and then, because her fingertips are still tipped with heat, she reaches out and pushes the girl, just slightly. "You're in my way."

CHAPTER SEVENTEEN

The women won't stop feeding Justine, and for the first time in months it doesn't make her gag or choke. Justine holds up her hand to refuse another bite of homemade green curry. The woman serving it—*did she call herself Eris, or Eros?* Justine isn't quite sure—tuts and asks, "Are you sure?"

Justine knows that to look at her gauntness is to assume either anorexia or terrible illness, so she can't blame the woman's uncertain gaze.

"Keep the food out," another woman calls. "We've got more."

What these women have together is like nothing Justine can ever remember experiencing. It is like family—particularly when they gather here in this house and share meals and joke like they aren't also conducting serious work. Not that meals in her own were ever like this, her father dead of an aneurysm when she was barely a year old. Her mother, the kind to play classical music at a meal, not engage in conversation. Not even with Nate, the two of them working so often late into the night, that even after Willa came along, dinner was most often eaten over a couch cushion with a slew of papers spread out before them. This is like a sisterhood—like if sororities weren't the toxic soup of white girl posing and binge drinking of Justine's own college memory, and instead forces for good. It is also like something else, a sense of being connected to a larger purpose, that she only got a taste of last year when she interviewed them. She doesn't let that thought go much further. Chasing them in the past cost her everything. Chasing them now is the only thing she has left.

When the doors burst open again, bringing in the fresh smell of night air, Justine is surprised to see Zoe blow in behind Persephone and Artemis.

"I want to see Hannah," is all Zoe says, before glaring at Justine.

Hecate, picking up on the meaning behind Zoe's glare, emerges from a back room, chin tilted up. "You know it's thanks to Justine that we got Hannah away from those idiots, right?"

"I owed you that much, Zoe," Justine says.

Zoe's eyes widen. She looks apologetically at Justine. "I didn't know. Thank you."

Justine merely nods. She doesn't expect congratulations. Zoe has every right to hate her right now.

A rustle of women drift to another room and then Hannah emerges. Zoe stands staring at her daughter as though she can't believe it is really her. Hannah's eyes fill with tears, but she doesn't move toward her mother.

"Oh honey," Zoe says, and steps toward her, arms outstretched.

Justine isn't sure, but it looks like Hannah flinches for a second, and in that moment she relates to the girl. Justine's mother Helen was an overbearing presence in her own youth, bigger than life, opinionated, never making much space. *Does Hannah feel dwarfed by Zoe?* The two women hug, and Zoe lets loose big tears and holds her daughter too tightly. Justine has to look away—her heart clenching, her arms tingling with a visceral ache of what it feels like to hold your child like that.

When mother and daughter part, Hecate sighs. "What are we going to do with you three? You're not as useful as you think. You come with a lot of baggage, to be honest."

Zoe pulls off her sweater—she is always taking things off, Justine notices. "Talking to my husband isn't going to get us anywhere. It never has, why would it work now? We're not at a good enough place in our marriage. I'm too..." she waved at herself... "volatile. I don't even think I could find any diplomacy inside me if I tried. And even if I could, as far as his business partners and shareholders are concerned, I have no voice in anything."

Hecate looks thoughtful, so Zoe presses on. "And you didn't help matters any by pulling Hannah into this. He thinks she's just part of your radical agenda, now."

Hannah's lips tighten, and Justine suddenly wants to comfort her. *She shouldn't have to deal with this shit.*

"Well, we're not criminals. We can't say we kidnapped her," Hecate says, a sharp edge in her tone.

"I know," Zoe says. "I know."

"The trail will dead end with the Defenders of Freedom. They'll try to pin it on us, but we're not an 'us' that's easy to trace. Like Antifa, we have no website or headquarters or central hub. We show up when we're needed, we do our thing."

Justine stands up, her skinned knees and broken rib throbbing. "So let's *do* something. Let's stop sitting around while these companies plunder the earth and leave toxic refuse behind for poor communities to die in."

Hecate's lips tighten. "Some of us have been doing this work since before you were born, Justine."

Her tone is a slap, but Justine can't just keep sitting around anymore. Even at the moment when the Defenders had her in arms, when she was thrown to the hard ground of their little lair, her future uncertain, the very blood pumping through her veins had intention, her heart beating like an old car that has finally gotten started. *It's like being alive. Like giving a shit again.*

"So...give me a task."

Hecate makes eye contact with Persephone and Artemis, and then at Calliope and Ariadne, the silent, stoic ones who speak less, but always show up.

"You want a task? You can help me with an errand. We need to take young Hannah on a little visit. We need to lift some veils off her eyes."

Justine groans. "Sounds scintillating."

Hecate frowned. "You've got a broken rib, what do you expect me to do with you?"

Justine won't admit it aloud, but there is something comforting about the constant throb in her ribs. In the same way that all the discomforts of pregnancy—a foot in the bladder, baby's midnight hiccups, the constant tug of gravity on her nether regions—were also a joy; they'd meant that her baby was alive.

At the thought of Willa, a fresh pain stabs her, but not in the rib. She lurches forward with a feeling like she might vomit, but instead, one single, punctuated sob erupts from her mouth. It is tearless and violent, but it passes through her quickly.

Hecate simply raises a brow. "All right," she says, as though Justine has passed some test. "Now get dressed. Zoe, this is where we part ways again. What I want you to do is go home and see if you can get into any of your husband's computers, iPads, etc. You are looking for information that we can use to impress upon him the seriousness of our request. Hannah will stay with us until then."

"I want a guarantee that Hannah will not be harmed!" Zoe says.

It's Hannah who responds first. She shakes her head at her mother—their features such an echo of each other's. "There are no guarantees, Mom. I'm an adult now, and I want to help Nemesis. You need to let go."

Hecate and the other Nemesis women give awed, approving grins in Hannah's direction.

Zoe's face reddens, and she opens her mouth as though to protest. Closing her eyes a long moment, and inhaling hard, she reopens her eyes, steps forward, and hugs Hannah again.

"Be careful," she says.

CHAPTER EIGHTEEN

Hecate instructs Hannah to tuck her voluminous dark hair into a slouchy dark cap. "If I tell you to stay in the car, or get down, you do just that." Hannah is surprised to feel... excited, energized. *Maybe I don't have to go all the way to Kenya to do some good in the world.*

Justine looks sullen and gloomy, eyes on a distant horizon. Hannah has noticed Justine doesn't have a Greek name. *She must not really be one of them. Does it bother her?*

The road Hecate takes them on is full of potholes. Justine makes little gasping sounds every time the car jounces, clutching at her ribs. Hannah can't help herself—she presses a hand lightly on Justine's shoulders and rubs. Justine smiles at the tenderness of the gesture.

Once the car finally stops and they can take their blindfolds off, the three of them step out of the electric vehicle to an instant assault on the senses. Hannah claps a hand to her mouth, cringing, "What's that smell?"

Mentioning it only seems to make it stronger. It manages to smell both organic—rotting and fishy—and synthetic—the punch of chemical fumes that make her start coughing. Like she is trapped in a port-a-potty that has spent days baking in the sun.

"That's the smell of chemicals that shouldn't be leaching into land or water but are. From one of your father's plants," Hecate says simply. "His safety team will tell you it's just a smell, that there's no physical component, but people's health says otherwise."

Hannah scans a row of run-down apartments, their exteriors peeling and faded, a couple of windows missing and replaced with crudely nailed boards. "Nobody lives here, right? Who could live with that stench?"

Hecate frowns. "Oh yes, people live here. Work here. Raise their babies here, who play outside because their apartments are so stiflingly hot in the summer that at least outdoors they can get an occasional breeze."

Hannah claps a hand to her mouth again, feeling sick from more than just the smell.

Hecate gestures them toward one of the apartments around the side and knocks. The sound of children screeching and the shuffling steps of a larger body greets them, until the door is at last flung open by a teenage girl with a long dark braid. Before her, twin toddlers around the age of two with sticky faces, dressed only in diapers, babble.

"Hello sweetheart," Hecate says. "Not at school today?"

The girl smiles at Hecate, then frowns and shakes her head. "Mama had to get a second job." Justine glances at Hannah still cringing against the smell and gently pokes her. Hannah works hard to soften her face to normalcy.

"We brought a few things for you," Hecate says. "These are my friends. You might see more of them in the near future."

The girl's face awakens at Hecate's words, and the toddlers reach for the bag at Hecate's side.

"Ah, ah, ah, *niños*, patience." She holds it up high above their heads. "May we come in?"

"Oh, of course," the girl says.

"You know me better than that, sweetheart. Call me Sarah."

Justine raises an eyebrow and looks at Hannah as though to say, could that be Hecate's true name? *No. She probably doesn't give out her real name very often.*

The girl leads them into a cramped apartment, too small for three children and the absent mama. It is tidy, despite a small tumble of toys on the floor, and smells of recently cooked food, maybe chili. Hannah only catches the echo of food for a moment, like an ethereal top note, before the toxic fug from outside rises up aggressively, as though infused in the fibers and wallboards of the place.

Hecate sits at the tiny kitchen table, which only has two chairs, and pulls out her items. "Freshly baked bread, your mama's favorite. Persimmons for baking." The fruit looks almost obscenely fresh, gleaming and rounded like breasts. "And this..." Hecate slides across an envelope.

The girl opens the envelope and smiles in the way of someone who doesn't expect to be happily surprised. She makes a little hiccupping cry, and then closes her eyes altogether.

"Thank you," she whisper-cries, over and over. The toddlers, who have been clacking loud toys, stop suddenly and stare at their sister, faces tensed up by a decision whether to cry or not.

"The way you can show your gratitude is to tell your mama to quit that second job so you can go back to school. Understood?"

The girl holds one hand to her mouth, but nods vigorously.

After they leave the girl and her siblings, back out in the foul scented air, Hannah asks, "What was in the envelope?"

Hecate starts up the nearly soundless vehicle and doesn't look at Hannah. "A very big money order. One that will pay their bills for some time. Allow them to resettle outside of this toxic sludge. Project Nemesis doesn't exist as an entity on paper anywhere, but some of our members are lawyers, researchers, financial professionals. We've been able to...negotiate small settlements for individual folks."

Hannah notes how she lingers on the word *negotiate* and suspects she doesn't mean between men in suits and over tables with lawyers.

Hecate continues, "This apartment complex is actually soon to be torn down, its residents resettled. Do you know why?"

"Because of that...smell?" Hannah holds her nose.

"That's right. That smell is the result of toxic chemicals leached into the nearby stream. The chemicals have found their way into the water table, since most of the properties out here are on wells. A lot of the folks that have lived here have gotten very sick. Or will."

"That's terrible," Hannah says.

"Yep. And do you know which company is responsible for this?"

Hannah feels Justine's eyes on her. Both women are waiting for her to understand something. She knows, but she doesn't want to know. Tears prick at her eyes—she fights them back.

"My...my dad's company?"

Hecate sighs heavily and nods.

They repeat this scenario at half a dozen other places, driving from the South Bay area to the Central Coast and back.

"And how are you deciding who to help?" Hannah asks at one point. "How do you choose?"

Hecate's silences are weighted and pointed—Hannah can almost feel what isn't said like a dense fog that wraps around her. "We help those who need it most, the ones without the power, the money, the resources."

Hannah falls silent, considering.

Their last stop takes them up a long winding private driveway to a house that is many times bigger and in much better condition than any they've seen that day. Hannah shoots Justine a quizzical expression, but Justine just shrugs. Surely the residents of what is just shy of a mansion don't need help paying their bills?

They park, but rather than approach the front door, Hecate leads them around a side path, flanked by rose bushes, to a back gate, with a keypad. She enters the code and they slip behind the gate into a lush back patio, landscaped in billowy grasses and climbing vines, following a neatly paved stone path to a back door. There, Hecate enters another passcode and lets them into the bottom floor of the house, which is cool and unlit. A set of stairs leads to a basement complete with a pool table, a mini fridge, a couple of couches, and a DVD player.

"What is this, why are we here?" Justine asks.

"Your new safe house," Hecate says. "You wanted a task, Justine? Watch over little Miss Ready to Save the World until we figure out how she can be most useful. If Daddy turns over that video, well, she'll be wanted for a crime she did not commit."

"What?" Hannah says. "What are you talking about?"

Justine opens her mouth as though to say something soothing, but Hecate presses on. "You need to know the kind of man your father is, sweetheart. He threatened to turn that video you made over to the police."

"Are you kidding me?"

Hecate shakes her head. "Everything has its price."

"I thought you said I could be useful," Hannah cries, her voice straining, sounding embarrassingly young to even her ears.

Hecate reaches out a motherly hand to Hannah's face. She smooths a lock of hair away that escaped from the cap. "You can be the most useful by staying out of the way. There's food in the fridge, water, a toilet. You can't go upstairs. Clothing and blankets in the closet."

"How long are we supposed to stay here?" Justine asks sharply.

"I can't say," Hecate says.

"You're not going to just lock me up!" Justine all but shouts.

"You're not locked up, Justine. You can walk right out of here no problem, both of you. We'll park your car only blocks away. But if you do leave, not only will you no longer be able to count on our protection, but don't expect to come strutting back into our midst again. We won't return your calls anymore."

Hannah doubles over, thinking she might puke.

"You're missing an opportunity in me," Justine spits out at Hecate, who is already moving for the door.

Hannah stands dumbly by.

"We never miss an opportunity," Hecate says simply, then lets herself out the door, which closes with a final sounding snick.

Justine paces the room like some kind of caged wild cat. "I gave these women what they wanted! I have nothing to lose and now they're going to just cast me aside?"

"Justine, let's just, let's just think," Hannah says. "We'll figure something out."

Justine looks up with startled eyes. "I'm so sorry about all of this, Hannah. It's all my fault."

Hannah doesn't understand how that is true, but Justine looks so sad she just goes and hugs her. Justine squeals in pain.

"Sorry," Hannah says. "I forgot."

"Don't be sorry," Justine says. "You have nothing to be sorry for."

CHAPTER NINETEEN

A light fritzes over the construction scene. In its strobing Zoe can make out mounds of dirt, like giant anthills, massive cinder blocks, construction debris, trucks, red cones. She paces the perimeter, as close as she is able to get. In weeks cement will harden over earth, pillars will rise, receptacles will form to hold the most dangerous material on earth—enriched uranium—and her husband's hand has helped to shape all of this. She's not sure why, but she just had to look at it, all formlessness and possibility, just like her. An intrusive thought enters: a vision of the whole thing exploding in flames, the women of Nemesis standing back with expressions of satisfaction, and Zoe at the center of them.

She can see it from Phil's point of view—he is building possibility: the possibility of light and heat and industry. Schools and hospitals and grocery stores. But he is also killing possibility: the waste remnants of this plant will be death itself —with millions of years to break down uranium fuel. And the rest of his business, petroleum bound, steadily contributing to the death of the planet that offers up resources with little choice.

Zoe shivers. She no longer knows who is a friend and who is an enemy. Even her own daughter confuses her.

Am I being used, or willingly lending myself as a tool? Nemesis takes care of people, but they threaten everything I have —all I've gained. Justine was a friend, but her loss has split me apart, hardened me.

You're still on his side—says a voice in her head that is something like Justine's, but not entirely; it is her own voice, from a long time ago. *Maybe I was a broken thing then, but wasn't I a more authentic person at least? I've sold myself into the soft comfort of Phil's padded life. Who was I before?*

* * *

In a time when they'd first started dating, in the weeks before he learned that she was lying about being in college and living in the shiny campus dorms, Phil had joined her at the coffee shop where they'd met and found her deep into a sketch.

"Wow, that's...dark," he said, leaning over her from behind, wafting a breeze of his gingery cologne. He always smelled aggressively fresh and clean, like he showered every few hours.

She jumped, not having heard him arrive. The sketch had taken on a life of its own—they did that—and she hadn't even really noticed what she was drawing—an emaciated man, curled into a fetal ball, except for his bottom arm, which was limp and flat, a needle protruding from it. She'd drawn his skin taut over muscle, his face little more than skin over bone.

She quickly covered up the drawing.

He sat down beside her, warm green eyes fixed on her. "Don't do that, don't hide it. You're really good."

No one but her high school art teacher had ever really seen

her work. And he just thought she had "Goth tendencies" due to her subject matter. Nobody knew about her home life. She kept all friendships at arm's length, acquaintances only, so nobody ever asked to come over.

She shrugged. "Better to get the dark stuff on the page than keep it in my head," she said in what she hoped was an airy tone.

Phil laughed. "You're not dark. You're..." he put one hand on her hand that was still chalky and coated with charcoal. "... raw. Different from anyone I've ever met. I like it."

And then they'd gone back to his apartment and had messy sex, the only time she could—or would—really let her guard down. She loved the helpless look in his eyes when she knew he was going to come and she was responsible for that power.

Afterwards, curled nakedly together, he said, "What do you plan to do with that art degree you're getting? Teach or something?"

She still didn't have the heart to admit she wasn't actually in school. "Just be a starving artist, I guess," she said. "Live in a little studio in the woods and live off the food of my own garden. You know, go into town once a month or something."

He laughed. "God, I wish I had your freedom."

"What do you mean?"

"I'm my father's son. That means the family business. Rasmussen energy. MBA, then a Ph.D. Work for the company. Probably run it. That's my fate."

"I'm sorry," she said, snuggling into his neck. "We could just run away together. There have to be lots of run down cottages in lots of forests."

He'd laughed and held her. "I really wish I could."

* * *

Zoe returns to the present when a sharp chill threads its way through her jacket. She can hardly remember either of those people they used to be.

What would our lives have been like if we'd just run away as I'd suggested? And now? What if I she can't go home? If the cars and the clothes and the access are all denied? Where would she go? What would she do? Bernard? Would he still hold her in high regard, let his old boss sleep on his couch, or would even EarthWorks prove to be a house of cards built upon Phil's allowance? Should she join her mother on the street somewhere?

Why worry about having nothing? I've had nothing before.

It hits her that she isn't really sure who her friends are— because some part of her is still that same girl who doesn't trust anyone, who doesn't let people close. Everyone who plays a significant role in her life is there because they have to be: Karina. Bernard. Fernando. The myriad staff. Lorraine, the wife of Phil's CFO. Their friendship mostly comprised of standing, stiff-smiling at their husbands' events, drinks in hand as they pretend to have a few things in common. *Sometimes it feels as though Phil has paid a cast of people to make me feel like I have a real life. No, I can't blame Phil.* She latched onto the life he dangled before her with so little thought. She slipped into the skin of the woman he needed her to be because, at the time, it felt so much better than the one she'd come crawling, wretched and terrified, from.

The faces of the Nemesis women rise to mind. Artemis, with her long red braid and her thoughtful face. Stern, serious Hecate. Powerful Persephone. She wonders about their real names and who they were before they were warrior goddesses. She considers who she might become if she remains surrounded by such women on a regular basis.

That shiver returns. She has the strangest sensation of

having left more than just a suit behind in the woods that day when Justine dragged her into their midst, and that if she were to look at her face in a mirror suddenly, she wouldn't recognize herself.

The Lyft finally slides into view and she slips inside, suddenly feeling she can't go home tonight after all. That it will be like walking into a dream she's unsure if she wants to wake from. She picks the closest, cheapest motel she can find. Then she texts Phil:

Staying late at the office to do a lot of catch-up work. Don't wait up. May just sleep here.

To her surprise he replies right away:

Don't work too hard.

When did their marriage stop containing these sweet and normal exchanges? Like so many things in her life, she missed the moment when everything changed, and now...now, it's too late.

CHAPTER TWENTY

"Can you drive a stick shift?" Justine asks Hannah. "I need something for the pain. I don't want to go out, but I'm not going to be able to sleep without it."

"I mean, I can drive an automatic, but I don't really drive."

"Of course you don't. You have chauffeurs," Justine says sharply.

Shame washes over Hannah. When Justine says it like that, it sounds...disgusting. How has she never questioned it before?

"It's not hard, I'll show you," Justine says through gritted teeth.

"Are you sure? In the dark, at night? I mean what if we get pulled over?"

"It's that or we walk back. I don't think I should drive right now."

Pity wells up in Hannah. "You're not okay. Should I take you to the hospital or something?"

Justine shakes her head. "Just be a big girl and drive this *goddamned* car, Hannah. I'll walk you through it."

Hannah suddenly feels like crying, though she knows it's

stupid, childish. She was planning to go to Africa and start a school? Who is she kidding—she can't even think of driving a car without panicking.

"Okay, okay," she says, coming around to Justine's side. "I can do this."

Justine hands over the keys, walks to the other side and gets in.

Once she is in, before she starts the car, Hannah turns to Justine. "Do you think my mom is mad at me for that video?"

"Push in that pedal—all the way. Turn on the car, lift the brake there and turn the headlights on."

Hannah does as she's told. "I don't know what's happening," she says more softly than she intends. "I feel like my life as I knew it is over."

Justine's laugh is dry, strained. "Oh kid, your life is just beginning. And maybe your mother's is, too. End of one thing, start of something else. Now, take the gear shift through the diagram—one to four. Get a feel for it."

"I'm scared," Hannah says, as she moves through the gears —first, up into second, down, over, and up into third, down into fourth.

"I used to be scared," Justine says. "Take it back into first."

"And you're not now?" Hannah asks, almost afraid of the answer. She knows that the worst possible thing has happened to Justine. It seems like the kind of thing that only happens to women on crime shows. She doesn't know how anyone survives that.

"Now I just want to leave a lasting mark on the world. Give it a little gas—not much—then slowly let the clutch out."

"What's the clutch?" Hannah asks, giving the accelerator too much gas and making the engine rev too hard.

"Easy," Justine says. "The clutch is the left pedal. When you let it out, you will be in gear."

"Does this have to do with my dad's new plant?" Hannah says. Her body feels numb to her—her own voice sounds far away, like she's shouting down a long tunnel.

"I think someone needs to teach your dad a lesson that money doesn't buy you everything."

Hannah eases off on the gas pedal while slowly letting the clutch out. She feels the car lurch forward, thinking about the different versions of her dad. The man in his power suits behind closed doors who she doesn't know at all—someone who wheels and deals with other powerful men. And the version of him at holidays, grandiose and loudly laughing, always with a drink in hand. And the one she doesn't remember very much anymore, who used to come running to her room in comfort when she woke with those childhood nightmares.

"Give it some gas. When you hear it and feel it whine, push the clutch back in, and shift up into second gear, and then let the clutch out."

"Will he get hurt?" Hannah asks, following Justine's instructions.

Justine sighs again. "Not physically hurt. Just hurt in the bank account. And believe me, your daddy's got plenty of bank account to spare. Push the clutch in and shift down, over and up into third. Then let the clutch back out."

Hannah wants to defend him, to point out that this is a country where you are allowed to make whatever money you can, that's the whole point. But she knows something else: that her dad was born into money even before he made it. That he started at the top and had every advantage, and as a result, so has she. Her mom, on the other hand, that isn't true of her, but that's all she knows.

"Clutch in. Pull it down into fourth; clutch out." Justine says. "Learning something new is as easy as that. You just have to be willing to grow."

Does she mean driving a stick shift or letting go of a life?
Both—most likely—both.

* * *

By the time they return from the drugstore with a big bottle of ibuprofen to the safe house, Justine is groaning in pain. Hannah props herself beneath Justine's non-injured side and helps her down the path—grateful that Justine remembers the passcode, because she's forgotten it. She is a shit activist, or whatever it is these people are. But as they limp around the back toward the basement entrance, a woman with neatly cropped blonde hair emerges from the house.

"Excuse me, who are you and what are you doing on my property?" she demands in a high voice, tinged with fright.

"We're..." Hannah begins, but doesn't know what else to say. Hecate didn't prepare them for this scenario. But then again, they were meant to stay put.

"We're friends of, uh, Sarah's," Justine croaks.

Hannah's glad Justine remembered the pseudonym Hecate gave; she would have said the wrong thing.

The woman's eyes narrow upon them even more tightly. Lasers in on the way Hannah's propping up Justine, and Justine's pinched, tight face.

"Are you on drugs?" she asks.

Justine makes a pained sounding laugh. "I wish," she says. "Broken rib."

The woman lifts her chin and pulls herself back upright. "I told Sarah she can't keep bringing people over here. I'm sorry, but you can't stay."

"Please," Hannah tried. "She's hurt. She just needs a place to rest."

The woman takes a cell phone out of her purse. "There's a Motel 6 just down the road," she says tersely.

"One night?" Justine's voice is croaky with pain.

The woman's skin tightens across her cheeks as she frowns. "Do I need to call the police?"

"No! No, please don't do that," Hannah all but shrieks. "We'll go, please."

The woman nods but holds out her phone as though it were a weapon. Justine mutters something under her breath, possibly a curse. Then they turn back around, limp-walking back to the car.

"*Fuck!*" Hannah beats her hands against the steering wheel. "What if Nemesis won't help us anymore? And what if my dad really turns over that video? I could get arrested..." Hot tears roll out of her eyes. She presses the heels of her hands into her face.

Justine slams her palm down onto the dashboard of the car. "Stop it. We're not helpless. I just need some ibuprofen. We don't know that your father turned that video over to the police yet. Even if he did, they have no idea we're connected to one another. We can go back to my house. No one's there."

Hannah tries to calm her breathing, to stop the tears, but they are already turning to hiccups. She nods, but she doesn't think she can see well enough to drive just yet.

"Shit," Justine says, but without any anger. Then Justine's slim, cool hand snakes around her shoulders and rubs her back lightly. "Breathe, Hannah. Just breathe. You're going to survive this. It's going to be okay."

Somehow, Hannah collects herself enough to drive to Justine's house. They park a street over, though, at Justine's insistence, even though it means she has to limp-walk extra distance.

Justine's house is small, but cozy, though it smells musty,

like nobody's opened a window in months. In every room boxes are piled up against walls.

"My husband's stuff," Justine says simply when she notices Hannah's eyes lingering on it. "He's having a hard time really making the separation."

"What about you?" Hannah asks. "Did you want him to go?"

Justine begins rattling through cabinets until she finds what she is looking for, downing additional Tylenol to accompany the ibuprofen pills with a gulp of tap water.

Justine slumps into one of the worn kitchen chairs. "No. Maybe. We love each other, but I couldn't open myself to him... after..." she says.

Hannah isn't entirely sure what Justine means, but she gets the gist.

The kitchen isn't as lonely as the rest of the house. A few bright landscape paintings hang on the walls. A water cooler stands in one corner, empty. It is a nice, homey space, but Hannah's eyes are drawn to what is missing; no colorful kid drawings on the fridge, no roughly made ceramic mugs or child plates in evidence.

"I'm sorry...about your daughter," she says softly, tentatively. She doesn't want to hurt Justine, but how can she not say it, here in the place where the little girl lived?

Justine swallows hard. She looks at her hands, picks at a fingernail, then her eyes snap up in a purposeful sort of way, seem to assess Hannah. After a minute, Justine rises, walks down the hallway, and Hannah hears the soft snick of a door opening.

She senses that Justine means for her to follow. Hannah finds Justine standing before a bedroom. She peers past Justine's shoulder, half afraid of what she'll see.

The room is empty of children's things or bedding. No

stuffed animals, no bookshelves full of board books like her mother used to read to her. No colorful wallpaper or toddler bed. Just a futon mattress heaped in blankets, some magazines cast about the floor, a mug of some abandoned beverage. The only evidence a child has ever called this home are four *Dora the Explorer* stickers, half peeling, on the door itself.

"Tonight, you can sleep here."

"Her room?" Hannah asks.

Justine stares blankly at a far corner for a long moment, then nods.

Hannah looks at her, nose wrinkled. *Does she want me to sleep in her dead child's room? But of course, Justine can't sleep in here. Of course she can't.*

"Sure, thanks. I'm kinda hungry though."

Justine is the kind of thin that makes you think she has an eating disorder, and Hannah, having met her before when she looked healthy and normal, wonders if there's even food in the house.

"I've got some frozen pizzas, if you can stand that?"

Hannah allows a little laugh. "What do you think I've been eating all year at college?"

Justine's tiny smile doesn't last.

They eat their frozen pizza at the little kitchen table, and Hannah tries to pretend that everything will be alright. She'll talk to her mom, and her mom will talk sense to her dad, and they will make this nightmare of Nemesis and the fate of her future hanging in the balance go away.

"Have you ever thought of having another...?" Hannah blurts.

Justine presses her lips together hard, and Hannah wishes she didn't ask it. She doesn't know how to talk to adults.

"I didn't think I wanted any to begin with," Justine says after a moment. "My husband talked me into it."

"What was his argument? Like, why did you after all?"

Justine smiles slightly. "He told me he knew I'd want to leave a legacy." Her laugh is bitter. "That the journalist in me craved leaving a trace, so to speak."

Hannah can't swallow her bite suddenly.

"I felt like shit at it. I didn't have those ethereal impulses women are supposed to have. And maybe some part of me knew that."

"I doubt you were," Hannah says softly. "Shit, I mean."

Justine looks at her sharply. "I didn't feel an immediate bond with her when she was born. I mean, other than that instinct to protect that comes through you the minute that baby is in your arms. I felt like we needed to be introduced. That we needed a chaperone who could teach us to each other. When my milk came in, I grew closer to her, when she *needed* me, my body, for survival, I guess. But I had a hard time, physically, mentally, with the lack of sleep, but..." Now, a tiny warble entered Justine's voice, the suggestion of tears, "I chose my work over her time and time again."

"I..." Hannah starts, but she doesn't know what to say, how to comfort her. Hannah can't really imagine it anyway—her own mom was annoyingly present. Joined the PTA at every school, organized a million mom's group outings. They had Mommy and Me classes and girls' spa weekends. The first time Hannah felt like she could just be herself, figure out her way in the world, was the day her parents dropped her off at her college dorms. The moment her mom's back had disappeared through the door, Hannah took the biggest breath of her life.

"It's okay," Justine says, wiping away a tear. "I wouldn't know what to say to me either."

When they stand there, awkwardly looking at each other for too long, Hannah wishes she'd directed the conversation somewhere else. Justine finally shakes herself and says, "I'll get you something to sleep in." She brings Hannah a pair of her own flannel pajamas that are a bit short in the legs and arms, though cozy, and Hannah takes her cue, lying down in the room that holds so much sadness.

Hannah is still lying there, hours later, mind churning, when Justine creeps back into the room and hunkers in the doorway for a long minute. Zoe put her to bed every night for years, first a comforting thing, and eventually a smothering thing. By the time she was thirteen, she had to practically yell at her mom to leave her alone. She'd seen her mom's eyes fill with hurt, but she couldn't stop herself. But now, Hannah doesn't mind the woman in the doorway—there is something comforting in Justine's presence, though she doesn't really know why. And she can almost picture the little girl, Willa, who she'd only met once, lying beside her now, her hair sweaty and tangled across her forehead, Justine looking in on her fondly. Justine's breathing is loud in the stillness, a hitched and heavy sound. Hannah wants to put out her arms to her, as though asking to be held, but she does not.

CHAPTER TWENTY-ONE

Justine doesn't know what possessed her to go look in on Hannah as she slept. She isn't a child, really, certainly doesn't seem in need of mothering, and yet...Justine will never get to know what sort of young woman Willa would have become. She imagines that her toddler's fierce will would have stayed with her, made her a formidable woman in the world. *Like you are trying to be?* The critical voice had simply emerged one day after Willa's death. *She is the price you paid for pursuing your desires.*

She grasps her head even now and crushes her fingers into her skull to stop it. For an entire year she has lost complete touch with reality. But now reality is so heightened and sharp, it could cut her with its simplicity.

She could not save her own daughter, but she can save Hannah from this mess she's inadvertently been drawn into. She can do this and teach the girl's father a lesson in the process, and maybe, just maybe, the women of Nemesis will talk about her in fond memory. They'll say her sacrifices were worth something.

Just the knowledge that the girl is sleeping in the other room makes the house feel different. Full.

She takes her laptop to the kitchen, makes herself some tea, and sets to doing some simple research.

* * *

Justine is jarred awake by the sound of footsteps. She lifts her head from the kitchen table. Bright morning light carves away shadows. She fell asleep at the table over her work just like so many nights of her life. For a brief moment she imagines that the person coming toward her is her tiny daughter, padding in to climb into her lap as Justine finishes an article. Her heart pounds with anticipation of the soft limbs clad in plush footie pajamas...until memory catches up and she is cold again, hollow. Instead, Hannah stands there, messy haired and curious, peering over Justine's shoulder at her laptop. Realizing what she'd been looking at last night, Justine slams the laptop closed.

"Hungry?" she asks the girl who, in her sleep rumpled state, looks much younger than she is.

Hannah nods.

"I hope you like frozen waffles and instant coffee. I threw out pretty much everything else."

"Sure," Hannah says, and Justine is overcome with the strangest urge to hug this girl.

Instead, she busies herself preparing food and boiling water, things she hasn't done in almost a year. There was always someone else fussing over food, trying to cajole nutrients into her body for those long months—her mother at first, her meals leaning toward nutrition over flavor. Nate, of course, until his own emptiness grew too great and he stopped trying to fill hers, too. Zoe, briefly.

For the first time in months, Justine thinks she should call Nate, reassure him that she is okay. Ask after him. The painful silences between them or the awkward forced attempts at normalcy have been nearly as bad as the loss itself. But every time she thinks of picking up the phone, she doesn't know what to say.

She watches Hannah eat her toaster waffles with jam unselfconsciously, voraciously, with bemusement. She can't remember inhabiting her body in that sort of way in a long time. If she hadn't brought Zoe out to Nemesis, then the Defenders would not have identified her, targeted her husband, found Hannah. Just as always, Justine indirectly caused harm to others, and now she has to make it right.

I can't take back what happened to Willa. I can't ever make that right again. But this I can.

Can't I?

If she lets herself, when she closes her eyes, she can still see the tight, closed look on Nate's face when she'd come running to the hospital, hours after it had happened, after it was too late, after she'd made her way back from that encounter with Nemesis, when she'd finally believed she was getting close to something big, that they were letting her *in*.

"You were supposed to pick her up," Nate had said on the phone with such an awful tinge to his voice. "You were supposed to be there, Justine."

"Are you okay?" The voice now seems to be coming from far away, tinny and small. For a moment Justine is disoriented. Her own kitchen looks strange to her, like those early days when they'd first moved in and she kept making her way to the hall closet when she meant to go to the bathroom, or bumping into things that aren't where her mental map remembered them.

The girl is looking at her with Zoe's dark eyes and that mess of dark curls and sorrow in her face.

Justine tries to smile reassuringly, but her lips are rubber, they won't comply.

"Maybe it's too much to be here?" Hannah asks. "We could go somewhere else."

Justine forces her lips into a smile she doesn't mean. "I'm going out to run some errands, get a little more food. You need to promise me you'll stay put."

Hannah looks stricken.

"No one knows we're here, Hannah. I promise. And I'll keep a low profile."

Hannah nods, but her face is full of clenched muscles and tight lines. "Can you drive?"

"I'm better. I'll be fine. You can watch TV or surf the internet, okay?"

"When do you think I'm, like, free to go?" Hannah asks in that same small voice that makes Justine aware of just how young she really is. Perhaps younger than her age by the shelter of her privilege. "I'm supposed to be on a flight to Kenya in four days."

Justine finds sudden strength now. She stands up and places a gentle hand on Hannah's shoulder. "I'm working on that, okay? I promise. I will make it right."

Hannah chews her lip, as though she wants to say something, but does not.

Justine takes her cue, grabbing her coat. "I'll be back very soon."

CHAPTER TWENTY-TWO

Hannah holds her breath, listening. Now she is torn between an anxious thudding of her pulse at being alone and a kind of relief. When she hears the car engine rev and pull away, she releases her breath. She thinks about calling her mother. It would be so easy for Zoe to come pick her up, and Hannah would be back in her bedroom in less than a half hour, and they'll figure something out. She'll tell her mom she was coerced. She'll apologize to her father for that video that makes her look complicit. Except...she can't shake all that she's seen. Those poor families living near a toxic slurry. Her father's company's part in it. Allegations of worse things within his company.

She thinks about the way Justine slammed her laptop closed when she'd seen Hannah standing there. There was something in the hurried way she'd closed it that makes Hannah want to know what she was looking at. Something guilty about the actions.

She lifts the lid with two fingers only, as though she is trying to leave little evidence at a crime scene. There are dozens of tabs open, so many she feels defeated at even bothering to look, but she tries a few. There is one in particular, a PDF Justine downloaded with a recipe for making a simple bomb. *What the hell! Was Justine responsible for the bomb at my parents' house? But then why would she be looking up how to make them? Something doesn't make sense.*

Nothing makes sense, in fact. Except that Justine is determined to send her father a message. Hannah can't imagine how she is going to get back in his good graces after that video. But... bombing her father's new plant in the making? *That is a criminal act. Does Justine really mean to do something so final, so serious?* But then Hannah thinks about the way Justine looks at her—her eyes are haunted, and she moves through this lonely house like a woman with nothing to live for. Hannah knows what she needs to do: she needs to thwart Justine's very bad plan. But she's learned one thing from growing up a Rasmussen: you get people to change their minds by going along with them, making them believe you are on their side. Then, you redirect them.

CHAPTER TWENTY-THREE

Morning carves razor-like through Zoe's sleep and, for one heart-pounding moment, she doesn't know where she is. No thousand thread count beneath her outstretched hand, just overly starched sheets. No purified air or subtle scent of oranges in the air, but the meaty scent of a breakfast buffet down the hall.

She is overcome by a sudden, strange exhilaration. She has nothing with her but the clothes she wore and her small purse. She can smell her own night-sweaty, unshowered funk rising up from the sheets. But she does not have to explain herself to anyone. Doesn't have to deal with Phil's frowning disapproval or convictions about their daughter-as-terrorist.

She gets a Lyft back to the house, knowing Phil will be at work. A security guard is now stationed outside the gate. He is young enough to be her son, but powerfully built and armed. Her reflexive response to any weapon is an instant cold sweat.

"Name and ID, ma'am?" he asks as she approaches.

She laughs. "I live here."

"Still need to see your I.D."

173

With a smug smile, she produces her I.D. The woman in that photo is poised and coiffed, her gaze commanding the viewer, *Don't you know who I am?* Zoe feels as if she is looking at a relative, not herself. Even the security guard seems to have his doubts about the version of her on the I.D., and the unkempt woman standing before him, her long hair a mass of tangles, no crisp suit, no make-up. He looks between them several times, but he finally nods and lets her through.

She showers, dresses in a sleek silver gray suit with high heeled booties, and pulls her hair up. The lump on her forehead left a slight bruise in its wake. She won't cover it up—let everyone at the office think she's been *through something*. She needs everyone to cut her a little slack. She gathers her work briefcase and, rather than calling on Fernando to drive her, helps herself to the keys to one of the cars. Today feels like a day for being in complete control of herself.

* * *

She thinks her assistant Bernard is going to cry when he catches sight of her. He neatly extricates her from gushing staff and escorts her into her office, tightly closing the door behind them.

"Good lord, woman, you could have warned me about your midlife crisis," he says, though not unkindly. He is tall and lean, hair always slicked into obedience, suits impeccable. He does look a little dark under the eyes. His worry touches her.

"That's not how midlife crises work—they take everyone by surprise, throw things asunder."

Bernard's cheeks flex, but he doesn't smile. He is still mad.

"Are you sick to death about Hannah?" he says first.

Zoe's stomach does drop, even though she knows Hannah is, in essence, okay. This act of pretending is getting harder.

And Hannah is only okay so long as Phil does not make good on his threat to turn that video over to the cops.

"You even have to ask?" she says, filling her voice with motherly concern. "But I trust the police. I have to focus on other things in the meantime to distract myself."

He stares at her for a long moment, then extracts his tablet and stylus, pecking at his screen like a hungry bird. "Well, we've got shit to get done, Zoe. Not the least of which is figure out what to do about the massive donation we received from Rasmussen Energy."

Zoe's head snaps up. "What?"

Bernard's dark green eyes widen. "Three million dollars. Think of all the solar panels we could fund! But...I know, I know..." he holds up his hand.

"We can't accept it. It's a blatant conflict of interest for me, for one, and worse, it's Phil's way of exerting control."

Bernard pouted slightly. "I knew you were going to say that. So, I gather he didn't tell you in advance?"

Zoe drops heavily into her desk chair and sighs. "Of course not. If it's possible for someone to revenge-donate money, that feels like what my husband just did."

"Damn, could he revenge-buy me a trip to the Caribbean while he's at it?" Bernard says.

Zoe is too incensed to laugh. She reaches across the desk and grasps one of Bernard's neatly manicured hands. "I'm sorry to have bailed on the grant ceremony. I won't do that again, leave you high and dry. I promise."

Bernard looks at her hand as though he might slap it off, but then heaves a sigh. "You better not. And it's not me you need to apologize to, but the board."

Zoe sighs. "There will be time for that later. Now I have six thousand emails and five hundred calls to return, right?"

"At least," he says. "And you're Em-Ceeing every awards ceremony that we ever have in the future." Now he smiles.

"Deal."

Bernard finally lets her be after briefing her on all that she's missed in the past three days, and Zoe locks her office door behind him. She boots up her computer and thinks about that moment in the clearing when those men—defenders of what, exactly—showed up en masse like boys playing cops. Vigilante justice. She can't help but think of the one story she'd heard from her Oma before she'd died—about the day she'd encountered German boys she'd gone to school with, newly outfitted in their SS uniforms coming through town. At first sight, she'd said, "They looked so handsome, so impressive, I swooned a little at first sight." Then they'd trashed Jewish-owned storefronts, hooting in glee, calling out slurs and threatening violence on anyone bold enough to stay out on the streets and, she said, "I knew then that terrible things were to come.

"Even though I saw it with my own eyes, I didn't want to believe it," she'd told Zoe and her mother. "I didn't want to believe that anyone could hate us so much."

These angry terrified boys, they have the typical arrogance of men for whom everything has always been handed to them with little fight. But she isn't going to let her daughter take the fall for either end of that continuum, not the scared little men, nor the big hungry powerful ones.

"Everyone has a weakness," Phil is fond of saying when discussing negotiating a business deal.

Yes they do.

And for the first time she wonders what her husband's is. She, clearly, is not it. His own daughter may not even be. What is the point of all this wealth and power if it doesn't protect or guarantee the family you've built?

Well, rejecting his donation will be a start. She cancels the automated payment through their online payment system.

*   *   *

That night, Zoe does something she hasn't done in a very long time: she cooks dinner for her husband and meets him at the door with a kiss and a tumbler of scotch.

He eyes her with surprise but clutches her tightly in a hug that feels almost conciliatory.

She's roasted a chicken and some vegetables, made a nice butternut squash risotto, and pulled out the Rombauer Chardonnay. She sets the table with the second-best China and relieves all the staff who are likely to try and take over serving or cleaning up after them.

"What's all this?" Phil asks as he sits down at her urging.

"Peace offering?" she says.

"You're saying it as a question," he says, but his mouth tilts up in a grin.

"I'm tired of fighting," she says.

Phil sighs and nods, though he doesn't say that he is tired of it too. He shrugs off his suit coat jacket and moves his place setting beside hers rather than across.

He cuts into his chicken, which bubbles over with juices, and sighs contentedly as he bites into it. One part of her is pleased, another annoyed; this is the version of her he likes best. The accommodating wife who makes him dinner, as she did in the early years before they lived in a compound with staff. But did she really ever offer another version of herself to him? She'd wanted escape—rescue—and he'd given that to her. She had failed to ever ask for more.

Until now.

After he's had a second glass of scotch and finished most of his meal, she keeps her voice light as she says, "EarthWorks won't be accepting your donation."

Phil's eyes are the only things to move toward her, a flick in her direction, almost as though he hasn't heard her.

"I appreciate the gesture," she adds quickly, "but even *you* know I can't."

"Can't? You mean *won't?*" Phil says, an edge entering his voice. "I thought this dinner was a peace offering."

"Well, actually, I *can* accept your money, and would be glad to, just not for EarthWorks."

Phil rumbles a laugh. "Tell me there's anything you actually want and you can have it, Zo. You know that."

Zoe pushes her own plate away, drains the wine in her glass. "I *want* the three million. But I need it to be given freely, no questions asked, made out to cash, not to EarthWorks."

Phil's bald pate gleams with the sweat of too much drink. His mouth is caught between smiling and frowning. In moments like these, she wonders if he's terrifying as a boss. "It's those terrorists, isn't it? They think they can get ransom for radicalizing our daughter?"

Zoe closes her eyes. An electric charge is looping up her spine. Her limbs tremble slightly. She opens them again. "You think I wouldn't tell you if they...if anybody were trying to extort us? You say I can have whatever I want. You say you're reasonable and generous. So, prove that to me, by giving me that money, no questions asked."

Phil tosses his napkin down hard on the table. "Given all of your behavior of the past week, given our daughter's behavior...you're asking a whole lot of me, you realize that? You're asking me to be reasonable when you have been anything but."

Zoe inhales, steels herself. She wants to rage, to tell him that he is selfish and boorish and that whoever tossed that newspaper with the words planet rapist over the fence was right. *Focus on the prize,* she reminds herself.

"I know," she says. "I'm getting my shit together, Phil. And I'm going to get Hannah to come to her senses, too. I promise you. I have a pet project, and it's not EarthWorks, but I promise you that it won't hurt your stock profile and it won't come back to bite you in the ass..." Okay, there she may be lying just a bit. "It will feel like you have some faith in me. That would count for a lot."

Phil stands and pours himself a third scotch. He spends a long moment with his back to her, swirling the liquid in his glass. "On two conditions," he says at last.

She can barely breathe with hope that he is agreeing.

"Name them."

"Hannah does not go to Kenya with that idiot boyfriend. Instead, she goes back to school, but not art. She gets a bachelor's in economics, then an MBA, then she comes to work for me."

Zoe can't swallow for a moment. *The cost for doing something good is to crush our daughter's dreams? Okay. We aren't signing a contract, inking anything in blood. This is a verbal agreement between spouses. How binding can that actually be?*

"Fine. But she'll hate you, too, you know. She won't see it as my fault."

Phil shrugs. "Sometimes the best things for us are the things we are forced to do, for our own good."

Zoe looks down at the remnants of her dinner, no longer hungry.

"If you say so. What's the second condition?"

Phil looks at his hands for a moment, as though afraid to meet her gaze. She is going to have to start attending more of his high profile events. Play the good wife much more effectively.

"Step down from your little organization," he says. A slight sheen of sweat has broken out on his forehead, as though from heavy exertion. The sight of it makes her own neck begin to sweat.

"My *little* organization?" she says roughly. "You mean the non-profit I built with my own sweat that makes energy afford-able for hundreds of people every year? Way not to seem like the villain here, Phil!"

She rises, lays her palms flat on the dining room table as though she could flip it over with just the momentum of her rage. He just stares at her.

"And yet you refuse to see yourself as keeping me on a leash," she seethes.

His face pinches into angry points, and suddenly he looks foreign to Zoe, not someone she has ever loved, surely not the man who fathered her child.

"You want my money, that's my demand."

My money. She homes in on his choice of words, aware that the line between them has been redrawn.

"That terrorist group has infiltrated your organization, whether you want to admit it or not. That is affecting my busi-ness. My home. I can't have my wife involved. It looks bad for everyone."

"I'm so glad you're finally admitting it's *your* money. That I am just an appendage to your life. That I am a bad look for you!"

Phil slams his hand down on the table, rattling the remaining dishes and her composure. "You can't have it both ways."

"Fine," she spits, her body a torch, sweat trickling down the back of her neck and in between her cleavage. *Is it worth it? That money can get Nemesis to take the heat off Hannah. And Earth-Works can appoint a new Director, and it will go on without me, so it will still be doing good in the world. And Hannah is young, she has time to pursue her dreams.* Still, she can't help but see the faces of those young girls who accosted her in the café, suggesting she should *do something.* Doing the right thing comes with a cost sometimes, she assures herself. It's worth it. It has to be.

After dinner, Zoe locks herself in the bathroom and texts via Signal.

> *MUST meet. Have something you'll want*

No reply, as usual.

Phil works so late that she doesn't hear him come to bed. Only notices he is there, his back turned away from her in slumber, when she awakes in a pool of her own sweat, unable to sleep. She wanders to the kitchen for a cool glass of water and is pleased to see she's finally gotten a response.

> *Tomorrow.* With an address and a time.

* * *

In the morning Zoe finds two things on her dresser: a pre-written resignation letter to EarthWorks that she merely has to sign, and a cashier's check for three million dollars. She isn't sure which item makes her catch her breath more. The letter sounds ridiculously unlike her. Though she is tempted to rewrite it, she hopes the tone will hint to the board that she's been pressured. All that has happened in the last week, from the newspaper flung over their gate to the bombing and Hannah's kidnapping, should have been the worst week of their lives. For Phil, it has added up to circumstances working in his favor. And the irony isn't lost on her that what Nemesis wants from him, to step down from his company, he is getting from her.

She signs, scans, and emails the letter to her board, copying Bernard. She should have told him in person—he won't forgive her for that—but she can't face him.

She takes the check and drives to the meeting place. Once inside, it turns out to be a little cottage, an Airbnb, she surmises, by its crisp lack of personality and potent air-freshener scent.

Hecate is waiting in a rocking chair, in a big fuzzy sweater and fingerless gloves, looking like some kindly grandma. Zoe laughs at the idea of Hecate doing grandmotherly knitting or baking.

Hecate raises an eyebrow at Zoe. "Long night?" she asks.

Zoe exhales heavily. "You don't even know."

Hecate smiles as though Zoe's exhaustion is a good sign. "Anything worth doing is worth losing some sleep over," she says.

Zoe passes over numerous retorts but knows it's hopeless to expect sympathy from Hecate.

"I got Phil to give me, well *you*, something that can make a big difference to Nemesis. And in return, I need you to make it clear that Hannah did not record that video of her own accord. I need you to get her to take that back."

Hecate raises a challenging eyebrow as she receives the envelope and opens it.

Zoe can't help the elation that rises in her as she waits for Hecate's expression to light up when she sees the check.

Hecate pulls it out, stares at it for a long minute, rubs her thumbs over its edges and then looks up at Zoe with hard eyes. "We don't need a revolving bank account; we need to change power structures. Your husband feels generous every time he donates or gives money away. But it doesn't change anything."

Zoe reels back as though Hecate has slapped her. "This is

three *million* dollars. Think of what you can do with it! No strings attached. Cashier's check. No one has to know where it came from."

Hecate looks away. "I appreciate that you know how to patch up holes and bridge gaps, my dear. But that's not what we asked of you."

Zoe wants to wrench the check out of Hecate's hands and tear it to shreds.

"Do you know what I sacrificed to get this? I stepped down from Earthworks. I traded on my daughter's future!"

Hecate raised her eyebrows, looking infuriatingly amused. "That's not what we asked."

Zoe stands up. "So, you want me to weaponize myself like Justine? Bring you my husband so you can hold him for ransom?"

Hecate smirks. "There's a thought." Perhaps at the sudden stricken look on Zoe's face, she holds up her hands. "I kid. As for Justine, at first I didn't think she was going to be anything more than a loose cannon, but I've since changed my mind. I was right to appoint her to watch over your daughter. Justine is a person who just needs to be sent in the right direction, given the right impetus. She'll make something happen. I can feel it."

"What do you mean you appointed her to watch over Hannah? Are you crazy? Justine is suicidal or homicidal, I'm not sure which..."

"Those of us with the least to lose often make the best soldiers."

"My daughter is 19! You need to do something about that video!"

"On the contrary! Perhaps you can get your husband to see your daughter *has* been radicalized, but not by us...but by a woman out of her mind with grief. And together they want only one thing—the destruction of economic patriarchy and environmental racism, but they'll start with your husband's company. Or else, I fear Justine and Hannah might not be able to promise to keep their actions nonviolent."

"What have you done?" Zoe all but hisses, backing away from the woman. "What have you done with my daughter?"

Hecate frowns. "We haven't *done* anything with her. I do hope, however, that something has catalyzed inside her that was already there, ready to awaken. Isn't it the nature of children to surpass their parents? To do bigger, bolder, greater things than we ever could?"

"Tell me where she is," Zoe demands.

Hecate shrugs. "I don't know. We sent them to a safe house, but they disappeared."

Zoe hands begin to crimp into claws. She senses herself moving toward the woman before she knows what she is doing, but suddenly arms are grasping her, pinning hers behind her. Calliope. Ariadne. They materialized out of nowhere in the little cottage—though she is vaguely aware of a door opening.

"Get her out of here," Hecate says.

These women who look so slight now manage to muscle her backwards. Hecate holds up the check and flaps it in her hands. "Thank you for this."

"You used me!" Zoe shouts.

Hecate's brows meet in befuddlement. "We did nothing to harm you. *You* keep coming to *us*. Perhaps you need to take a good hard look at what really matters to you, Zoe. A woman with a history like yours."

"What's that supposed to mean?" Zoe shouts, heaving herself forward against the momentum of the women dragging her backwards.

"You know what it means."

Then she is pulled out the door.

"God damn it!" she shouts. "I never asked for any of this."

Hecate's parting words are, "Nobody is a victim here."

But I am a victim. If Justine hadn't dragged me into this bullshit, I'd be living the same comfortable life, no worse for wear.

She shakes herself free of this line of thinking; it will get her nowhere. She stomps off to her car, heaves herself into the seat and sits there, breathing heavily for a few minutes, trying to calm her pounding heart. Her phone buzzes with texts. The board has clearly read the letter. She glances at the phone quickly but can't bear to read them. Except for the last one, from Lorraine, she of the stiff blonde chignon, who rarely ever texts her anymore.

Say it isn't true!!!

With shaky fingers, Zoe opens the text.

Lorraine has sent a link to a news story. Her heart thrums high up in her throat. Nausea flows into her, sharp and sudden.

"Energy Magnate Daughter Suspected in Terrorist Bombing of Family Home."

Zoe feels first like she'll vomit, and then like she could tear her own hair out and turn it into a rope to strangle her husband with. Phil has thrown their daughter under the bus *after* she gave him what he wanted. *Why?*

Now she has to exert pressure back. She has money and power, too, peripherally. She can use it. They are not going to take her daughter down.

She remembers the one man called Spencer, the name spit off his buddies' lips too easily to have been fake. Can't be too many Spencers in the county. Her car is suddenly too warm. The heater isn't even on. *Fuck this.* A fresh gout of sweat breaks out between her breasts. She will not endure menopause in silk, that is for sure. She throws the suit jacket off and unbuttons the top few buttons of her blouse, stuffing a tissue into her cleavage.

She has an image of herself suddenly as a woman made of fire—like something she once fantasized about as a teen, when the flimsy lock on her door had not been a strong enough barrier against her mother's nighttime visitors. If she could burst into flame, she could always be safe. Maybe there is a similar mechanism to her body's changes now. She is pricklier —her temper is shorter, more volatile, sending off messages to the world: *Leave me alone or regret it.*

She knows who to call to find the aggravating Spencer and his angry little group. The very person that Phil hired after they'd tidied up the details of the homicide in her mother's house.

"We worked so hard to make it go away," she'd said to Phil more than 30 years ago when he'd told her about hiring the PI. "Why would you try to dig it up again?"

Phil had taken her hands in his, gently. "I need to know that even if someone looks very hard, they won't find out. It's to protect you."

The PI had said that the details of the murder—not that he'd used that word—were as buried as money could buy. Yet he had been able to turn up every horrifying detail of her mother's past—her traumas, her substance abuse, even some of her whereabouts in the stretches of days when she didn't come home at all. A list of them all laid out, page after page, for Phil to see. She'd felt worse than naked—as though her very internal organs were laid out on a table.

At any rate, she'd kept his card all these years as some sort of insurance, as though by holding onto it, the past really, truly could not come back to haunt her.

But, of course, the past lived inside her, no matter how far from it she believes she's come.

The man who answers the phone sounds far too young to be Frank Turner, P.I. But the phone still works, so that's something.

"I'm looking for Frank Turner," she says.

"I'm Jackson Turner, his son," says the voice.

"Oh, I suppose that means he's retired," she says glumly. "It has been a long time."

"He has passed away, unfortunately, but I run his business now, how can I help?"

And that is how Zoe finds herself hiring the son of the man who helped confirm that one of the worst days was truly behind her. Now, she embarks on preventing a worse one.

At the end of the call Jackson has agreed to track down the elusive Spencer, and turn up any criminal activity she can use against him. She mentions that he is a possible person of interest in the attack on her home.

Then, she leaves the house and takes one of the many cars at her disposal, a slightly less ostentatious Mercedes, and drives without thinking, almost on autopilot, though it has been months since she's been to Justine's house. *Is it still Justine's house? Does she even live there anymore?* She parks down the street so that she won't be seen.

Zoe knows she should try to cleave apart this strange new version of Justine, who is fierce and violent and wants to destroy, and remember her friend beneath it all. A woman who spent her career chasing meaning and truth, a woman who lost everything that mattered to her. Who blames herself for that loss.

But right now Zoe is just frothing with rage and fear.

My daughter is in danger, one way or another, from Justine's madness, Nemesis's wild agenda, Phil's betrayal, and possibly the police—who are probably trying to track Hannah down at this very minute.

CHAPTER TWENTY-FOUR

As Zoe approaches Justine's house she is surprised and not surprised to see movement within. A silhouette in the kitchen, staring out the window. Too tall to be Justine. *Hannah? How stupid can they be?* She'd driven here in a fit, not really expecting to find them, only hoping. *Is it possible they don't know, yet, either?*

"Son of a bitch," she mutters aloud.

Maybe they haven't heard the news. Do I storm in there and take Hannah away? But where will we go?

If they went home, who knew what Phil would do. Turn her over to the police? If Zoe confronts her, Hannah might rebel, digging in harder for her cause. Who knows what Justine has been saying to her, what ideas Nemesis had planted in her mind.

Zoe paces out of sight of the window, chewing her cuticles, thinking, thinking. Distracted as she is, she doesn't see the person coming her way until they are suddenly behind her, calling her name.

She squeals and jumps, twisting around to find Justine standing there, warily.

"What the hell are you doing with my daughter?" Zoe demands.

Justine's face no longer holds that fierce intensity of the day she took Zoe at rifle point. She still looks gaunt and tired, but there is color in her cheeks. Life in her eyes.

"I'm not *doing* anything with her. Just trying to keep her safe and out of the public eye."

"So you saw the news story then?"

Justine gives a small, tight nod. "She doesn't know yet. But she suspected Phil would turn that video over."

"Nemesis knew it, too. They are using us. All of us!" Zoe says. She's too embarrassed to tell her about the money she all but threw away.

Justine frowns. "I don't think they mean her any harm."

"It doesn't matter what they mean...she's not safe here at your house, Justine. What are you planning?"

Justine's eyes narrow, her face sharpening for a second and then she releases it all, exhales. "Just trying to buy her a little time before her world crumbles. The kid was already terrified that her father was ready to wash his hands of her. Maybe she's afraid you will, too."

Zoe steps backwards, a tide of defensive anger crashing over her. But she takes a deep breath. Throws her face into her hands. "I guess I can't blame her for that. I don't even know what Phil is thinking right now. He must really believe she's been radicalized and he barely trusts me, either."

Justine opens her hands, palms up. "She's trying to figure herself out, and frankly there are worse causes she could get behind."

Zoe clenches and unclenches her fists. "What are we going

to do? The police are going to look for her. Hecate sounded convinced you're up to something."

Justine looks away for a long second, then shakes her head. "I thought I could make myself essential to their plans, even use you to do so, but I was wrong. So, my new job is to keep Hannah safe."

"How?"

"There's somewhere safe we can go for a little while."

Guilt is a spike to Zoe's heart. *I should be the one to figure out how to protect Hannah.*

Justine gestures at the house. "You can go talk to her."

Zoe looks up. Hannah's figure has disappeared from the window. She steels herself. What if she fucks it up?

Justine digs something out from beneath a fingernail, and at last looks back up at Zoe, brows deeply furrowed. "I didn't mean to hurt you, Zoe. I didn't mean for any of this..."

Zoe holds up a hand, but not in anger. "You haven't been in your right mind, shall we say. For good reason. But I'll tell you something I'm loath to admit..."

Justine stares at her curiously.

"You woke me up from a long sleep. I didn't even know I was sleeping. And now that I'm awake, I want more. I want to be more than Phil Rasmussen's little pet project, you know?"

Justine smiles, the most genuine smile Zoe has seen in as long as she could remember.

"And maybe I could use your help. I need to clear Hannah's name from this stupid act of terror. We both know that Nemesis didn't bomb my house—those fucking Defenders did. And I've already got a jumpstart on some information I need on them. But you found them once, right? You tracked them down the other night when you rescued Hannah. I need to do that again."

Now Justine's face positively radiates light. Zoe knows it is dangerous to tempt Justine with a plan of this sort, but she needs all the help she can get. And her heart lifts knowing her daughter is in that house right now, that she can just walk inside and hold her in her arms again.

"I'll help you," Justine says. "Of course I will."

Inside, the house is so much emptier and quieter than the last time Zoe was there, she almost doesn't recognize it. Fewer paintings on the wall, all family photos gone, half empty bookshelves, even a couple of open cupboards in the kitchen hold no food. And Justine has been living here in its lonely bones all these months. Her throat constricts. *I've been a terrible friend.*

Justine calls after Hannah, but she doesn't come. Justine frowns and makes a small circuit of the rooms in her house, calling Hannah's name. With each room that comes up empty, Zoe's heart beats a little faster.

From the back of the house, she hears Justine mutter, *"Shit."* Zoe walks on leaden legs to join Justine. The back door is wide open.

"Shit, she must have seen me through the window," Zoe says, running down the back steps and calling her daughter's name.

"She can't have gone far," Justine says, running after and then past Zoe. But even after running up and down the street and several side streets there is no sign of her.

"Why would she do that?" Zoe says. "She can't think I'm here because she's in trouble?"

Justine leans forward, hands on her thighs, panting slightly. "But she is in trouble, Zoe, and maybe she doesn't know who to trust right now. Your husband called in the video, after all."

Zoe nods. "He must really believe she's in on it. He thinks he's saving her from them. But *I'm* her mother, I should be the one protecting her."

Justine shakes her head. "Maybe she doesn't know that."

Zoe wants to protest that Justine doesn't know anything about Hannah but is caught short. "*Shit*," Zoe says.

Justine chews on her lip. "She's a smart girl. The worst-case scenario is that she gets arrested. Your husband and you have the means to get her a fair trial, and there won't be any evidence that she had anything to do with that bomb going off. Or she finds her way back to Nemesis."

"You might have the worst-case scenarios backwards," Zoe says with a sigh.

Justine smiles slightly. "Maybe she just needed some time to cool down. Let me help you with your other problem in the meantime."

Zoe follows Justine back inside and sits down with her at the table beside her laptop. The house feels like a place that is being prepared for sale, no one living wholeheartedly inside it anymore.

But there is something slightly different about Justine. She's lost the dissociative sheen of the day she showed up with her rifle at Zoe's home. She seems brighter, somehow. *Dare I say, purposeful?*

Justine maneuvers her way through a dozen tabs open on her screen and pulls up a site that Zoe isn't familiar with.

"This is called 8Chan," Justine says. "On the surface it's a place to go and chat with your very particular, unique set of friends about, well, frankly any damn thing you can imagine. But the deeper you go, the darker and stickier and creepier it gets."

Zoe laughs. "Right up my alley."

Justine shakes her head. "No, not in a good way. In a 'I wish I could scrub my brain after' kind of way."

Zoe grimaces. "Well, it makes sense we'd find those spineless dicks in a deep dark hole, then, doesn't it?"

Justine nods. "Indeed. But they think they're so smart, so

stealthy. When I wrote about them last year, it took me all of about two weeks to infiltrate their groups, to pose as one of them, to mimic them. In a way I'm glad I never got to finish the article that I was working on when I first started investigating. I felt dirty just brushing up against their edges."

"Why'd you stop?" Zoe asks.

Justine's silence is long, and Zoe realizes too late what she's stepped into. "Oh god, Justine, I'm sorry. I didn't think..."

"No, it's okay. I don't expect people to tiptoe around me for the rest of my life."

For the first time since this whole ordeal has begun, Justine holds Zoe's eye contact, and Zoe doesn't break it.

Within an hour, Justine had helped Zoe create her own account, and her own moniker: GoWhite71. She's shown her three threads that are especially active, and how to lurk more than chat, not calling much attention to herself while participating just enough for the others to trust her. Most of the chat is innocuous and stupid—a ridiculous amount of time spent talking about video games, occasionally women they are trying to fuck, and, less frequently, comments disparaging specific racial groups, throwing their favor for the most heinous political candidates and adding the offensive suffix "tard" onto as many words as they can.

She learns the names of websites exclusive to white supremacists. Power Stormers. White Might. We Are Legion.

Now she just has to find "Spencer" and threaten to air his dirty laundry if he doesn't clear Hannah's name.

CHAPTER TWENTY-FIVE

I n such a way that she doesn't incite suspicion, Justine makes five different stops to buy everything she needs. Though would anyone really bother to report suspicious shopping when you can walk into a Walmart anywhere in this country and buy an automatic rifle and all the ammo you can dream of?

Unexpectedly, Hannah's presence in her life has centered Justine, brought her back down from the fugue she entered the day she took Zoe at rifle point to Nemesis, unable to face the anniversary of the worst day of her life. She doesn't feel quite as hopeless as she has the past year. She can almost envision a future again, where basic tasks bring meaning, maybe even joy.

But it doesn't change what she has to do.

The question is not if, but when. When will it have the greatest impact? Rasmussen Energy already had their groundbreaking. The bare bones of the plant have been laid out, but building won't begin in earnest until the coming weeks. She has to maximize the damage to structure and minimize the damage to human casualties. *So convenient of Nemesis to have changed their tune against destruction now that I am honed and ready for just such a cause.* Dry outrage swirls with her thoughts.

When she first wandered into their midst, they'd still been frothing over with the neatly targeted anger that she so resonated with—hitting the power brokers where it hurt.

She still remembers that terrifying-electric moment when she stood looking down on the blown transformer, the thrill of it. She'd only realized later how necessary that had been. Simply telling her, in a little sit-down interview, was just not going to make her *see.* She thought they'd seen something in her that was like them: hungry for justice, willing to make sacrifices.

"Sacrifices are part of raising a child," Nate had said to her in those tough early months when Willa was a wailing, never sleeping, raging little creature. When sleep deprivation made Justine feel as though her mind had unmoored itself, and dark thoughts scarred the edges of her days.

She'd followed Nemesis' directions, stumbling through darkened forest, scared and tired and hungry, but also feeling like she was on the cusp of discovery, of something meaningful.

Why hadn't she let herself see, then, that raising a child, a person, was meaningful, too? Why had it always seemed like a choice with no winner: autonomy and independence and the pursuit of her career on one side, a healthy child, steeped in mother's love on the other? Either-Or. She'd never thought she could Have It All as the magazines promised, and since Nate was ever the Good Father, she had believed she could chase the career and the child would be there waiting for her. *God damn it, I should have been able to.*

* * *

When she returns home, her dubious purchases tucked safely into her garage, Justine finds Hannah seated at the kitchen table reading her old newspaper clips binder, as though the girl did not just run off hours before.

Hannah looks up at Justine with the crimped expression of a younger child, both guilty and self-satisfied.

"I can't believe he did it. Turned the video over," she says in a small voice. "I hate him. I hate her, too. She could have stopped him."

Justine sits down opposite the girl, trying to think of a way to console her before figuring out their game plan.

Justine closes her eyes a moment. *What a luxury to be able to hate your parents. What a luxury to be hated by your child.*

"I can't imagine what that feels like, Hannah, but I think your mom is pulling for you. I think you could have at least talked to her."

Hannah shrugs. "I couldn't deal with her drama."

Justine fights the smile that forms on her lips. Busies herself making a little salad.

"Here's something I know for sure, Hannah. We can't appreciate our parents until we become one, or have enough life experience, which you, I'm sorry to say, don't have yet. And maybe as parents we can't appreciate our children..." A sudden wave of vertigo takes hold of her, and she has to grip the countertop.

"You okay?" Hannah asks, always vigilant of Justine's every shift in mood.

Justine inhales deeply and the world comes back to rights. "We certainly don't appreciate our children while they're children—parenthood is too much about survival, unless you've got a huge family to help or can pay for nannies—wait..." Justine narrows her eyes at Hannah. *"Were* you raised by nannies?"

Hannah's pretty face wrinkles with disgust. "No! My mom

was really intense about doing everything herself. She hated that we have, like, housekeepers and staff, and my parents always fight about that stuff. She made all my meals and got me dressed and ready for school every day when I was little. That's kind of the problem—there was never any space away from her. I don't think she's really handled me being away at college too well."

They are both quiet for a long time. Justine eventually gets up and chops cucumbers into tidy triangles, and cherry tomatoes in glistening halves, and then Hannah says, very softly, almost too softly, "I bet you were a good mother."

Justine sweeps all the veggies into a big bowl and tosses in arugula and feta cheese before turning around again.

"I don't know, Hannah. I can't look at it objectively. I can't see through my guilt."

Hannah bites her lip, twists her fingers together as though trying to braid them. "Can I ask you how she...how it...? What happened?"

The salad bowl suddenly feels so heavy, like a lead weight as she carries it to the table. Swallowing is difficult.

Hannah looks ready to take back her words, eyes big whorls of concern. But Justine feels a volatile need to speak it aloud, as forceful and inevitable as a contraction.

"To answer that, I need to tell you about when I first encountered the women of Nemesis. I can't really explain it, but they electrified something inside me."

Hannah dishes herself out a small salad.

"Something about them called to me on a deep level. Maybe they remind me, even a bit of my own mother. I was drawn by the idea that a group of women were taking their values into their own hands and getting stuff done without men, without following society's approved rules. They were going against what women are supposed to do—no softness and silence and being some kind of vessel just for babies. That *spoke* to me."

Justine's body is jittery. She can't be contained in sitting. She stands, begins washing the few dishes in the sink.

"But I didn't understand that I was just a...spectator. That's what they wanted me to understand. I see it now. So, when they threw down a gauntlet—invited me to actually witness one of their...actions, with the promise, potentially, of participating in one, I leapt at the chance, even though I knew, in the back of my mind, that I couldn't be both a Nemesis member and a mother."

Hannah sits up straighter, as though she senses that this is going somewhere serious.

"I'd already made a habit of pissing off my husband running late. Making work a priority. What was one more time? Only this time..."

Justine's breath feels heavy in her chest, as though she were breathing gel or foam, not air, remembering the day—the electricity that rode the edge between thrill and terror, more profound than nearly anything she'd ever felt in her life. Like she was on the cusp of a great discovery.

"When I finally made it back to my car, it was an hour later than I should have gotten back. I was supposed to pick Willa up from the daycare center at 4. But I was late, again, and she had...she had become aware of my tendency to be late, and she had learned to read the digital clock and she knew." Her throat is too dry. She licks her lips and tries to swallow. "She knew her mother wasn't coming when she said she would. She knew because in her two short years, she'd grown to expect it."

Hannah has gone so still she looks almost farcical, her lips frozen, hands clasped together.

Justine can barely make out the edges of her own body. She feels as though she is narrating this story from a very great distance. Down a long corridor, or from the top of an empty theater.

"And when I didn't come, and didn't come, and before they called Nate to get her, Willa took it upon herself to go and look for me. I don't know how she did it. How she slipped past their notice, how she made it out the front door..."

Justine's voice falters. Hannah looks blurry through her tears.

"The SUV didn't see her, because she was so small..." Her voice simply stops working, her throat squeezing like a fist, her tears streaming, and her body wringing itself with hard wrenches torqued to get the truth—and pain—out.

Hannah is suddenly up and behind her, wrapping thin arms around Justine, who wants to shrug them off.

I don't deserve sympathy.

"That daycare center was negligent," Hannah says at last, when she pulls back, wiping away tears. "It didn't matter that you were late. *They* were responsible. They failed. Not you."

Justine's mouth forms words that her vocal cords can't quite produce. *Sure, easy to say now. But if I had been there on time, she would still be here.*

"Anyway," she wipes her eyes. "What's pressing now is *your* safety. Police could come look for you here. We can't stay here. You know that, right?"

Hannah considers her for a long moment, then nods very slowly. "Maybe I should just turn myself in. Make it easier on everyone."

Justine shakes her head. "No! Your mom and I have a lead to pursue first. And if you stay with me, and they find us, I'll say I held you hostage."

"You can't do that!" Hannah insists. "I don't want you to."

Justine's lips smile even though the feeling doesn't extend into her chest. "You have to let me. It's what I'm meant to do."

CHAPTER TWENTY-SIX

E ver since Justine showed up in her driveway, Zoe's life
has become a series of bad decisions. Bad as defined by
whom, though? *My alleged friends? Society? Truthfully, these
decisions don't feel bad; they feel exhilarating.* With each one
she throws off a shackle, a corset rib, revealing something
tender and real.

She stands outside Spencer's apartment with the gun her
husband gave her for self-defense (usually locked inside the
safe in her bedroom). This is only the latest in this string of bad
decisions. *Maybe, in fact, the worst of them all.*

And she doesn't care like the Zoe of even a week ago would
have. Phil won't absolve her of this, or make it go away. *Am I
breaking down as surely as Justine did?*

His apartment is, blessedly, at the very end and back of the
complex. It would be nondescript except for the biggest, most
garish American flag and a smaller confederate flag right on the
porch. *The audacity.*

Justine spent a couple hours teaching her to pick a lock, and
so long as the terror making her hands tremble doesn't thwart

her, she is going to do this. Lock picking, particularly on shitty apartment doorknobs, turns out to be surprisingly easy. *Maybe too easy.* She slips inside.

His apartment is dark, smells faintly of microwaved pizza and cologne. A series of empty beer bottles are lined up along the counter in the kitchen. Other than that, his apartment is neat, almost impersonal. A black leather couch in the small living room, with an entertainment center, a stack of porn DVDs—*no surprise*—and some action-adventure movies.

She moves to his bedroom. Double bed, covers tossed in a tangle. A dank, musty smell. Dirty underwear on the floor. The walls are plastered in posters of half-naked blonde women, with glistening fake boobs. She tries not to gag, imagining his bedside manner with the ladies. A couple of quick grunts and thrusts, and then passing out cold at the unlucky lady's unfulfilled side.

Also on his wall, a horrifying old cartoon, with Black folks drawn as caricatures. No personal photos except for one photo of a little boy holding a toy gun by his bedside. She can't look away from that photo for a long moment. It is hard to tell when it had been taken by clothing and location. *Is it him as a child? His son? A brother?*

It doesn't matter. She is not going to "everybody was somebody's baby" this asshole. She pulls open drawers, looking, looking, for anything. A camera. Prints. Something. She goes through his T-shirts and sweatshirts, digs beneath his clean underwear and socks. Nothing of note. From his closet she yanks out sweatshirts and shoes and is discouraged. Nothing. He has a lot of baseball caps. Must be thirty. Various sports teams and...a Rasmussen Energy cap identical to one that Phil and several members of his staff have. Her entire being goes cold and still. Phil had them made for an informal baseball league among his staff. They'd come and play games at his own private baseball field on their property. How many times did she stand at a distance watching them play, thinking Phil looked like a charming coach with his "boys."

How in hell does Spencer have one of these hats? He can't work for Phil. It's not possible.

She is busy turning the hat over and over again in her hands when the front door opens and footsteps thud inside.

Shit, that was a lot faster than I anticipated. I thought I'd have an hour before he came home. Though she is ready, her heart races, mouth instantly dry.

She pulls the gun from her pocket, tries to still her shaking hands.

She hears him crack open the fridge, then the hiss of a carbonated drink opening. It takes him a few minutes to make it to his bedroom, beer in hand, where he enters, slowly, distracted by his phone in hand, then spots her, his eyes widening. "What the fuck?"

"Spencer?" she asks, trying to sound important, like someone who might be carrying a court summons or news of a loved one's passing.

He squints at her for a long time, trying to place her.

It annoys her that he is not shrieking or shouting, does not appear to be freaked out by her presence. That if, in the reverse, she would be reaching for her pepper spray at the mere sight of a strange man, as women are taught to do. It annoys her that a man like him can walk so freely through the world, unafraid.

Then, finally, his eyes widen. "Youuuu?"

She smiles. "Me."

"You're a crazy bitch."

"I've been called worse. We need to talk."

"You have some fucking nerve," he says. "You want the press to get wind of this shit?"

"I think the real question here, Mr. Miller, is whether you

want the press, or anyone, really, to get wind of *your* shit." Rage shakes her voice then. It's bracing. "Your little game of vigilante in the woods. Threatening women. And worse...bombing my husband's estate. Kidnapping my daughter. You know the police have video of your face? Well, top of your head, your eyes, but *I* recognized you. I can identify you easy-peasy."

He shakes his head, then glances around his apartment as though looking for a weapon. Then he smiles. A sharp, smug smile that makes her want to kick him in the nuts right then and there.

"You don't remember me, do you?" he says.

"I just *told* you I remember you. Are you not listening?"

Now Spencer laughs. A big-throated belly laugh. *"Fuuu-uck,"* he says, still chuckling. "Not from the other day. From years ago."

So accustomed to being hot all the time, the chill that plunges through Zoe now is as bracing as a splash of cold water.

"What are you talking..."

"I remember you. Who you *really* are. White trash. Junkie mom. Probably a whore too."

"Fuck *you.*" Her mind is scrambling for purchase of a memory of this man during *those* years of her life. She can't recall it, no matter how hard she stares.

"Yeah, probably not. You were pretty fucked up. Now he mimics a woman's crying voice, "Phil, Phil, what have I done..."

The world tilts at its edges. She is hot, she is cold, she is... wet. Sitting at the bottom of a shower that Phil dragged her into to get her to stop screaming, to wash off the blood.

"You're going to be okay. We'll make this okay," Phil said, stroking her wet face. "Trust me. We've got this."

We. All these years she's assumed Phil was speaking in the royal "we" that night. But was there another voice? Another person there that night? Someone who helped them clean up the body of the man who had broken into their apartment seeking drugs, seeking more, from her mother, then from her. She can still conjure his clammy hands on her pajama bottoms, dragging them off, gooseflesh prickling her thighs as she kicked out. But he was stronger than her. He pinned her down. If not for the gun that her mother kept so haphazardly, thoughtlessly under her bed, that night could have gone much differently.

Spencer must see the realization dawn in her eyes. "That's right. It's me Philly called that night to help clean up your murderous little mess. You got that guy good. Brains everywhere. Your mom never even woke up from her heroin sleep. Doubt she knew what happened. For all she knows, it was just a bad dream."

Zoe shakes her head, as much to try and expunge the image as to deny it. Nobody is supposed to know. Least of all *this* man.

"How...why?"

"Philly and I go *waaaay* back. Prep school—ha, I know, I don't look like I come from money. I wasn't rich like him, but he doesn't hold that against me. My grandparents put up their house to pay my way to keep me outta my poor sad mother's hair. Such a troublemaker. But I was useful to him. He's generous like that. You do something for him, he does something for you."

"You...work for him?"

"Something like that."

Zoe remembers she is holding a gun. She's let it dangle slightly, but now she raises it again.

Spencer's eyes and posture sharpen. "I'm betting it's been a long time since you shot one of those."

She shakes her head. "I've done my time at the range."

"Look, I don't know what you want. I walk into my house and find you here with a fucking gun. I should call the cops."

"But Phil wouldn't like that, would he?" she says. "I'm betting this whole life of yours—if you can call it a life—is financed on his dime."

"What the fuck do you want?"

"I want my daughter exonerated! I want you to take responsibility for what you and your little fuckheads did, bombing our house, blaming Project Nemesis, when it was *you.*"

Spencer's glib grin returns, and this time Zoe can't take it. "Stop fucking smiling."

"Your daughter was never the intended target. *You* were. You are just fucking lucky your crazy friend got there first."

Zoe narrows her eyes.

"Yeah. And at first, even I thought Phil was being...over the top, and all. No way was his own wife associated with a terrorist group. Then I fucking see you in the woods with them! I couldn't believe it."

The room is quaking. No, it's her body trembling, all over, as though a fever has set in. "You're making no sense. You're making it sound like my husband engineered that whole thing. The bombing. The kidnapping. Blaming Nemesis."

"I guess you're smarter than you look," Spencer says.

"That makes no fucking sense! What reason would he have..."

And then it lands. Of course it makes sense. He's been gunning for her to detach herself from EarthWorks. So convinced that people would start to associate Nemesis' acts of sabotage with her organization. He was incensed by that article about energy companies and climate change, by the newspaper tossed over the lawn.

"You're going to record a video that says my daughter is an innocent pawn, a victim, whom you forced to make that video incriminating herself. Then you're going to turn yourself into the police."

Spencer considers her, nods slightly, and before she can even think to be prepared, launches himself at her. It is an awkward lunge more than a targeted one, and she merely stumbles backwards. She drops the phone but holds fast to her gun and aims a well-placed kick to his nuts.

He drops, whining, his face pinched with pain and red with rage.

She points the gun at his head and releases the safety. "That was stupid," she says, panting. "You, of all people, know I'm capable of shooting a man in the head."

He is panting, too. The air in the room is seething with his rage at being humiliated, caught off guard, as though this sort of thing never happens to him.

Spencer doesn't look at her, instead he scans his apartment, scoping out where he's stashed a weapon—she follows his line of sight—and spends a long moment just staring at the wall behind her head. This begins to make her nervous.

"Fine," he says through clenched teeth. "Start recording."

She has to fumble with one hand to squat, pick up her phone, and prepares the recording function, all while keeping an eye on him. She tosses it over to him and he grasps it off the ground.

He hits the record button and holds it to his face. "My name is Spencer Miller, and I am a member of the Defenders of Freedom, a proud brotherhood of men who know the true face of this country, a white face..."

"Ah-ah, nope!" She angles the gun down at his head and motions for him to say what he is supposed to say. Instead, in one swift motion, Spencer rushes her again, like a football player with his eye on a touchdown, knocking the gun from her hand and tumbling atop her. She stupidly stopped preparing for an attack, let down her guard. *You've grown soft and easy in all these comfortable years.* That voice that is indistinguishable from the girl she was, patched together with ragged survival defenses, or her mother.

"Don't you understand," he says, now having turned the tables and holding the gun on her so tightly she can feel her pulse in her neck. "He'll ruin me just for having told you as much as I have...My life is as good as over."

Zoe can't swallow, or breathe, or move. Her entire body is clenched like a fist. *So this is how it ends. Poetic justice, maybe. A life for a life?* She closes her eyes.

When the gun goes off, it takes her a moment to realize it's his head he pressed the gun into.

She is not sure how long she sits there, crying, moaning, shaking—her eyes a blur of blood spatter and prickles of light. She knows that blood speckles her face and clothing, that she can't just simply leave the apartment, satisfied with what she's gained, having one-upped this guy. Her DNA is here. She will have to call someone. Explain. Time is warping in on itself, twisting around to a time more than thirty years ago. She is that girl in the shower, sobbing, hoping that Phil will show up and tell her what to do.

This time, I can't call Phil.

This time, I don't want to call Phil.

She keeps half expecting a neighbor to come pounding on the door at the sound of the gunshot. Forces herself not to look at the garish remains of the man whose life may have been figuratively ruined moments before but is now actually ruined... and *she* did that.

Somebody is dead because of me.

Again.

CHAPTER TWENTY-SEVEN

J ustine studies Hannah's profile as she drives the rental car. The girl has tucked her voluminous dark curls up into one of Nate's old baseball caps and wears a jacket with a high collar pulled up around her neck. The look is capped off with dark sunglasses.

Justine lets Hannah drive, because she is tired more than anything. An intense weariness has come over her, like in those old days when she'd stay up until 3 a.m. working on a story and then have to get up for work at 7. She briefly forgot about the pain of her broken rib, or rather, doesn't qualify it as negative— it is almost a relief to have a physical ache to center her mind.

They had left Justine's car behind at the house and taken a Lyft to a rental place, now ensconced in a bland, mid-sized sedan. Thus, Justine isn't surprised when her mother lets her big Doberman, named, in her mother's ironic way, "Sally," greet the car with her ferocious barking snarl at the end of her long driveway. That dog won't let them come any closer to the house, which makes Justine happy. This dog was Justine's idea, after reading a terrible story in the *New York Times* about a woman, living alone in a rural part of upstate New York, who was randomly murdered by men who robbed the first house they encountered.

"*Shit,* that's a big dog!" Hannah wails, cowering back against the seat.

Justine laughs and eases out of the car. Sally's barks instantly turn to yips of delight, and she nudges her big head up against Justine's thigh and licks whatever she can reach.

"She's a big baby," Justine says. "You can come out."

Hannah reluctantly emerges from the car, frowning at the dog.

A lump forms in Justine's throat at the sight of her mother ambling down the dirt road toward them. Her gait is slower, her bad knee likely acting up from hours spent kneeling in the garden. Her hair is so much whiter than the last Justine saw her. *Jesus, how long has it been? Can't have been more than a couple months, can it?*

Her mother grabs hold of Sally by the collar. "Didn't recognize the car, Teeny. I'll take her back to the house, you can drive the rest of the way in," she says. She glances at Hannah, then at Justine, her hazel eyes full of questions.

Justine feels so many things just looking at her mother. Images, unbidden, began to rush into her mind. Her mother's pale hand reaching to smooth a wisp of Willa's hair away from her face in the hospital. Waking from drugged sleep every few hours to find her mother's silhouette in the chair by her bedside, sometimes reading, sometimes gazing out the window, sometimes peering desperately at Justine as though willing her to rise from her bed. Then her mother's slow retreat back to her garden and her volunteering, giving in to Justine's stonewalling, her silence. Nate, making excuses for her. For himself. Then all of them slipping away.

Except, Justine considers, *for Zoe.*

Zoe kept coming around. Kept calling. Showed up with fresh cut flowers and tidily prepared meals in little glass containers.

It's only when Hannah says, "Justine?"— her name demanding direction—that Justine realizes she's been standing there silently too long, staring after her mother, who's already turned and gone back up toward the house, fingers wrapped tightly beneath Sally's collar.

They follow her in the car and park. The little yellow house where Justine grew up looks much the same as it always did—paint in need of retouching, stone statues of fairies and female deities in various states of repose, and her mother's beautiful garden in rich bounty even for October. Willa loved coming here, running through the untamed beauty like a wild thing.

When they enter the house, her mother has put out teacups and is setting the kettle on the stove. Hannah stands in the cozy living room that overlooks the kitchen, clutching her hands together as though she doesn't know what to do with them, hair still tucked up inside her hat and glasses.

"So, this is the fugitive then?" Her mother says over her shoulder.

Hannah gasps slightly.

Justine is surprised her mother figured it out so quickly.

"You know she's innocent of any crime," Justine says, finding her voice. "And her name is Hannah. Hannah, this is my mother, Helen."

Hannah nods slightly and lets a wisp of muscle movement provide a hint of a smile. Helen smooths hairs away from her face and sets to chopping pears and apples into neat slices, then pulls out a soft white cheese from the fridge.

"So...you're still after them, then?" Her mother says. The words sound light, but Justine can feel the edge beneath them.

"Not...exactly." There is no way to explain everything without sounding like a woman crazed, a woman who's lost all sense of direction or purpose in the last year, which, she supposes, she has.

"She's helping me," Hannah says.

Helen arranges the cheese and fruit on a big white plate and slides it onto the counter toward them.

"So, if you're not guilty of a crime, why are you hiding?" Helen asks, popping one pale yellow slice of pear into her mouth.

Hannah takes off her glasses and hat and sighs heavily.

"She's been set up. Wrong place, wrong time, and we need a little bit more time to bring the actual perpetrators to light," Justine says.

She didn't expect her mother to run to her with open arms, exactly, to comfort her, but she also didn't think it would be a challenge to convince her to harbor Hannah for a week or so. But then, she'd never really been able to predict her mother. Helen, having to play both mother and father, could run hot and cold.

"Have a bite," Helen extends the plate to Hannah, who glances at Justine as though for permission. Justine nods and Hannah steps forward, takes one of each item on the plate and then retreats a few steps, nibbling at them like a hungry mouse.

"Surely isn't anything to eat at your place," Helen says, scorn in her voice as she turns off the roaring teapot.

Justine doesn't take the bait.

Helen makes brief eye contact. "Nate called about a week ago. Says he's worried about you. Thought you might be... returning to your obsession."

Justine shakes her head. "Wish he wouldn't do that. Bring you into it."

Helen purses her lips, chews. "Some things are better left alone, Justine," she says.

Justine has a reflexive urge to stomp her foot. This is the thing her mother always did best—lay down rules and lock down choices. Maybe it's why Justine was so reluctant to become a mother herself, if that was the job.

Hannah suddenly takes a step closer, as though sensing the tension between mother and daughter. "It isn't Justine's fault," she says stridently, urgently. Such a young thing to say, it warms Justine more than she cares to admit. "What happened to Willa."

Helen presses a hand to her mouth.

Justine looks away, wishes she could just storm outside, but that seems petulant. She came here for Hannah's safety, not a loving reunion.

Helen silently arranges and rearranges pear slices and cheese for a long moment, then, in a thick voice, says, "Of course it isn't Justine's fault. Good god, who could think it is?"

Justine has to set down the teacup she'd just lifted to her lips, her hand is trembling.

"I got that sense, just now," Hannah insists. "Calling Justine obsessed."

Helen's eyes widen, and Justine is about ready to call this whole idea stupid, take Hannah out of here, and find a Plan C when Helen drops onto one of the bar stools at the counter.

"I never meant to suggest that, Justine. I only meant that this particular group, this cause, it took you over. It preoccupied you in a way that never seemed quite healthy to me. Like you were punishing yourself for something even before Willa..."

Justine drops onto one of the other stools, suddenly so very tired. Like she could close her eyes right then and sleep sitting up. "Proving something to myself," she says in a small voice.

Both women looked at her, waiting for more.

"Nate had the biological urge. I never seemed to have it. I loved him so much I was willing to get pregnant. For him. Even though what I loved most of all was my work."

Helen shakes her head slightly, but rather than a reprimand she lets out a soft, sad, "Oh Justine, do you really think because you wanted a baby less than Nate that you loved her any less than him?" Helen keeps shaking her head, tears now forming in her eyes. She stands up from her stool and moves toward Justine, but Justine holds out her hand.

"If you hug me right now, I will break," her voice cracks just slightly, but she holds it together.

"Well, you're already broken," Hannah says. When Justine and Helen both shoot her sharp eyes, she amends, "Your rib, I mean!"

Helen gapes. "Broken rib?"

"Justine saved my life," Hannah says proudly.

"You give me too much credit."

"Don't listen to her. She *did*." Hannah's head shake is hard, emphatic.

"Looks like you have a tale or two to tell me," Helen says, and sits back down. Her voice has lightened.

Suddenly Justine is hungry. Ravenously hungry. She feeds herself several pieces of cheese and apple, sips her tea. "Can we move to a couch? My side does ache," she asks.

And there, she unfurls the details of the past week, telling them everything except for how she took Zoe at rifle point. Makes it sound more like she'd strongly encouraged her to come despite her better judgment.

When she is done, her mother sits nodding to herself, deciding something. "The basement still has that little bathroom and sink and cot from when your dad thought Reagan really was going to get us all nuked," she says.

Justine can't help but laugh. She remembers so few things

about her father. Though she remembers hiding in a cabinet in the basement when her mother called her for chores she didn't want to do or for dinner she didn't want to eat. Could still hear Helen's exasperated, "Teeny, get your butt up here!"

Hannah wrinkles her nose as though imagining life in a dank basement.

"If it comes to that," Helen adds, turning to Hannah. "Otherwise, Justine's old bedroom is very comfortable."

Justine's heart lifts. Hannah smiles hesitantly, then says, "Thank you."

Helen nods. "Life has been a little bit too predictable around here," she says.

They look at each other, mother and daughter, and though neither moves in for a hug, Justine feels, for the first time in a long time, held.

CHAPTER TWENTY-EIGHT

Zoe wore gloves, so there are no fingerprints on the gun. Or any other parts of the house. But hair? Shoe prints? There is probably something to incriminate her beneath black light. To leave is to flee. Leaving demonstrates guilt. So, when her vocal cords work again, when her hands stop shaking, she does what she was unable to do thirty years before: call the police. She calls them with the awareness that from this point forward, everything will change. Irrevocably. She is keenly sure that the thin thread that has been holding her and Phil together will snap. He will wash his hands of her. Lament the thirty years he gave away to her. Prove his mother right that Zoe was nothing but trash, and he was a fool to have married her anyway.

Maybe, though, since her "crime" is so much worse than Hannah's alleged one, he won't be able to hold onto his outrage at his daughter.

By the time the police arrive she has shucked off as many layers as she can and still be presentable—the cardigan, the jacket, the gloves (tucked into the jacket pocket). The officer who meets her at the door frowns slightly at her, but she can't read exactly what he is frowning at.

Sweat has beaded up between her breasts, behind her neck and the backs of her thighs, and her camisole clings damply to her. She wonders if it will look like a lover's quarrel gone awry. She is still shaky, as though she hasn't eaten, yet she calmly lets them in. She sits primly on the nearest chair, pushed forward to its edge so she won't smear blood on it.

She answers questions as simply as she can without telling them too much.

—*She'd simply come expecting to have a conversation.*

—*She doesn't know him personally, no, only through a* mutual friend (which is not exactly a lie).

—*She did not expect Spencer to take his own life, only brought the gun as a reflex of self-defense, for being a woman in a strange man's house discussing a heated topic, but he became threatening.*

She is waiting for the questions about breaking and entering, about what right she had to ask him such questions when the slightly older detective asks her name a second time, as though he'd been chewing it over in his head for a few minutes.

"Zoe Rasmussen."

He squints and looks at his partner. "Rasmussen? Any relation to Phil Rasmussen?"

In her out of body state she hadn't thought twice to answering, "His wife."

The detective closes his notebook. "I recommend you call your lawyer, ma'am. Why don't you go on home and make that call."

Zoe and the younger detective both stare at the older detective in the same surprised way. Years ago, Phil simply came and made it all right. And now, at the mere mention of her husband's name, this cop is willing to let her go home? She is relieved, but keenly aware of the injustice of it.

"Okay," she says softly, though she doesn't move.

The older detective pulls something out of his pocket and holds it out to her. She stares at it for a long moment before realizing what it is. A handkerchief. How old fashioned. "You might want to clean yourself up first," he says.

The younger detective clears his throat heavily, and then, when his partner doesn't react, takes him by the crook of the elbow and leads him out of her earshot. But Zoe can tell, even in her disassociated state, that they are arguing. That the younger detective is shocked by the behavior of the older.

With a shiver she backs out of the room and finds the bathroom just next door. Her own face is a Jackson Pollock painting of blood and...*oh god...is that brain matter?* The physicality of it now suddenly comes rushing back in and she gags, hot bile rising into her throat. She drops to her knees before the toilet, pukes once, violently, hotly, sweat now plastering her hair to her head. When she can stand, she wets the handkerchief, and wipes her face and hair as clean as possible. Her camisole is ruined, but she doesn't care. All the heat of the past twenty minutes is suddenly swept away as though someone opened a big window onto a frigid night. She is shivering. She braces herself and goes out to gather her cardigan and jacket and purse.

The younger detective is no longer in sight. The older one simply nods at her. "Take care, Mrs. Rasmussen," he says, and she rushes out the door.

She finds the younger detective waiting by his car in the parking lot, arms folded, staring bitterly off into the night. He looks at her with such contempt she can't bear to hold eye contact.

She spends the drive home terrified of how to explain the

sight of herself to her husband. But he is not home. The house is quiet, except for Karina's steady presence, tidying the kitchen after a meal that no one was there to eat.

"Phil isn't home?" Zoe asks, keeping her dark jacket wrapped tightly around her torso to hide the blood speckled camisole.

Karina frowns at her, as though she's said something strange. "Mr. Rasmussen is gone to San Francisco for the Power and Energy Conference." She says it the way you might remind a child that they still have homework to do.

Zoe stares at Karina. *He is gone? How did she forget that?* This followed by a rush of relief so significant she could drop to her knees. What Spencer had said...it can't be true. Yet what man would go out of town when, as far as he knows, his daughter is caught up with people he considers terrorists? She steadies herself with a hand on the countertop, then quickly excuses herself to her room, where she strips off the offending clothes and wads them into the nearest garbage can.

She can't get the shower hot enough to cleanse away the feeling of Spencer's death lingering on her body. She stays in until the water runs lukewarm, and she knows that Karina is likely pacing nervously around the house wondering what is wrong with her, but her body has locked into inertia.

When she finally emerges, her skin is pink and tacky. She dresses in her coziest and thinnest jersey knit pajamas, surprised that the stress hasn't triggered a hot flash already. One will come, most likely in the middle of the night, when she'll wake plastered to her sheets.

She bids Karina good night, but soon realizes sleep is not going to find her anytime soon. She makes herself some chamomile tea, then her mind skitters back to all that Spencer told her. Not to *the* moment, though that will repeat behind her eyes for years to come, she suspects, but to the question of who he is—*was*—in the larger scheme of things. He seemed insignificant to her—just a cog in a machine. What he intimated about her husband...*could he just have been lying?* She takes advantage of her husband being away and slides into his office, booting up his home computer.

The usual tabs are open: stocks, energy markets, political news, all of which she has no interest in. She can't access his email or anything personal, so she begins rooting through his drawers. *What am I looking for exactly? A signed confession saying, "Yes, I bombed my own home, kidnapped my own daughter because she looked like my wife?"* She'd love to find that.

She traipses downstairs, to the meeting space where many of his employees congregate during the day. Computer stations and iPad blink in stasis, and she proceeds to go through them, one by one, turning them on, like opening giant white eyes, and looking for...something—looking for...anything.

She wastes an hour. Two. Nothing.

Frustrated, and finally feeling the tug of fatigue, she is about to leave, when she thinks about that horrible website Justine had her browse—8Chan.

She opens up 8Chan on the big computer, preparing to use her own newly created credentials when she sees that the computer is already logged in. At first, she tells herself, she shouldn't be surprised. Phil and his employees are far more on top of things relating to the Internet, to information, to connecting with others than she is. Maybe it's not what she thinks.

But something stops her from logging out and logging back in as herself. She maneuvers her way to the thread Justine taught her to find and then she looks twice at the login name. *WhiteMight69.*

It feels as though her lungs are squeezed between two plates compressing tighter and tighter toward one another.

No. It can't be. I'm reading it wrong. It could be any of the men who work for him.

WhiteMight69 was one of the more outspoken, aggressive commenters in the threads when she last delved into their sickening depths.

It can't be Phil. It can't.

She searches for posts from WhiteMight69, trying to think of answers that point to anything other than her own husband being a white supremacist. *Surely this is just one of his employees. His assistant du jour, the obsequious and kowtowing Todd? It must be. It has to be.*

And then she reads WhiteMight69's posts.

He blames the Jews for stealing money away from "real" whites.

He suggests that slavery should never have ended.

He suggests that those who demand equal rights, an end to police brutality will "get what is coming to them soon enough."

Though the words are horrifyingly new, the tone and cadence sound so much like him, like the worst of him, when he is angry and petty and barking out threats he will never follow up on. Her body begins to ache.

Her husband is not who she thought. Whether he never was, or he has slowly transformed from someone she thought was decent into...this, she doesn't know. *What does it make me?*

What else might he be hiding?

Surely he isn't keeping more secrets from her?

Is he?

He is.

Of course he is.

She doesn't want to read further, but she has to, because now that the crack has appeared in the veneer, she needs to widen it, to make it possible to do what she knows she has to do next.

WhiteMight69: *It is all worth the sacrifice at the homestead.*

Love2Hate489: *Get that fixed yet?*

WhiteMight69: *Oh yeah, and so many other little problems fixed, too. Sometimes even your own family needs a lesson.*

She doubles over, muscles and nerves clenching in spasms inside her. It is so much worse than she'd thought. *He engineered an explosion—he blew up our home—to hurt me? And so little concern for Hannah?*

She screenshots everything, sends them to her phone, then retreats to her bedroom, head in hands, dense with thought fragments that won't quite coalesce. Marriage and meaning, murder and death, and the level of hatred that live in some men. *Her* man.

How did I not know? Or didn't I? Didn't I write off some of his subtler comments—a racist joke here, a sexist note there? Look the other way at his classist ideals about who deserves resources? Wasn't there a reason that I never, ever mentioned my Jewish origins?

His scent rises up from their bedroom—that spicy body spray she once thought was sexy now smells cloying. The spacious room feels suddenly too small, constricting. Before she really thinks it through, she goes to her walk-in closet and digs through, way in the back, until she finds it, the only thing she has kept from before, a single suitcase—ratty and battered, which Phil threatened to throw away, but hadn't, because most of his threats are empty—except when they are not.

It's time to unbury her past.

CHAPTER TWENTY-NINE

Hannah didn't miss her mom much when she was at college. Or only in a vague way, since she knew she'd see her at the holidays. But even then, her mom was mostly tense and cranky and snappy, and it wasn't like they would have some beautiful mother and child reunion anyway. Her parents had been fighting more and more. Her mom is often distracted and on her phone. But Helen's brusque nature—which does not seem maternal in the least other than how she keeps trying to feed Hannah—makes her miss her mom for the first time in a while.

She passes time helping Helen weed and trim her garden, fold laundry, and complete other mundane, but also meditative, tasks.

"Not like that," Helen barks out, no matter how Hannah is doing it. "Plants are hearty but also delicate. It matters where you snip them. Do it the wrong way and you cut off a limb. Do it the right way and you encourage it to grow back."

She vaguely feels as though Helen is trying to teach her some kind of metaphoric life lessons, but she can't grasp the meaning, she's too anxious. Her chest is like a cage of birds all trying to get out at the same time through a tiny door.

What will happen if the police find me? What will happen if they don't find me? Am I a fugitive? Will my mom and Justine find the men responsible and clear my name in time?

And what about Colin and Kenya?

Then Helen calls her for lunch, or asks her to do a crossword puzzle, or some other mindless, physical task, and she forgets about it for a while.

But today, perhaps taking pity on her, Helen asks if she wants to watch the news. She asks it nervously, as though she isn't sure how much Hannah knows about her own story, and whether she wants to learn more about it on the local news. When you are the daughter of one of the richest men in the country, you *are* news whether you like it or not.

Hannah, without her phone, cut off from her best friends and social media, has begun to feel like she's missing a limb.

"Yeah, let's watch the news."

"Let's do something productive at the same time," Helen insists, and so they angle the TV so that they can watch it from the kitchen counter where Helen instructs Hannah in baking several kinds of bread and a batch of cinnamon rolls.

Hannah has forgotten how depressing the news is, how it emphasizes only the worst of everyone and everything. She gets into the rhythm of combining ingredients and kneading dough as Helen looks on, when the sound of her parents' names startles her out of her zone.

The heavily made up, dark-haired anchor woman is frowning seriously into the camera. "Energy Magnate Phil Rasmussen is having a terrible week. First, his daughter is linked to a domestic terrorist group that may have bombed his own estate. Now, according to an anonymous tip, his wife, Zoe Rasmussen, is linked to the death of a local man. The deceased man, Spencer Miller, age 56, may have worked as an independent consultant for Rasmussen Energy. He was found dead of a gunshot wound two nights ago in his own apartment. It is unclear if his death has been ruled accidental or homicide at this time. The anonymous source has indicated she was at the scene but did not say how she knew the victim."

The male anchor makes a sound of awe and then adds, "Even more shocking, Mrs. Rasmussen is also linked to the murder of a man in her mother's apartment some thirty years ago. The source suggests that police may launch an investigation into any connections between the two deaths."

The female anchor tidies and taps a stack of papers before her. "In addition to the recent bombing at the Rasmussen estate, that's a lot of drama for one family, wouldn't you say, Jake?"

"I would indeed, Amber."

Hannah's entire hands are encased in dough she's forgotten to keep kneading. Helen says nothing, simply drags the dough off Hannah's hands and puts it back in its bowl, washes her own hands, then turns the TV off with one sharp flick of the remote.

"Oh my fucking god," Hannah says.

CHAPTER THIRTY

Zoe packs two suitcases full of essentials, feeling a sudden and surprising lack of attachment for the things she is leaving behind. The house—god, how ludicrous to even call it a house—this estate, Phil's domain—has never truly felt like hers. It had taken her more than a year when she first moved in with him to stop expecting to find roaches scurrying through the pantry. To not expect the black mold squeezing its way through cracked bathroom tiles. She hadn't gotten used to not having to sniff the crotch and armpits of all her clothing to find the cleanest thing, or even to having an in-home laundry. It always felt like a resort, with round globes of fruit in the kitchen, not penicillin projects, and fresh slabs of meat, endless boxes of food so that you could not shop for weeks and still not starve. An obscene amount of enough. Hers on borrowed time. In Phil's world, wanting was reserved for desire, not yearning to fill emptiness.

She won't miss 90% of the staff, most of whom were hired by Phil, most of them career-climbing young men anyway—

only Karina, who stands at the bottom of the stairs with sad eyes as Zoe lugs her two suitcases down, sweating and puffing.

Zoe changes into sweatpants and a sweatshirt she's forgotten she owned but found way at the back of her closet, from years ago, before she'd begun to wear the skin of Mrs. Rasmussen so well she could shapeshift into it without thought. Phil always sneers when he sees her in comfortable clothes, because their house is not a home—it is a meeting place for Men of Great Importance, an extension of his business, a museum to everything in the world that matters to Phil.

When did I stop being part of that collection?

Karina doesn't try to help, but she looks as though she desperately wants to: biting her lip, wringing her hands.

"Where you will go, Missus?" Karina asks, reverting to her Russian syntax in this moment of stress when Zoe reaches the landing in the big, marble-tiled foyer.

"I don't know," Zoe says, flipping hair out of her face. "For right now, a hotel."

"You are really leaving?"

Zoe nods. "I really am." She knows what it means. Divorce equals leaving everything she's acquired in these thirty years behind. Money, prestige, fine things, power by association. People to do things for her.

Things that were never mine to begin with.

She stops in front of Karina, whose eyes are dark and wet. She takes the woman's hand. "You've been a wonder. Every person should be lucky to have a Karina in their lives. Ask for a raise when I'm gone, will you? He'll be so overwhelmed he won't deny you that."

Karina shakes her head. "You will keep in touch?"

Zoe smiles slightly, looks down at Karina's shiny black Louboutin pumps, but doesn't answer. Today she will begin telling only the truth, no matter what it costs her.

She drags her suitcases out to the driveway, lifting their handles, engaging their wheels, and rolls them to the newly repaired front gate—Phil wasted no time protecting his assets. She drags them farther down the road, to the lamp post where the Lyft driver will see her, and waits. She knows if she looks back she will find the estate intact and standing. With her back turned toward it, it feels as though it is on fire. Maybe because she is burning her life down.

Hours later, ensconced in a cheap motel that smells of bleach, the text blast from Phil begins.

What have you done?
Where are you?
You better be coming home.
We have serious damage control to do.
Do you know what this means?

She waits, longer than is normal. Longer than he is able to stand, she hopes. Watches shitty TV and drinks two cups of tap water. And then she writes back, at last:

The minute you were willing to sacrifice our daughter
I knew you were not the man I thought
Then I found out who you really are
And what you did to your own family
Isn't that right, WhiteMight69?

Silence. A beat. Then, his reply:

I will ruin you.

She doesn't text back: *I was ruined a long time ago.*

CHAPTER THIRTY-ONE

Zoe fills the Styrofoam 7-11 cup full of bitter smelling coffee. It isn't $30 gourmet coffee shat out of a rare jungle cat's anus, but somehow it tastes better than any she's had in years. It reminds her uncannily of the instant coffee her mother used to make, often left to cool and thicken into a dense syrup on a counter or bookshelf.

After she pays and steps out onto the street, walking back to her motel, she is surprised, and then not at all surprised in the same beat, to find a woman with a thick red braid suddenly walking in lock step with her.

"Don't acknowledge me," Artemis says. Though it is hard not to pay attention to the striking redhead, she doesn't make eye contact. "I'll follow you back to your room."

Zoe bristles. "If I let you," she says, more sharply than she intends.

Artemis snorts. "Fair enough," she says. "Though we already know where you're staying."

Zoe sips her coffee, walks a little faster, a strange sense of giddiness that makes her want to belt out laughter. She could run off with Nemesis if she wants to. She could get a job as a barista. She could do anything.

She arrives at her room and steps inside but leaves the door ajar. A few minutes later, Persephone, accompanied by Artemis, walks in and shuts the door quietly behind them.

Zoe sinks onto the bed, staring Persephone down.

"What?" she says. "What could you possibly want? You didn't respond to my requests for help, and I didn't deliver my husband on a silver platter, so what?"

Persephone nodded slightly. "We understand your frustrations, your lack of trust, but we have some information here that you need to know."

"Your husband is...*part* of the Defenders of Freedom. He's a white supremacist."

Zoe takes a long sip of her mediocre coffee.

"WhiteMight69," she says simply.

Artemis raised a pale brow. "You knew?"

Zoe shrugs. "I found out last night, surfing his computer, why do you think I'm in this hotel room?"

Persephone frowned. "He just left that information up on his computer?"

Zoe shook her head. "Not exactly." She recounts how she found her way to the 8chan account, how she recognized him in the posts, put the pieces together. "I could *hear* him in them."

She yelps as coffee spills into her hand from the cup she is unconsciously crushing. She sets it on the nightstand and wipes her hand on the bedspread.

"That's not everything, Zoe," Artemis says.

"He bombed his own house. Our house, to teach me a lesson," Zoe says. "To get me to step down from EarthWorks— but then I wound up making that easy for him. I'm complicit in so much, I know. But not that."

Artemis raises shocked and admiring eyebrows. "Your supporters really are a liability for him?"

Zoe nods. "Like a lot of men of his ilk, he can't tell the difference between an actual anarchist and people who just care about the earth. No offense."

Artemis barks a laugh. "Well in our case, we're the same, you know. But I get your gist."

"I am somehow not surprised about what he did to me, but that he set up his own daughter, too, that he put her in danger and is using her now..." She speaks the words but they feel as though they are coming from a radio at a distance down a long corridor from her. "I can't forgive that."

Artemis's strong features don't soften with any pity or tenderness—she looks like the mythical goddess she is named for, strong and ready for whatever might come next. Then, for this one moment, her face eases a moment.

Zoe stands—her body a wire pulled taut. She feels like she could run, or leap or do something big and wild. Instead, she bends forward and she screams, no, she *roars*, into her hands so hard her throat scrapes raw.

Artemis simply sits, watching her, like a curious corvid. Or like a woman who's already seen so much human misery this is nothing to her.

"I discovered all of this last night. How do *you* know that?" Her voice is thick.

"You still underestimate us," Artemis says.

Zoe shakes her head, as though to cast off this horrible truth. "I'm done underestimating women," she says. "And over-estimating men."

"We saw the news...about you and the man who died. Spencer. Did you kill him?"

Zoe laughs because she might otherwise cry. Her mind tried to protect her from that reality by pushing it aside. "I didn't," she says. "But I was trying to get him to confess, to absolve Hannah. And now that I've let my past out of the bag, I expect they'll be coming for me, soon, too."

"You mean for the other man you killed from years ago?"

Zoe cringes a little at Artemis' forthright words, looks down at her hands, which have begun to tremble, just as they had all those decades ago, blood speckled and sweating.

"Self-defense. My mother was a heroin addict who often traded sex for drugs, and that means we had a very low life element often coming by. He came for me...to rape me, I feared. I defended myself. Soon, I hope, everyone knows. And then I hope they know that Phil helped me to cover it up."

"You didn't have to throw yourself under the bus to take him down," Artemis says. Her voice contains the first inkling of tenderness Zoe has heard. "That's not what we had in mind."

Zoe sighed. "I have lived nearly my entire life waiting for this other shoe to drop. You already know what a lie my life has been. You all were trying to tell me that when I wasn't ready to hear it. So I let it fall apart. What I need is to make sure my daughter doesn't take the fall for the sins of her parents."

"Your daughter is wiser than you think. But so are you. I believe your husband will be too busy trying to patch up his reputation to bother with this farce he's set up."

Zoe smiles slightly. "So, you've told me all that I need to know about my husband. Now what?"

"We have a good lawyer who can help you out."

Zoe shakes her head. "Are you serious? You have lawyers in your midst?"

"We're everywhere. Playing the long game. Slowly and steadily." She stands up and comes toward Zoe, holding out a card. "Here's her name."

"What does she charge? I don't have a lot of liquid funds these days."

For the first time since she arrived, Persephone stands up and smiles, showing perfectly straight white teeth. "I think your husband's three-million-dollar deposit will more than cover her services."

Artemis rises alongside Persephone and both women turn to go, then Persephone stops and looks back over her shoulder. "Tell Hannah we'll do the same for her."

Zoe hugs herself after the women leave, standing there, rivulets of feeling coursing through her.

After Zoe gets off the phone with the lawyer, awaiting a call from the police now that she no longer has Phil's protection for any of her "crimes," she takes a shower. When she gets out, she finds an urgent text from Hannah:

Call me now. Justine's about to do something stupid.

CHAPTER THIRTY-TWO

I n one version of reality, Justine stays at her mother's house with Hannah, playing the kind aunt, or the unofficial godmother—maybe teaching Hannah some of her former journalism skills, something the girl can use in the world. In this version, Justine still works as a journalist, in fact, is not living off the 401(k) she cashed out when it was clear she was not going to be able to go back to work. Maybe this version of Justine, who gains twenty pounds back by eating healthy foods and caring about her physical body, starts going on jogs, redecorates Willa's empty, untouched bedroom and lets Hannah know she'll have her back no matter the outcome of her fate.

But Rasmussen Energy, Phil Rasmussen, needs to learn that even men at the top of the world are not invincible. And she still wants to prove something to Nemesis.

And that is why, instead of doing any of those things, she slips out into the night, wrapped in C-4.

For once she doesn't have to try to hide who she is. She needs as much incriminating information as possible. She drives her own car, makes sure she leaves her wallet with ID inside of it, and puts several credit cards and her insurance card into her pants pockets, if any of them survive the night.

There are only two other things she needs to do first. The first stop is the one place she has consciously avoided going except for the family spectacle over a year ago, where she couldn't even look at the tiny casket lowered into the ground, where Nate had been torn between fury at her acting out in front of all his family, and compassion for their shared grief. It manifested as an inability to look at or touch her that entire day. That was the first night that Zoe came and curled around her in bed, held her until the Ambien kicked in enough for her to sleep.

The thing about cemeteries is that they are strangely cheerful places to visit if you don't think about their inhabitants. The lush lawns, the bouquets of flowers, well-trimmed trees, and pretty stone benches. Against her wishes, Nate affixed a little enamel photo of Willa to the headstone, and this is the first time she's gazed upon the sweet, dark eyed face of her daughter since the last time she saw her in person. She's been unable to look at photographs.

Her daughter's gravesite is, as expected, tidy, wiped clean, and freshly minted with a bouquet of marigolds, her favorite. Justine experiences only a slight pass of guilt that she hasn't been the one who came to tidy it. In fact, it probably wasn't even Nate—but Nate's mother, Maureen, who eventually stopped trying to coax Justine back to life with casseroles, chocolates, and chiding.

Justine expects to be pummeled by a wave of grief, a knock you sideways kind that kicks your feet out from under you and freezes the air in your chest, but what arises instead is a single, shiny moment of joy—remembering the shape of her daughter's body as it fit into the curve of her lap when, some nights, she'd slip out of the story time comfort of her father's nighttime routine and join her mother while writing.

The memory is so potent she can viscerally feel the weight and heft of her daughter against her own skin, smell that slightly gamey, slightly sweet smell of her body, feel their two hearts beating, one beside the other—Willa's fast like a wild bird, Justine's in its dull and predictable thudding while she worked.

She takes out her cell phone and dials Nate's number. He might not answer. *I can't blame him if he doesn't.* Now that there is no *her*, and there is no *them*, he's likely throwing himself into work, doing the very thing he spent three years trying to urge her not to do.

But Nate answers, sounding only slightly surprised. "'Tine?"

"Hey," she says.

She is relieved that his next words are, "Are you okay?" rather than, "What do you want?" This tone suggests he is still mostly himself, someone who nurtures, who cares about others. Their loss has not stripped him of everything. *He will be okay.*

"I am okay," she says. "I'm here. At the cemetery."

"Oh 'Tine, you should have called me before..."

"No," she says, quickly, interrupting, but not harshly. "It's okay. It's the right time. Thank you and your mom for taking such good care of the site."

He says nothing, but she can hear him breathing, feel him thinking.

"I just want to say that I'm sorry."

"You don't have..."

"I do. I'm sorry for driving you away instead of bringing you close. I'm sorry for giving up. I'm sorry for making false promises to you, and for believing we had all the time in the world with her."

He is crying now, and...so is she, but the tears are gentle, cleansing. She has almost forgotten the feeling of crying freely like this, with cheeks publicly wet. But she doesn't feel like her chest will break into pieces, at least.

"It's okay," he says at last, sniffling.

"I just want you to know that I do love you. Even if I'm not capable of doing much about it, even if I'm still broken, I want you to know that."

"I love you, too, 'Tine. Always will. You don't need to sound so fatalistic about it. We have time. We can heal as slowly as you need."

She suddenly wishes he were there, so she could feel the solid density of him against her one last time. The reason she went against her own better judgment of herself, of her desires, and had a child was because she loved *this man* so much. That counts for something.

"Okay," she says, softly, hating the lie on her lips, but unable to dash his last, tender, flimsy thread of his hope.

"Okay," he says.

And before he can ask her to make up any other lies, or offer false promises, she ends the call, leaving her phone there on the grave site. She wants to, but cannot, call her mother. Her mother will know immediately that something is wrong. Her mother will do stupid things like call the police or instruct Nate to come find her. She has to trust that her mother will forgive her. Might even understand. She plants one kiss on her daughter's enamel face and sits there a while longer, gathering her strength, hoping beyond hope that she will, in some form or another, see her again.

CHAPTER THIRTY-THREE

I f there is one thing Justine learned in her years as a journalist it's that people who lurked behind monikers and computer screens secretly yearned for attention. And it is easy to draw them out. Their egos are fragile; it takes very little to threaten them.

Assuming the screen name she adopted several years ago to infiltrate these groups, she slips into the virtual cesspool and plants her seed:

Those nemesis cunts are tryin to pull some shit in our name at the big Rasmussen Energy plant tomorrow night.
not on our watch
we'll show those bitches we're serious

It feels fitting to wear the explosives, sewn into the lining of an old vest of Nate's. She wants to be sure of the finality of this moment, to feel the moment when she slips out of her skin and dissolves. There's little fear as she nears the outline of the plant's early construction, which looms like a creepy man in an alley, dominating space. She won't be able to get close enough to do any damage to the structures, but if her calculations are correct, she'll make exactly the kind of statement, and bring attention to Phil Rasmussen and his company at precisely the wrong time for him, optics-wise; his daughter, a suspect in her own home bombing; his wife, guilty of possibly two murders; his secrets, frothing over. She'll paint the grounds with her blood. And, maybe, just maybe, take down a few white supremacists while she's at it.

She waits in the shadows, overcome by stillness. There isn't even a breeze tonight. Willa always sniffed out her solitude—as though she had a special sense for when her mother most needed to burrow into the quiet of her mind to work out the pieces of a story. What she wouldn't give now to hear that little patter of curious toes coming to find her. The urgent fingers prying notebook and pen out of Justine's hands to plant herself as the object of her mother's sole attention.

The night seems to bend toward her—embrace her even—as though giving her a last corporeal hug. Justine doesn't believe in heaven or hell or an afterlife, but she takes heart in the idea of that intangible part of her—energy or particles or soul—finding its way back to wherever Willa's went, too. Commingling again as they did when Willa was forging herself from her mother's very body.

Caught in her musings, Justine realizes she has overlooked sounds as being tied to the not-so-distant freeway, but now she recognizes them as boots on ground, perhaps those of people attempting to be stealthy, or maybe her senses are on high alert. She peers around the pillar connecting a chain link fence and sees four men stalking the property's perimeter, hands at their belts where she imagines the outlines of guns.

With a hand on her own explosive trigger, she steps out

into the sallow floodlight, preparing to make her way toward them, when someone claps a hand to her shoulder.

All four men turn at the sound of her shriek.

Justine doesn't move or turn, but someone whispers harshly in her ear, "What are you doing?"

Zoe! Justine grasps Zoe's arm and pulls her behind her own body. The men have spotted them and have pulled their guns free, aiming in their direction.

"Zoe, you need to leave now," Justine whispers sharply. "Please!"

Zoe doesn't move, but whispers urgently. "No. I know what you think, that your life is worthless, that you'll hurt Phil or send him a message by doing this, but you don't understand...he doesn't care. Not about me or Hannah or you, not in the ways that count. You'll be hurting yourself for nothing."

Justine pats her vest self-consciously, as though to remind herself that she still holds the power here. Zoe inhales sharply. Had she figured out that Justine was prepared to make herself a more deadly weapon than these men could ever hope to be?

"Go now, Zoe, so you won't be hurt or implicated. Please!" Hot tears burn on Justine's cheeks.

"We know what you bitches are up to!" one of the men shouts at them. They are not so close as to make out facial features, but close enough that their bullets could be deadly.

"You wish!" Justine shouts.

To Zoe, she hisses, "You really want men like them to get away with their bullshit?"

"I don't care about them! I care about you. We need you, your skills. An intrepid journalist, an excellent mother..."

"No," Justine's voice is a lance.

"Yes!" Zoe says firmly. "Yes, you are, you are still her mother and you loved her fiercely and it was never your fault. Please, Justine, don't do this!"

The men shout obscenities, taunting them.

"It's Hannah who told me what you're up to. She figured it out—saw the supply list you'd made on your computer. She begged me to stop you. She cares about you, Justine, and her whole world is crashing down, in more ways than she even knows right now. She doesn't deserve to lose you, too. *Please!*"

Suddenly, Justine hears Hannah telling her that what happened to Willa isn't her fault.

Maybe Zoe is right, she doesn't have to do this.

"I can't just do nothing," Justine breathes. "Don't you understand that?"

Zoe nods. "I do, more than you know. I've just ruined everything in my own life because it's the right thing to do. I've learned things about Phil. He's behind all of this. The bombing, Hannah's kidnapping, pinning it all on Nemesis. There are other ways we can hurt him."

"What the fuck are you ladies doing?" One of the men calls out and strolls close enough to see.

Zoe gasps.

"What?" Justine asks.

"That little fucker...I've seen him at the house, too," Zoe says. "Justine, you can't take the fall for what these stupid little men are doing, have done, do you understand me? We can hurt Phil in other ways. Trust me!"

Justine stares at Zoe for a long moment, and then the men seem to decide something all at once, they rush toward them, maybe thirty feet away.

"Hurry!" Zoe urges.

Justine shrugs out of the vest. Zoe tentatively takes it from her. "It won't go off if I just set it down?"

"No, you have to press the trigger, which is in the pocket."

The men skid to a halt just feet away from them. There are four of them, of varying ages. "What are you doing?" One of the men shouts. "What is that?" He gestures at Zoe's hand where the vest dangles.

They creep slightly closer, as though improving their chances of a good shot.

Zoe tucks the vest into an armpit and holds her hands up high. "I'm just going to set it down," she says. She takes a few steps and places the vest on the ground between them.

One of the men gazes at it with narrowed eyes. "What's in there? A recording device? Is that what this is? You think you're going to catch *us* out at something? You're the bitches destroying property and shit!"

Justine can't help but smirk as she shakes her head. The speaker scowls and comes even closer. Justine grasps Zoe's arm and they back away.

The men close in on the vest, which they still can't seem to see, pointing at it like it is a ferocious beast. Justine pulls Zoe back into the darkness behind the pillar and then loudly shouts, "Boo!"

A gunshot goes off in the dark. Justine, acting without thought, shoves Zoe to the ground as the night explodes around them.

CHAPTER THIRTY-FOUR

THREE DAYS LATER

I n the worst week of Hannah's life, when her family has splintered, when the woman she's come to look up to has been arrested for bringing an explosive device to her dad's new nuclear plant, and her mom for being an accomplice, when she's missed her chance to fly to Kenya to start her new life, Colin only sent one text.

Sorry you won't be able to make it, babe.

They have Internet, and email, there's no way he didn't see the news. He must have known what happened. He made fast to distance himself from her. Is it her father's connection to the white supremacists?—she can't blame him for that, it still makes her sick to her stomach—but she wonders if Colin bailed because now he can't benefit from her family name and connections. Having a Rasmussen on board is now just a liability.

Stupid hurtful men. How could my own dad be so evil?

"Let's focus, Hannah," says Hecate's steady voice.

Hannah tries to focus on the moment.

"Your testimony is going to be very important on several counts," says the tall sleek lawyer who sits next to Hecate. Her hair is pulled up in a tight black bun and her slender little eyebrows are crafted out of little more than brow pencil and hope. She wears shiny black suit pants, sharp-toed black leather boots, and a soft white cashmere top. She looks like someone her mother would have mingled with at a bougie event.

"You can vouch for Justine, talk about how she tried to help you, rescued you, kept you safe. You can talk about her grief, what she shared with you, and how you firmly believe her only intention was to kill herself, not anybody else. We're going to shoot for temporary insanity borne of grief. Her own husband is willing to testify to that effect."

The way the woman says "kill herself" like she'd say "wash her hair" freaks Hannah out. These people, these power brokers of the world, they move through it like knives. Of course she wants to help Justine out. That's not a problem. It's her mom she's worried about.

"What about my mom? And my dad, what's going to happen to him? Can we prove that he is involved with the bombing?"

Hecate offers a rare smile, runs a hand through her voluminous hair, and Hannah hears the irrational soundtrack of an old commercial her mom used to sing in her mind, "I'm gonna wash that man right out of my hair."

"Your mom...is going to be okay, one way or another."

"She *killed* someone," Hannah says, stomach churning. *How could my mom have killed someone?*

"She'll explain it all to you, in good time," Hecate says. "As for the man who provided the other half of your DNA, we don't even have to prove his involvement. We just have to spook his stockholders, his board of directors. Well, frankly, spook them a little bit more. I think a radicalized daughter, a renegade wife who is present at the scene of a Rasmussen employee's suicide, and an explosion at the site of his new plant-to-be is a very deliciously destabilizing set of forces."

Hannah hopes so. She hasn't seen him since she was kidnapped. Whether he'd intended for her to be the one they took or not doesn't matter—he didn't consider the very real damage his actions had led to. *I don't think I can even face him.*

* * *

It's two more days before Hannah is allowed to see her mother in prison. It's not like the movies, there's no glass wall between them. They're allowed to sit across a little plastic table with institutional gray chairs, hard on the butt. She almost doesn't recognize her mom when they bring her in. It's not just the blue jumpsuit, which is like the farthest thing from anything her mother would ever wear, but the pale and blotchy skin, usually hidden under make-up. Her hair is pulled back into a loose ponytail.

"Hi, baby," her mom says when they sit down.

Hannah is speechless for a moment. She just stares at her mom. *How is this the same woman who tucked me in every night, sang me lullabies? Or the same woman in her crisp suits commanding a team of employees at EarthWorks. I don't know this woman at all.*

"I just don't understand," Hannah says.

"Which part?" Zoe says.

"Any of it. All of it. Like...why didn't you just tell me about your past?"

Zoe tips her head back and sighs at the ceiling. "I was ashamed. Afraid. We worked hard to seal everything up tight. I didn't know how to...unseal it. I was afraid of what it would cost me."

"Well, you weren't going to get in trouble for it, Dad made sure of that, right?"

Zoe's eyes pinch a little. She kind of hopes her words hurt her mom even though she isn't sure why she's mad.

"There are different kinds of trouble. I knew I wouldn't go to jail...ha." She looks down at herself and laughs darkly. "But you had an entirely different childhood from mine, and I wanted to keep it that way. Not taint you with it. I barely survived my own."

"You could have told me...something."

"I told you your grandmother had problems with drugs. That's why we don't really have a relationship with her."

Hannah shakes her head. "Why did you kill a man?"

Zoe looks at her hands. There are tears in her eyes when she looks back up. "He tried to hurt me. Hurt us. It was instinct. I didn't think; I just acted."

A relieved sigh leaks out of her. She didn't realize she needed to hear this. That it wasn't in cold blood.

She thinks of her childhood nightmares of someone breaking down her door, dragging her out of bed.

"You should have trusted me."

Zoe sighs. "I didn't trust myself. I didn't believe that my life with your...with Phil was real for a very long time. I kept waiting for someone to show up and strip everything away, including you."

Hannah's heart squeezes a little.

"Being a mom was the first thing I felt good at, natural at. I was keeping you safe. Or so I thought. I just could never find the words to tell you...what came before."

"I wish you had," Hannah said.

Zoe nods. "I wish I had, too. I wish so many things. But

there's freedom now in not having to worry about the past coming back to bite me. Not feeling ashamed."

"Can I meet her?" Hannah asks.

Zoe frowns. "Who?"

"My grandma."

Zoe goes very still for a long moment. "Yeah. She's complicated. She's not easy to find. But if you want to, we can do that."

"I want to. I want to know the full truth. Make up my own mind."

"Deal."

CHAPTER THIRTY-FIVE

When the arresting officer asked Zoe if she was related to "that Phil Rasmussen big energy guy" Zoe had said no. It was the first time in her life she disavowed that connection, and she had done it willingly. She said it reflexively, not really thinking. If ever there is a time that she needs all the power that comes with the Rasmussen name, it is this. And now she'll never have it again.

So, when they drag her to the visitor's booth this morning, where she expects to find Hecate or Artemis or her lawyer, she is stunned to look upon Phil's pale face.

And he does look pale. Like someone taken with a virus before they really know it. Dark circles under his watery blue eyes. Lips a thin line. Combover a little unkempt.

There is no glass between them. Zoe's heart gallops. He could just reach across the table and wrap his meaty hands around her thin throat. Could these officers be paid to look the other way? Her throat grows dry at the thought. He already helped disappear the evidence of one murder. Covered up a bombing.

She just glares at him, waiting for him to make the opening gambit.

He looks her up and down, assessing, like she is property for purchase. "I'm not paying for your bail," he says. "And per the guidelines of our prenuptial agreement, you are cut off. No trust fund. No clothes in your closet. Not even Hannah's baby book."

Zoe struggles to swallow on that. Nothing else matters to her. But Hannah's things—that's low.

She glares at him. "You have the audacity to bring up our daughter? What you allowed to happen to her..."

He inhales sharply and looks past her. Zoe fights the urge to look at what he is seeing. Can't stop picturing mafia movies— a guy moving in with a choking wire. A pistol to the back of her head.

"You associated with terrorists, Zo! What did you expect me to do? And I didn't know they would take Hannah. She wasn't even supposed to be home."

Zoe sits up straight. "You know what disgusts me most? Not just that you bombed your own home and attempted to kidnap your own wife..."

"Of which there is no proof."

Zoe ignores the smug self-righteousness. "What sickens me is that so many of these people who work for you have ties to those white supremacist groups. Because that's who you are. Isn't it?"

Phil's lips compress. His eyes tighten in an ugly way she recognizes from their worst fights.

Phil smiles then, traces a random pattern on the table between them. "Whatever you think you know, I'm on this side of the table, and you're on that side. I'm going to walk out of here, and you're going to stay in jail."

"I didn't do anything. They'll find me innocent. You, though? In the long run, it's you who will be ruined."

Phil stands up, smooths his suit.

I can't believe I ever loved this man. But did I—really? Or did I just confuse rescue for love?

"I'm no white supremacist, Zoe. I saw a means to an end. Those terrorist women were after me. Those men had a vendetta against the women. If there's one thing I've always been good at, it's moving players around the board where I need them."

Zoe can't stop the disgusted sound that escapes her.

"How can you not see that it's the same thing to weaponize hatred? That makes you complicit all the same!"

Phil sneers, sits back, hands on belly, like he's just enjoyed a lavish meal. "And what does it make *you*? I know that you were in one of those terrorist safe houses when you said you were just out on a hike with your journalist friend. I know that you lied to me. I knew within hours."

"I already know what I am," she says. "At least I feel bad about it. Anyway, I'd have thought you were used to the lies." She stands up and signals to the guard behind her. "Our whole marriage was, apparently, a lie, after all."

He shakes his head. "I thought you would be grateful. Given what you came from. That you would feel lucky. I should have listened to my mother who said you can't separate a person from the trash heap they grew up in. But what can I say...I was blinded by youthful lust. I forgot that everything fades: desire, a woman's beauty..."

"You're disgusting," Zoe says. "It's a blessing to be shed of you."

Phil's face compresses. He leans in, and *here it comes, the moment he'll snap.* "You don't know what I can do, Zoe."

And though a part of her wonders if she'll regret it even as the words are leaving her lips, she says, "I think I know exactly what you're capable of."

* * *

The trial is tedious, and Zoe's back hurts from sitting up so straight for so many hours. She refuses to so much as slump whenever Phil is in the courtroom; she still has her pride.

She isn't sure what makes her look behind her at the sound of the court doors hushing shut again, signaling an entrance. Probably someone coming back from the toilet or after a coffee break. Yet the very air feels charged even before she lays eyes on the woman. This is how her mind conceives of the person who has just entered. Not her mother, just "the woman." Because Tamara has managed to find a suit—or an approximation of one—a dark blue suit jacket and black pants, not even too thread bare and almost matching. A gray blouse. Clean blue sneakers. Her hair—what's left of it, cropped short and slicked back artfully. She's even wearing foundation and lipstick.

Zoe can't stop herself from staring. Catches Calliope's eye at the back of the courtroom—of course they sent her; cherubically blonde and blue-eyed Calliope is the last person anyone would suspect for an anarchist. Calliope raises a knowing brow at Zoe.

When Tamara is eventually called to the stand, Phil looks smugly at her. Yet Tamara glares back at him, holding his gaze until he finally looks away. Zoe can't help the rise of pride in her mother. Everything about Tamara seems to radiate: *what do I have to lose? Try me.*

Tamara is here as a character witness, to disprove the defense's argument that Zoe showed intent to bomb Rasmussen's new plant, to harm the men, because, as the prosecuting lawyer argued, she has "a history of violence." She's not sure what her mother can possibly say that will help, but she can't fight the swell of gratitude that she's here. The prosecution begins, "Your daughter, Zoe Rasmussen, killed a man in cold blood in your apartment thirty years ago. Zoe was also on the scene of a man found dead in his own apartment just a few weeks ago. You're her mother, so of course you're going to want to absolve your daughter, but how can you really say, Miss Gold, that your daughter does not have violent tendencies."

Tamara purses her lips, swallows hard, sucks her teeth. Zoe's entire body prickles, crawling with energy. All Zoe's gratitude dissolves. *She should not be up there. She'll say something rude or nonsensical. This is a bad idea.*

"What my daughter has, is bad luck," Tamara says, then clears her throat, loudly. "The bad luck of being in the wrong place at the wrong time, and that's my fault. I've struggled with substance abuse my whole life. Put her in a lot of bad situations. Like the night her father was killed. She didn't know it was him. I should have told them both long before. Would have avoided the whole mess."

Zoe feels punched. Can't get a deep breath. The entire courtroom murmurs. *Her father?*

"Yes, I should have told them both. Another fault of mine. Anyway, that's not the point." Tamara wipes her palms on her pants. "Point is, I attracted a low life element and the only good thing that came out of it was her." She points at Zoe.

Zoe is too busy reeling at the revelation to really feel the tenderness of her mother's words. The lawyer clears his throat. "Ma'am, please answer the question."

Tamara glares at him, as though she's seen much scarier things on the street than this slicked up lawyer in his suit. "The point is, Zoe didn't kill him. *I* did. Because he came after us. Would have killed one of us if I hadn't. She called her damn boyfriend for help, because she was scared. She did the right thing. But he—" here she points at Phil, "Phil, that man, Phil Rasmussen, came on over with his little buddy Spencer Miller, and they cleaned that murder up like not a thing had ever happened. And they didn't so much as get a smack on the wrist about it, but my Zoe is on trial?"

"That's bullshit!" Phil mutters, before his lawyer shushes him with a hand on his arm.

Zoe has to press her hand to her mouth to keep from smiling.

The judge bangs his gavel and Zoe's mother lifts her hands, flapping like small birds in front of her. "Thank you, ma'am, no further questions," the lawyer says in a stiff tone.

The defense asks a few questions, too, but Zoe has stopped listening. Her head buzzes with the new information, rewriting the event in her mind. Not some john. Not just another junkie. Her *father*. Or maybe he was all of those things at once. But still. Should she feel ashamed at her origins, or proud that she survived them? She can't decide.

Tamara gets off the stand, smooths down invisible wrinkles in her blouse, and then makes her way off the stand. On her way out, she stops beside Zoe. Her mother leans in close again and whispers, "I never thought he was good enough for you," before planting a kiss on Zoe's cheek and taking a seat in the row right behind her.

Zoe's cheek tingles. She's too surprised by her mother's presence, the awful revelation, and the look of glowering rage on Phil's face to respond. It's doubtful that Tamara's testimony will be any help to her case, but it means something to Zoe.

In the second darkest hour of Zoe's life, her mother showed up.

CHAPTER THIRTY-SIX

ONE MONTH AFTER THE BLAST

Hannah realizes she hasn't thought this through, especially. What she wants to ask. What she expects anyone to say. Her mom sits to her left, dressed uncharacteristically in sweats and a hoodie, no makeup, like some "before" version in a style makeover. Tamara—she can't quite allow herself to think of her as "Grandma" yet—sits to the right of her dressed in a pretty plum sweater with a high neck, with loud blush and bright eye shadow over pockmarked skin. Around them, mostly college students near her age bustle through the busy café as though everything is normal. Completely oblivious to the way Hannah's whole life has imploded, how she has no real idea what's going to happen next.

What she knows for sure: her parents are in the midst of an ugly divorce; she is not going to Kenya; Justine is willing to show her the journalism ropes; and maybe this isn't the worst moment of her life, after all.

"So, I guess I just want to know, like, more about you, and how Mom grew up and stuff," Hannah begins.

Tamara has just bitten into a poppyseed muffin, which

spills crumbs everywhere. Zoe's fingers twitch, as though she wants to clean up after Tamara, but she stays her hand.

"I grew up in New York," Tamara says between bites. "Middle class life. Perfect little family. The bees knees."

Her mom's eyebrow is ratcheted tightly upwards, like an arrow pointing to an exit.

"Except my daddy was a drinker. Everyone was then. My own mother drank and smoked while she was pregnant. He was the charming-for-the-friends-but-smack-around-the-kids-later kind of drinker. Got so mad one time he punched my brother in the temple. My brother, almost 200 pounds and full of muscle, hit the kitchen floor and he never got back up again."

Zoe gasps. "You said he was killed in a car accident."

Tamara sets down her muffin, wipes the crumbs off her black pants and shakes her head. "I told you a lot of wrong things, Zo-girl. Some things are just too terrible to say out loud."

Hannah looks between these women she comes from. "And what about...my grandfather. Why didn't you tell her about him?"

Tamara's face wrinkles. "Don't call him that. He didn't earn it."

Zoe is staring with keen intensity at Tamara now. In a thick, hushed voice she says, "I *killed* him. My own father. He tried to...well you know what he tried to do...to me."

Tamara looks away from them both, shaking her head slightly. "I was...so ashamed. How could I tell you?"

Zoe shrugs. "I don't know, just say, 'hey, by the way, that guy that comes every Thursday is your father. He's not a nice man. Stay away from him. Lock your door.'"

Tamara just looks at her hands. And despite herself, Hannah feels sorry for her...for her grandmother. Whose own childhood sounded full of pain and loss.

"Maybe there's no good answers," Hannah hears herself say.

Both women look quickly at her. "Just like there's no good answer for my...for my dad. For what he's done."

"There are answers," Zoe says, low, almost to herself. "Like stay awake, pay attention. Don't become complicit."

Hannah doesn't know what to say. She wants suddenly to go to Justine's, to sit and drink cocoa and talk about Justine's favorite stories she's written over the years.

Tamara reaches out and lays her chapped and callused hand on Hannah's own. "Don't let him take credit," she says.

Hannah wrinkles her brow. "Who...for what?" she says.

"Phil. That man who calls himself your father. Don't let him take credit for any of the great things you're going to do."

With that she stands up, wrapping her muffin remains in a napkin, briefly kisses Zoe on the head and then walks out of the café.

"Where's she going?" Hannah asks.

Zoe shakes her head. "I never know."

"I guess none of us do," Hannah says.

Zoe smiles, a big genuine one for the first time Hannah's seen in weeks. "I guess we don't."

CHAPTER THIRTY-SEVEN

TWO MONTHS LATER

Justine wiggles her ankle, cringing at the way the hard plastic of the monitor rubs up against the bony protrusions at the side. But other than the unpleasant feeling that someone knows her every move, her whereabouts, which are confined to the 1300 square feet of her home, there is a lightness in her chest she hasn't felt in...well, in more than a year.

She is just settling into the cushions of her couch to read when there is a knock at her door.

She doesn't think it is her probation officer with whom she's already met that week. She doesn't know who it could be, given that she isn't allowed to have visitors. Maybe Fedex delivering something.

She opens the door to find Zoe standing there, looking somehow smaller, shorter. No, that isn't it; the usual gleam and polish and shine about her—highlighted coif and her fancy suits —is gone. Changed. She looked just like a normal middle-aged woman you might pass on the street and not think much about at all.

"Hey," Justine says. "You aren't supposed to be here."

Zoe shrugs. "I know. But they aren't keeping track of *me*, only you."

Justine nods. There wasn't enough evidence to convict Zoe of any crime, past or present, for which she is grateful—especially for Hannah's sake. "True. Everything okay? Hannah sounds sad, but not broken. She's a special girl."

Zoe sighs. "She is. She was pretty broken-hearted about her dad, and that stupid boyfriend of hers ghosting her. Disappointed that the wheels of justice turn so slowly. Antsy. Having dropped out of school and unable to go to Kenya. But she's pretty excited about what you're teaching her. I think she's going to apply to journalism school." Zoe's breath makes plumes of cold air.

"God, why am I keeping you out in the cold! Come in," Justine says.

Zoe does, stamping off her feet on the little welcome mat.

"Tea?" Justine asks, already setting the kettle on.

Zoe nods.

"Are you going to try to get your job back?" Justine asks.

Zoe frowns and shakes her head. "If I'm honest with myself, I think maybe I did found EarthWorks just to spite Phil, at least unconsciously. I mean, it has done real good in the world, but that's not a good enough reason to do something. I've applied for a job with an organization in the tenderloin that needs a director, a program that advocates for the unhoused and tries to get them healthcare and housing."

Justine smiles. "I can't believe that at one point in time, not so long ago, work was everything to me, and now I feel like I can barely remember how to write a lede, much less an article."

"We're remaking ourselves," Zoe says. Her eyes suddenly cast about behind Justine. "Willa's photos. You put them back up."

Justine nods. She still can't look at them fully, head on, but she likes to see her daughter's wispy curls in her periphery every time she walks down the hall.

"She was real, here, mine," she says, annoyed by the catch in her voice, still unused to grieving publicly.

Zoe reaches for Justine's hand, and Justine doesn't pull away. "She was, Justine."

Justine clears her throat. "What brings you out, Zoe?"

Zoe purses her lips together, begins to fan herself, laughs. "It still boggles the mind that I can get hot as fuck in winter," she says. "I came to tell you some good news. Of a kind."

Justine can't imagine any news really sounding good, but she nods for Zoe to continue.

"It turns out Spencer Miller is the gift that keeps on giving. I mean, thanks to Persephone—I had no idea of her mad computer hacking skills. Phil was always careful to keep him as a contractor, never an employee, so there was very little paperwork linking the two."

"Ooh, there's always a trail."

Zoe nods. "Technically, Spencer worked for a staffing agency that contracted with Phil. But Spencer helped Phil clean up my...homicide...*before* Phil became the careful, savvy businessman he is today. Persephone found a very old email between Phil and Spencer—Phil's father's company was one of the first to have email, something called Lycos."

"Jesus, Lycos, that's even way before my time," Justine says.

"Yeah. They used it *only once* to communicate about the deed."

Justine laughs. "Once is all it takes, as they say."

Zoe nods. "Essentially, Phil blackmailed Spencer that if he ever said a word about what they'd done, he'd ruin him, and then he funded a lifestyle that Spencer would not want to give up. That is the thing he paid the private detective all those years ago to be sure could not be found. He was never protecting me–only himself."

Justine let out a small whoop. "Bet that's the last thing he expected to come and bite him in the ass," she says.

"Indeed."

Justine remembers herself—she is still learning how to be a person in the world again who cares about other people and their pain—she strokes Zoe's shoulder. "How are you feeling about...what your mother revealed in the courtroom? Hannah told me."

Zoe shakes her head. "I still don't know how I feel. I asked Tamara why she never told me about my father, and she just said she was ashamed. Of him, of how I was conceived, but not of me. It's sort of the same thing I said to Hannah about why I didn't tell her about that night. But secrets are poison. I don't want to keep them anymore."

Justine sits quiet for a moment, and then says, "I'm happy that you didn't wind up in prison, but sorry for all that you've lost. And for the role I played in it."

The teapot whistles just then, shrill and sharp, and they both jump slightly before Justine shuts it off and pours it into a teapot, then dumps chamomile and green tea leaves in.

Zoe shakes her head. "I'm not sorry anymore, Justine. I'm done being sorry."

EPILOGUE

6 MONTHS AFTER THE BLAST

Justine marvels at the symmetry of a full cabinet—big boxes and smaller boxes fitting into their spaces, asserting a future, an intention to go on feeding oneself and maybe others.

She's stocked up on things she personally won't eat; gritty sugar-coated Pop Tarts and frozen pizzas, things Hannah can snack on when she comes over for lessons in writing press releases and profiles in her role as EarthWorks' newest communications intern.

When a knock sounds at the back door, she wonders if it's Nate coming by with another excuse to fix something around the house, to test the boundaries of physical proximity, to see whether it's safe to be in the same space without combustion.

But it's not Nate who greets her. She almost doesn't recognize the woman. Hair in glossy waves around her shoulders, proud in a rich blue suit jacket over a silky white blouse. Justine can hardly reconcile this corporate woman with the world-weary warrior she's known.

"Hecate?"

"You can call me Carmen," Hecate says with a wide grin. "Welcome back to the world of the living, Justine. And back to work." She hands Justine a small digital recorder and a name badge for *The Clarion Courier*, her former paper.

"I don't..."

"I'm your new boss."

Justine gapes a moment longer, then she opens her mouth wide and laughs. "Are you still part of Nemesis?"

Carmen smiles. "Not on paper, but..."

Justine shakes her head.

"Look at the badge."

She holds it up. Her name, title, nothing unusual.

"No, turn it around."

On the back, just one word: *Niobe*.

"Niobe?"

"A bereaved mother, just like you," Carmen says. "A fitting name for a warrior goddess."

Justine closes her eyes, holds the badge to her heart, tears leaking out unbidden. When she opens her eyes again, Carmen nods just once.

"Let's get to work."

ACKNOWLEDGMENTS

This book was born from an intersection of my anxieties. The seed was planted not long after the devastating 2011 tsunami in Japan that breached the Fukushima nuclear plant. Unreliable clickbait-style "articles" suggested that nuclear waste had made its way via ocean currents all the way to the U.S. As a former journalist, I'm not typically alarmist and rarely prone to conspiracy thinking, but that article arrived at a time of multiple anxieties: I was a relatively new mother myself; a mother in my community was losing her daughter to an aggressive brain tumor; and my home state of California was in the grips of an epic drought, with one of the driest winters I could recall. I was consumed by thoughts of loss, not only of children and loved ones, but also loss of the natural world.

Around that time, I'd also written an article for *Scientific American* on the topic of "Environmental grief," a term defined by loss expert Kriss Kevorkian. Her work explores that one reason we may be so slow to respond to threats of climate change have to do with our inability to deal with our own grief, protected by the false comforts of capitalism and taught to avoid thoughts of death and loss.

In the almost 10 years between drafts, I went from a newish mother to a woman in perimenopause, and thus Zoe was born, in part, out of the transformations happening to me. Perimenopause ravages so many women/non-binary/gender-fluid folks and in a medical system that poorly studies these very normal and treatable health issues. Thankfully many of us talk to each other and reassure ourselves we aren't crazy—what we're experiencing is real.

Project Nemesis was born from a combination of my own desire for there to be true heroes of the downtrodden and the environment and inspiration of true eco-anarchists. I want it noted that true eco-anarchism does not promote violence typically, per se—and even my own made-up Project Nemesis comes to see there are many paths to change beyond it. I admire actual eco-anarchist groups, and hope that collectively we get our act together to preserve the future for our children. I am grateful to the Anarchist Library's "Ecoanarchist Manifesto" for defining some terms that ultimately gave voice to Hecate and the rest of Nemesis.

This book has experienced many incarnations, and I'm grateful to all the people who have helped me along the way. First, to *The Coachella Review*, which published an early chapter, giving me confidence to keep at this story, though that chapter no longer exists in the book.

Early feedback from my friend Laurel Hermanson helped me decide that this book was worth pursuing after I'd made some significant revisions. She was the one who firmed up for me that an all-women group of eco-anarchists was way more interesting than the alternative. And while my husband contends the only likable male in this book is Zoe's assistant Bernard, it is not intended to make commentary on men individually, but rather patriarchy as a system that hurts everyone.

This book probably would not be published if I hadn't seen that my friend and fellow Bennington alum, Kate Milliken, was teaching a novel workshop through the Center for Fiction toward the beginning of the pandemic. As a writing teacher myself, I realized I didn't feed my own writing enough. That workshop lit the fire under my butt to finish this novel. Kate's feedback was some of the most incisive, keen, and useful that I'd ever received, along with excellent additions from my workshop cohort: Lisa Ryan, Rob Del Mauro, Jenny Bolognese and Christina Tudor.

Of course, I wouldn't be here at all without the Running Wild Press staff: Lisa Kastner for taking a chance on me; Ben White for his keen editing eye and catching the kinds of "little things" that make a big difference; Evangeline Estropia for shepherding this book through the process and the intrepid design teams for my cover and interior design.

I'd also like to thank Stacey Parshall Jensen, an extraordinary writer and person, who gave generously of her time to read this, with helpful insights. Fellow writers Tracey Lander-Garrett and Martha Stromberg also read drafts when I was so close but didn't feel like I could do another draft and helped me take each draft to another level. My dear Dayna Bennett provided feedback, camaraderie, laughs, duck farts, and so much more. She, and my darlings Andrea Chmelik and Natalie Obando have made me laugh until I cried or peed myself on our annual writing retreat, forever my besties and darlings. Lesley Miles offered me sanctuary, accountability and support, as well as feedback, in her little airstream on the hill. Cindy Lamothe and Laura Bogart have long offered me moral support and encouragement in writing in general. And nothing would ever be possible without my greatest loves: Erik and Ben.

ABOUT RUNNING WILD PRESS

Running Wild Press publishes stories that cross genres with great stories and writing. RIZE publishes great genre stories written by people of color and by authors who identify with other marginalized groups. Our team consists of:

Lisa Diane Kastner, Founder and Executive Editor
Cody Sisco, Acquisitions Editor, RIZE
Benjamin White, Acquisition Editor, Running Wild
Peter A. Wright, Acquisition Editor, Running Wild
Resa Alboher, Editor
Angela Andrews, Editor
Sandra Bush, Editor
Ashley Crantas, Editor
Rebecca Dimyan, Editor
Abigail Efird, Editor
Aimee Hardy, Editor
Henry L. Herz, Editor
Cecilia Kennedy, Editor
Barbara Lockwood, Editor

ABOUT RUNNING WILD PRESS

Scott Schultz, Editor
Rod Gilley, Editor

Evangeline Estropia, Product Manager
Kimberly Ligutan, Product Manager
Lara Macaione, Marketing Director
Joelle Mitchell, Licensing and Strategy Lead
Pulp Art Studios, Cover Design
Standout Books, Interior Design
Polgarus Studios, Interior Design

Learn more about us and our stories at www.runningwild-press.com

Loved these stories and want more? Follow us at runningwildpublishing.com, www.facebook.com/runningwild-press, on Twitter @lisadkastner @RunWildBooks